THE WHITE SCHOONER

ANTONY TREW has spent many years at sea. During the 1939–45 war he served with the Mediterranean Fleet in the 22nd Anti-Submarine Group, and in the Western Approaches where he commanded the destroyer *Walker*, principally on Russian convoys. He was awarded the DSC.

He retired recently as Director-General of the Automobile Association in South Africa and now lives in England.

His highly successful career as a novelist began with the best-selling *Two Hours to Darkness* in 1963. Since then he has written nine novels, mainly about the sea. The most recent is *Death of a Supertanker*.

ANTONY TREW

The White Schooner

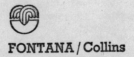

FONTANA/Collins

First published in 1969 by William Collins Sons & Co Ltd
First issued in Fontana Books 1971
Fifth Impression June 1979

Made and printed in Great Britain by
William Collins Sons & Co Ltd Glasgow

*Wheresoever the carcase is, there will
the eagles be gathered together*
ST. MATTHEW, 24:28

The characters and incidents in this story
are entirely fictitious and any resemblance
to living persons is coincidental

Chapter One

He was in the foothills now, clear of the terraces of almonds and caribs which led in giant steps to the valley below. The carpets of marguerites and poppies had given way to undergrowth, sparse at first but becoming thicker as he climbed. The sun shone from an April sky and straggling clouds threw shadows across the *campo*. The wind carried the scent of pines and junipers, and from the undergrowth came the tang of sage and rosemary.

It was warm so he sat on a rock in a small clearing and looked out towards the Mediterranean, enjoying the distant coolness of the blue water and wondering how it could be described without clichés and deciding it couldn't. From a fisherman's bag he took binoculars and scanned the valley. To his right lay the white cluster of buildings about San José where the road turned south at first and then east towards Ibiza, a grey line rising and falling, lost in the undulations of the landscape. To his left, perhaps half a mile away, a dirt road climbed through the terraces reaching up into the hills until it was lost in the fold of a ravine.

An occasional car moved along the road through the valley, but otherwise the landscape was still.

Above him a falcon hovered and he wondered if it were a lanner or a peregrine until he used the glasses and knew it was a peregrine. It was the first he'd sighted on the island so he took a book from the bag, found the peregrine and made a marginal notation, 'Nr. San José, 12/4/68.'

He put the binoculars and book in the bag, hesitating when he saw the bottle of wine. Better wait for lunch, he decided, and fastened the straps on the bag. He got to his feet slowly, slung it over his shoulder and set himself against the hill. There was no path and as the angle of the slope grew steeper he began to zigzag. It was hard work because the route he had chosen lay through thick undergrowth. At times he would find the way barred and then he would go back and try another.

Beads of sweat gathered on his face and rolled away to be replaced by others and dust, musty and choking, came from the shrubs he pushed aside as he climbed. It would be good, he thought, to be impervious to discomfort. But I am not. My left shoe hurts, I have this scratch on my forearm which smarts, the dust makes me asthmatic, I'm wet with sweat and have still a long way to go. I must make my mind a blank, he decided, and began humming *Up, Up and Away*. But he resented the tune because it had over the weeks and months become compulsive. So he changed to *Colonel Bogey* and felt better.

By late afternoon he had come to a gully which lay between the route he had taken and the dirt road. Opposite was a clearing, beyond it the road. Before he left the corner of the junipers he stood at their edge, making sure there was nothing on the road and no one in the gully. When he was satisfied he scrambled down the slope and worked his way slowly up the gully until he judged he was above the clearing. He could see on his right, ahead of him, the tops of pines, dark and menacing. He came out of the gully and went into them, choosing his way carefully, avoiding the dead branches which lay on the carpet of pine needles.

A bird called, a sharp *tjik-tjik-tjik*, and he started. God, he thought, even the call of a thrush shakes me. Must get a grip on myself. There's no law against being in this wood. But he knew that wasn't the point.

He set off through the plantation, still climbing obliquely across it until he saw the firebreak. Keeping to the trees he moved up the slope until he was abreast of thick undergrowth. Crossing the firebreak he went into it and crawled forward and when he'd gone like that slowly, perhaps for five minutes, he raised his head and saw the white splash of the *finca* in the trees on the far side of the ravine. It was ahead of him to the right, just clear of a jutting clump of pines. It was, he judged, four hundred yards away. He'd have to get a lot closer than that. He looked at his watch. There was an hour of daylight left. Slowly he crawled back through the undergrowth, reached the wood and, when he was well into it, moved up the slope again.

A part of his mind was analysing his emotions, registering surprise that he could at this moment be calm and objective.

Kagan should be here to see that you can be emotionally involved and yet retain your caution and judgment. Anyway, it was just a big white house, a container, so many superficial feet of wall, so many cubic yards of capacity; it was inanimate, without movement, that which might be in it remote, unreal, maybe not even there. He shook himself free from his thoughts and plodded on up the hill, to his right bright slats of daylight alternating with the dark trunks of trees.

Half an hour later he was in position, slightly above the *finca* and to its left, no more than a hundred yards from it and with a clear view across the ravine.

He was kneeling now, well shielded in a spinney of junipers and scrub, binoculars focused on the big house. It was magnificently sited, looking outward from the hills towards the sea. The architecture was Ibizencan, split levels, geometric lines, high white walls, windows trellised with cast iron, flat roofs, terra-cotta tiled, to collect the rain for the *cisterna* beneath the house. Castilian arches broke the wide frontal elevation and gave the house depth and character. On the terrace above the main house, two wings ran back into the excavated hillside; clustered about them, interspersed with clumps of cacti and figs, were the outbuildings for animals and farm equipment.

'So that's Altomonte. It's a big house,' he muttered to himself. 'They have not exaggerated.' He tried to identify its components, to establish by their windows and position the character of the different rooms, but it was not possible. And in all that sprawling structure where was the gallery? The bedrooms? Van Biljon's suite? Some things were self evident, like the barred windows. Others were not. Such as where the dogs were kept, and was there any break in the high stone wall which surrounded the *finca*, other than the iron-bound gate shut across the road from the valley.

For a long time these and other things occupied him and then the light had gone, and he put the binoculars back in the fishing bag. For some minutes he remained there, then, still on his knees, he started back towards the wood, going into the thicket where he rested until the moon had dipped beneath the hill. Then he went to the firebreak. He did not go into the wood again for he knew he would not be able to see the dried branches. So he kept to the firebreak where he could move faster and with less noise. Darkness would be his cover.

The ravine was on his left now, across it the lights of the *finca*, warm and inviting. As he watched those in the west wing went on, bright squares glowing in the high walls. Probably the gallery, he decided. With darkness had come a drop in temperature, and he buttoned the collar of his shirt against the cold. From the *finca* the smell of woodsmoke mixed with cooking came down to the firebreak. He sniffed it. Meat of some sort, mutton, perhaps with garlic. It reminded him of a night in the desert round a fire with bedouins: on the road to Damascus when his car had broken down. *On the road to Damascus.* It has a biblical ring, he thought. A biblical ring. He kept repeating the words, liking the onomatopeia.

His thoughts flung away as he tripped over a stone. He tried to break the fall with his hands but his forehead struck the ground and he heard the stone rolling into the ravine, breaking through dry brushwood, and he was appalled at its noise.

Predictably the silence was broken by the barking of dogs. Still clutching the ground, he turned his head and looked back. Faintly, in the distance, he could hear men's voices and presently he saw the beam of a flashlight travelling along a white wall.

'You bloody fool,' he gasped. 'You bloody fool. You weren't concentrating.' He waited, tense and upset. But his common sense told him that those in the *finca* could not at that distance have heard the noise of the stone. The dogs, yes. But not the men.

Presently it was silent again. The dogs had stopped barking, and the voices ceased.

He got up and dusted himself, found there was blood on his hand where the gravel had torn the skin, and a lump on his temple, raw and tender. He set the strap of the bag across his shoulder and started down the hill. Gingerly this time, concentrating, determined to do it efficiently. Half an hour later he reached the first terrace. Only then did he relax. He stepped on to it and followed its curving contours to the east where it met the dirt road.

The croaking of frogs led him to a small spring inside a stone surround. From it a trickle of water ran down a concrete furrow. He tasted the water, decided it was good, and scooped handfuls into his mouth. Then he washed his face and hands and rested by the spring. The fall had shaken him. Feeling

8

cold again, he took up his bag and set off down the road.

In the west a waning moon was setting.

As he walked he was aware of two things: the pungent smell of sweat and the warm stickiness of blood on his left hand. After a while he stopped and bound the hand with a handkerchief. It was not serious but it was uncomfortable, even painful. Pain is relative, he thought, *gurus* preclude it with mental disciplines. I shall presume that the pain in my left hand has always been there. Therefore it is normal, therefore I do not feel it. But it was no good. The hand still hurt.

An hour later he was nearing the foot of the hill and he knew that soon the dirt road would join the tarmac between San José and Ibiza and he would set off along it. The chances of a lift were not good. It was almost eleven o'clock, there would not be much traffic, and to car drivers he would seem a dubious risk. It promised to be a long night and he was already tired, but he could see no alternative. It reminded him of another night, long ago, when he had been alone in a strange country, on a fearsome journey.

The distant sound of a car travelling along the main road broke into his thoughts and soon its lights swept across the foot of the dirt road. Then they were gone and the noise of the engine faded. Soon afterwards he heard behind him the sound of a car starting, and as he turned its headlights came on and blinded him. It was parked just off the road, not more than fifty yards back. I must be tired, he thought, to have been so close without smelling it. The car started down the road and he stood aside to let it pass, but it drew up alongside him and he saw it was a jeep of the Guardia Civil. There were two uniformed men in it.

The driver said, '*Beunas noches, señor.*'

He replied, '*Beunas noches, señor,*' and knew that they were sizing him up, wondering what he was doing there at that time.

'It is late to be walking here,' said the driver in Spanish.

'Yes, indeed. I was in the hills to-day watching birds and then I fell.' With his bandaged hand he indicated his forehead. 'So I rested.'

'You are English, señor?' said the policeman in the passenger seat.

He nodded. 'Yes, I am English.' His Castilian Spanish was good, but his English accent always came through.

9

'How do you mean you were watching birds?' said the driver.

The Englishman took the binoculars and the bird book from the canvas bag and passed them to the driver, and while he and his companion examined them by torchlight the Englishman explained bird watching.

The policemen thought this was funny and they laughed to each other; but they were satisfied, and passed back the book and binoculars.

'In Spain we shoot birds and eat them,' said one of the policemen. 'They taste good.'

'I believe so,' said the Englishman. 'I have never tried.'

'You must do so, señor.'

'I may do so.'

The driver had an idea. 'Next time you should watch the bird first, then shoot it, and afterwards eat it.'

'This way you will have everything, señor,' said his companion.

'Quite so,' said the Englishman. 'It is worth considering.'

The earlier tension had gone. They were satisfied and when they offered him a lift into Ibiza he accepted.

They put him down at the Paseo Vara de Rey just as the crowd was coming out from the Cine Serra. Anxious to avoid them, he hurried down Calle Vincente Cuervo and then, by way of the harbour first, he went up into the old town.

He had told the police that his name was Charles Black and that he lived in a room in Señora Maria Massa's house, in a lane near El Corsario.

Chapter Two

Streaks of cloud scudded across the Aegean sky above Patmos, and from Chora looking across the bay to Scala the wind could be seen to strike the water in eddying gusts, while billows of smoke from the island steamer coming in from Leros were snatched from the funnel and blown low over the sea.

'It's a squally place in a northerly wind,' said the lanky young man sucking orange juice through a straw.

The girl with freckles and red hair nodded but didn't look up.

'Glad *Zuletha*'s snugly alongside,' he said.

'Famous last words.'

'What time did they say?'

She sighed and put down the paper. 'You're determined I'm not going to read this, aren't you?'

'What time did they say?'

'At, 'ow do you say, meeday,' she mimicked. 'We shall be 'appy eef you weel veesit us.'

He shook his head. 'Not very good. You could do better.'

She dropped her voice and spoke hoarsely. 'Ve haf not too much variety, but plenty good Sherman bee-er. *Ja wohl.*'

He laughed. 'That's better.'

'What was his name?'

'Helmut.'

'Helmut what?'

'Don't know,' he said. 'He was the character with the bushy beard. The one with a faceful of fuzz, whiskers, and brass rings in his ears was Francois.'

'You didn't tell them our names,' she said reprovingly. 'Very gauche.'

'They didn't ask.'

'They were nice. Picking up my scattered veg like that.'

'Pretty obvious, wasn't it?' He stifled a yawn.

'What was?'

'The way you dropped it.'

'Rubbish.' She flicked at his nose with a straw. 'You're

11

jealous. That lovely schooner. My dear, they must be rich. *Rich, madly rich.*' She sang the words.

He looked at his watch. 'Come on. It's a quarter to go. Let's go.'

He beckoned the waiter and paid the bill. Gathering their parcels they went across to the taxi, a tired looking Renault, and told the driver to take them to Port Scala.

As they walked down the quay to the schooner the lanky young man looked at it with a critical eye. 'Staysail schooner, Bermuda rigged,' he said.

The girl looked at the long white hull, reflected sunlight dancing on it, the masts standing high above the water. 'She's beautiful,' she said. 'No wonder they call her the *Snowgoose*.'

The name was on the stern transom, below it Piraeus, the port of registration.

'Look at the size of the exhausts,' he said. 'She must have bloody great auxiliaries.'

He could tell from the coachroofs and portlights that the schooner had crew space forward, the main accommodation amidships, aft of that a well-equipped cockpit and aft of that again more accommodation, probably the owner's suite.

A man with leathery skin and a greying beard was in the cockpit polishing brightwork. When he saw them he called down the forward companionway. Soon afterwards two young men appeared.

'*Bon*. You 'ave come,' called the Frenchman.

'Of course.' The girl smiled. 'I don't think we told you our names. I'm Ann Alexander. This is my husband, Dougal.' She felt she was being over formal and grinned to hide her embarrassment.

The Frenchman pointed to his companion. 'This is Helmut. I am Francois.'

'Yes,' said Dougal Alexander. 'You told us this morning.' His wife frowned at him.

'Welcome on board,' said Helmut. 'Meet the *Snowgoose*.'

'She's beautiful,' said Ann Alexander.

They followed the German down the forward companionway and along an alleyway between cabin doors to a small saloon. It was simply furnished with settees, a central table, a bookcase and lockers. There were signs of interrupted industry: two typewriters, a litter of typewritten sheets, note books, cameras, paints and brushes, and sketches in water-colour and pen-and-ink.

Helmut gestured with his hands. 'Excuse the rubbish, Always it is like this. We cruise to work.' The deep voice and hoarse German accent gave the words weight.

Drinks were produced, formalities soon forgotten, and the talk became general. The English girl explained that they lived in Athens where her husband worked for an oil company. They were spending their holiday cruising in *Zuletha*, a ketch which belonged to friends in Athens. There was chatter about cruising in the Aegean, about the islands they had visited and their boats.

Dougal Alexander looked round the cabin. 'What's the size of this monster?'

'Fifteen metres on the waterline. Thirty-five ton's displacement,' said Helmut.

'And three of you manage her?'

'Four. We have two paid hands. Dimitrio, a seaman, and Kamros who cooks and looks after the engines.'

'Big ones, aren't they?'

Helmut drained his tankard. 'Big enough. And your ketch. You have a motor?' He looked at Ann Alexander.

'Yes. A mini one. Keeps us out of trouble, though. When we can start it.'

She looked round the cabin and saw the typewriters. 'You say you cruise to work. Is this it?'

Francois made a face. 'I know what you think. Is this work? Yes. Very much. We have been commissioned by a publisher in Berne to make a yachtsman's guide for the Mediterranean islands. They have chartered this schooner for us. We have her for six months. There is much to do. *Beaucoup de travail!*'

'You lucky so-and-so's.' Dougal shook his head slowly. 'What a marvellous job. Were you always yachtsmen?'

'Of course,' said Helmut. 'It is not possible otherwise.'

'What language will it be in?'

'English, French, German,' said Francois.

'When will it come out?' The girl turned to her husband. 'We must get it, Dougal.'

The German hunched his shoulders and puffed his cheeks. 'Who knows? We have just started. Only one month already. After six months at sea then, well—we must do much ashore. In Berne they say to finish in December. This is fantastic. It is not possible.'

'Are you doing the Aegean or the whole Med?'

'Everything. The lot.'

'Blimey,' said Dougal. 'No wonder you've got big engines.'

Francois switched the subject to Patmos and wanted to know when they'd arrived and where they were going. While her husband was explaining, Ann Alexander was thinking how striking these two men were with their thick dark hair, acquiline bearded faces and quick intelligent eyes. The Frenchman's mandarin moustache, the gold rings in his ears, the red handkerchief knotted inside the blue denim shirt, reminded her of a character from *Treasure Island*. The German, brooding and phlegmatic, was the bigger, heavier man. She picked up a watercolour sketch which lay on the table.

'Where is this?'

Helmut leant over her shoulder. 'Leros. Port Lakki, from the south-west.'

'Memorise it, Ann.' Her husband held out his tankard for the Frenchman to fill.

She put down the sketch. 'It's jolly good.'

Helmut groaned. 'Don't say that. He is already too conceited.'

She looked at Francois. 'So you are the artist?'

'Also the photographer,' he said. 'I illustrate, he writes. Naturally the illustrations are better than the writings.'

Several beers later Dougal Alexander noticed the two men looking at their watches, exchanging glances. He consulted his. It was nearly half past one. He signalled to his wife and stood up.

'I wish,' said Francois to Ann, 'that we could offer you lunch. But we have very much to do and—' He looked round the cabin in a melancholy fashion. 'No facilities.'

'Sweet of you to think of it,' she said. 'But we couldn't have stayed. Anyway it was lovely and I think you have a most beautiful schooner.'

When they had said their good-byes and were walking down the quay towards the *Zuletha* she said, 'Nice, weren't they?'

'Quite pleasant.'

'Especially Helmut,' she said.

'The way the Frenchman looked at you, I think he'd have liked to paint you.'

14

She smiled at him shyly. 'Oh, do you really think so, darling?'

'Yes,' he said. 'In the nude.'

'What a mind you have. Lovely boat isn't it?'

'Yes. I'd have liked to look round it.'

'Me too. Funny they didn't offer to show us.'

'Oh, I don't know,' he said gloomily. 'I suppose they only asked us down to see you.'

'Nonsense,' she laughed, hoping he was right.

When their guests had gone, Helmut and Francois went back to the saloon. The German unlocked the port door in the forward bulkhead. Inside was a small well-fitted radio cabin, its equipment more extensive than was usual in a boat of that size. Putting on headphones he sat on the stool in front of the console, switched on the receiver and made adjustments on the control panel. Then he took off the headphones, looked at his watch and turned to his companion. 'I thought they would never go.'

'Yes. I also began to worry.'

'He is lucky to have such a crew,' said Helmut.

The Frenchman made a circle with his thumb and forefinger. 'Fabulous. Even in trousers. I would like to paint her.'

'*Ohne Hosen*—without trousers?'

'If you like.'

'I like.' The German looked at his watch. 'Two minutes more.' He swung the stool back to the console and put on the headphones.

From outside came the cries of seabirds fighting for scraps in the harbour, the lap of water along the hull, and the whistle in the rigging as the northerly wind came gusting down the slopes above Port Scala and the schooner strained at her moorings. There was a smell of beer in the cabin, and through the starboard door cooking odours drifted in from the galley.

Francois lit a cheroot and sprawled on the leather settee watching the German huddled over the radio set, ballpoint poised over a pad.

'Ah!' said Helmut. 'This is it.' He leant forward with sudden concentration, turning the volume control. The sound of the incoming signal was just audible in the saloon. The German wrote steadily. Then he switched off the set and removed the earphones. He had not switched on the transmitter, nor acknowledged the signal. They knew it would be repeated three times: on the hour, and at ten and twenty minutes past.

'We go,' he said, passing the signal to his companion.

The transmission had been made on an ultra high frequency; the originator's call-sign was ZID; the message read:

Contact established Paris. Indication favourable but not conclusive. Prospect travels flight UTA-783 Nice to-morrow, thence Ibiza via Palma following day. Proceed repeat proceed Ibiza.

Helmut locked the door to the radio cabin and soon afterwards Kamros, a swarthy thickset man, brought the lunch. Dimitrio was called and the four men sat down together to eat.

Chapter Three

At the desk there was no one about so he pressed the plunger marked '*Atención.*' The *receptionista* came from the inner office and peered at him through thick lenses. '*Señor?*'

'*Puedo tener la Cuenta ... *may I have my bill?' he said. '*Numero doscientos tres.*'

'*Ah, Señor Black.*'

'*Si, señor.*'

When he'd settled the bill he said he'd call back for the raincoat and suitcase, and walked out on to the Plaza de Cataluña, into the cold air and warm sun of a spring day.

The steamer for Ibiza was not sailing until seven so he had three hours to get rid of. He did some mental arithmetic. Passengers must embark half an hour before sailing. Allow half an hour to pick up the suitcase and take a taxi down to the docks. That was one hour. And the other two? He knew Barcelona too well to go sightseeing, and anyway he wasn't in that sort of mood. He was suffering, he knew, from loneliness. If he'd had a constant companion in the last three months it had been loneliness. Humbly he realised there wasn't anyone who was missing him. Rael? Not really. There were too many other things and people in her life. Maybe she thought of him occasionally. Perhaps even with affection. The uncommitted affection of an old love long dormant. A Pompeian affair. An ancient volcano, never again to erupt.

There would be perhaps half a dozen people thinking of him professionally, wondering what he was doing, and waiting. Sharing his task vicariously, but waiting: to congratulate him if he succeeded, to repudiate him if he failed. But that was not unique to him or his situation. It applied to many people doing many things in many places.

Two hours to get rid of. He crossed the Ramblas and the bright colours of a news kiosk drew him as the flash of a kingfisher draws a fish. He read the titles. *Il Giorna, La Stampa,* the *Daily Telegraph, Kurio, La Nazione, Il Messagio, Bolero, Wochen End, Stampa Sera, ΚΥΓΡΣ, l'Humanité, Politiken,*

17

Corriere Della Sera, Tribuna Illustraka, ΧΑΡΑΥΓΗ, Life, Ya,
Newsweek, Elle, Quick, Paris Match, Der Spiegel, The Times,
Das Neue Blatt . . . Heavens, was there no end to them?

After the newspapers, the paperbacks. He compared Spanish, French, German and English titles to see if there was any
pattern of literary tastes and decided there wasn't. Presumably
they represented demand. Or did they? It was cheaper to
publish two hundred thousand of one well-known name, than
twenty thousand each of ten not so well-known names. He
flipped through the glossies, bought *Art International* and
Studio and felt good because he hadn't disappointed the tired
looking woman in the kiosk, and they were the latest numbers
and it was important he should read them.

He walked to the centre of the plaza, on to the red, white
and blue of its paved geometry, and watched the tourists
feeding the pigeons. The Plaza de Cataluña, Trafalgar Square,
St. Mark's, Times Square, St. Peter's, Notre Dame and the
rest: pigeons, tourists, seedy nut salesmen. '*Look, honey!*'
'*Oh, look, daddy!*' Photographers, cameras, cinés. '*Stay right
there, honey!*' '*Hold it!*' '*Wait till he settles, darling!*' '*Oh
poof!*' '*Gee that's lucky, I do declare!*'

Later he went up past the fountains and then down the
Metro steps to clean his shoes at the slot machine. Then up
again and across the Ronda Universidad to the café on the
corner. He chose a table where the sunlight struck through the
glass.

A waiter brought him black coffee and he stirred it un-
necessarily, looking round the room and noting on the edge of
his mind that Spaniards drank more wine and beer at that
hour than coffee and tea. The insistent clamour of traffic
drowned the speech around him and muffled his thoughts,
leaving only a visual awareness: the blue and white neon
sign on the corner, *El Corte Inglese*, beneath it a department
store; *Banco de Vizcaya* on another high building; *Venticolor
Champi* on a passing bus; and way across the Plaza, in big
letters, *Uve Pana Supiel*. But he knew he was looking for
something else that should be there. No square of importance
was without it. Like pigeons and tourists. *Coñac y Jerez*, very
nice too, but that wasn't it. *Bertola*. No. Ah, there it was . . .
Todo va Mejor con Coca-Cola. He felt reassured. The traffic
was not yet at its peak but getting that way. He started counting makes. Few big cars, mostly small, and Seat had it all the

way. Even the stream of black and yellow taxis, numerous as Smiths in a London telephone directory, were Seat. He ordered another coffee and with his mind coasting he stared at a passing girl. Their eyes met momentarily and she switched hers away, tossing her head. He grinned.

In front of him a slim smart woman knocked her glove off the table as she poured tea. He leant forward and picked it up and she turned and thanked him in Spanish, her brown eyes using the brief moment of communication to read his face.

The glove dropping wasn't intentional, he decided. But after it she was classifying him as women did. I'm no good to you, he thought. I'm not rich and I sail—he looked at his watch —in one hour and ten minutes, and I cannot be deflected from what I have to do. The waiter came across and gave him the bill. As he went out he smiled at the owner of the gloves, and with the smallest movement of eyes and lips, gravely discreet, she acknowledged him.

Back in the Regina Royale he collected the suitcase and raincoat, tipped the porter and walked out through the glass doors, waving away the commissionaire who tried to take the bag and refusing his offer of a taxi. Absurd, he thought. Why have I to use an intermediary who has to be rewarded for a service I don't require of him. He walked down the Calle de Pelayo until a taxi set down a fare near him, and he got in and told the driver to take him to the harbour, to the steamer for Ibiza. Wrapped once again in his thoughts, he sat back as the taxi pulled out into the traffic.

At the end of the warehouse the taxi stopped and he paid it off. He took the steamship ticket from his wallet and when he reached the head of the gangway showed it to an ageing bucolic sailor who blinked a '*Bueno, señor*,' at him and exuded the smell of raw wine and garlic. The cabin number was on the ticket, and he went to the foyer and then down the staircase. He stopped at the bottom and checked the arrowed numbers. Twenty-seven was at the end of an alleyway on the starboard side. It was a dingy little cabin smelling faintly of disinfectant and urine and stale vomit. Two doors down a lavatory gave off the same odours more pungently. God, he thought, I mustn't try to sleep until I'm dead tired, or drunk. A typed ticket over the right-hand bunk read *Señor Charles*

Black. He put the raincoat and suitcase on the bunk. The ticket on the other bunk read: *Señor Juan Bolle.* He wished Señor Bolle no harm but hoped he'd miss the ship.

He went up to the deck lounge. It was crowded. Mostly young people, a few old, Spaniards and foreigners in equal parts, and a sprinkling of soldiers. Some of the faces were familiar, people he'd seen on the island, but most were strangers. Not one so far whom he really knew. He bought a Campari and soda and stayed at the bar. The tables were full. Near him a young German painter he'd often seen outside the Montesol was talking quietly to a girl in a sheepskin coat, pale with unkempt flaxen hair, a baby on her arm. Wife? Girl friend? Sister? Who cared?

Next to him a young man with dark glittering eyes, tall and elegant, rolled up the left sleeve of his black jersey and caressed a hairy forearm as if it were a girl's. A red silk scarf accentuated his darkness, and the blue denims stretched tightly round his thighs were like muslin round a ham. There were two Frenchmen with him and an English girl. Their clothes, their hair and ornaments, typed them. Drop-outs, hippies, flower people, maybe junkies. But they were all right, he decided: quiet, unpretentious, unconcerned with the other passengers. *Make love not war.* They believed that. But it was pure fantasy. Everything in his experience contradicted it. The next megalomaniac who came along thinking he was God wasn't going to be bought off with flowers. I'm thirty-five, he thought, they're not much more than half that. He sighed for lost youth.

A middle-aged man and his wife came up to the bar beside him. She had calm grey eyes and a skin like alabaster. He wore a high-necked jersey, a black beret, and a necklace of shark's teeth. It was Jan Ludich, a Czech painter, and his wife. The Czech saw him and grinned. '*Hola*, Charles. *Qué tal?*'—and she said, 'Hi, Charles, where've you been?'

'*Muy bien*,' he said. 'Madrid. For de Salla's *vernissage*.'

'What was it like?'

'Good, I thought.'

'You writing something about it?'

'Yes.'

He didn't know the Ludichs well but it was pleasant to have someone to talk to. They stayed at the bar chatting until the ship had cleared the harbour and the Czechs said they were going down to their cabin before dinner. By then he'd swallowed a good many Camparis.

The steamer was feeling the wind and sea and when he got to the dining-saloon it was less than half full. He sat at an empty table laid for four and divided his attention between the *Art International* he'd bought in Barcelona, the menu, and his fellow travellers. The chief steward showed a young Spanish couple to an adjoining table. Black nodded to them briefly. Later, from their shy inhibited conversation, he gathered they were going to Ibiza for their honeymoon. In a detached way he wondered if he would ever have a honeymoon.

A steward came up with the wine, balancing the tray against the roll of the ship. Black tasted the wine and nodded, and the steward filled his glass.

The Ludichs came by and soon afterwards he heard Kyriakou's loud voice and the Greek came in, large and florid, looking like a caricature of a bookmaker, brash check suit, cigar in mouth, red carnation in buttonhole. Kirry Kyriakou interested those who didn't know him, who thought they saw a colourful personality. Those on Ibiza who knew him well feared him, for he was influential and ruthless. It was whispered—whispered because he was rich—that a recent suicide—a girl's—could be attributed to him.

With Kyriakou was a younger man, Tino Costa, a tough Cypriot recently acquired by the Greek and rumoured to be his strong-arm man. Costa was big and craggy with hooded eyes, deep-set in a rubbery face. He claimed to have been a croupier at Las Vagas before he came to the island, and spoke with a North American accent.

Predictably, the third member of Kyriakou's party was Manuela Valez, a Puerto Rican, dark, fragile and handsome. They went to a table ahead of Charles Black, and the Greek and the girl sat facing him, but his view was partially obscured by Tino Costa's broad back. Black watched them with detached irony. Everything the Greek did was flamboyant, from the way he shot inches of starched white cuff—heavily weighted with gold nugget links—to the exaggerated ceremonial as he tasted the champagne, to which Tino Costa insisted on adding vodka. Kyriakou made a fuss because there were no flowers on the table, and when the chief steward explained that it was because of the weather, he brushed this aside and demanded flowers. When the chief steward gave in and had organised them, supporting the vase with sugar bowls, the Greek flourished a snake-skin wallet, peeling crisp one hundred peseta notes from it, each coming clear with an audible *zip*, to be passed to the chief steward with a grandiose flourish. As if he were knighting him, thought Black.

Though he had not met her, Black had, during his time on Ibiza, heard the island gossip about Manuela Valez, just as she had heard that about him.

Like him she was a comparatively recent arrival, a painter of sorts. He'd seen some of her pictures and thought little of them: crude attempts at a Miro-like spideryness, unconvincing abstractions, indifferently executed. She lived in a flat in the *barrio* sa Peña on a scale which, though modest, could not have been supported by the proceeds of her painting. Some said she lived on remittances from a well-to-do father in Puerto Rico, others that she had good alimony, but the rumour favoured was that Kyriakou supported her. She admitted to being on hash and LSD, but her detractors suspected more, notwithstanding her denials, and since the Greek was thought —or so the whispers went—to be involved vicariously in drug trafficking, her dependence on him seemed logical.

Black had been on the island long enough to know that the rumours which circulated in its café society were often inaccurate, often malicious, and he wondered how much of what he'd heard was true. And it happened that Manuela Valez was at that moment thinking about him and making much the same reservations. Since she faced him, she was obliged to look at the sun-bleached Englishman with the hawkish bearded face whom she had seen at times sitting outside the Montesol, sometimes with members of the artists-writers colony and their hangers-on, but more often alone. None of her friends seemed to know him well, and in her three months on the island she had not found herself in the same party. So while she talked to Kyriakou a part of her mind recalled what she had heard about Black: that he was artistic, charming but shiftless, drank too much and existed on a modest remittance from England supplemented by the proceeds of occasional contributions to art journals.

Not surprisingly, because he was seldom seen with women, he was rumoured to be a homosexual. She wasn't interested and so didn't care, but it had occurred to her that he wasn't often seen with men either, so perhaps he just didn't like people. Which wasn't difficult for her to understand, because she wasn't at all sure she liked people. At least not those she seemed to see most of these days.

Her last thought about him was interrupted by Tino Costa who was pawing at her knee under the table. She pushed away his hand, glared at him and turned to Kyriakou who was filling the Cypriot's glass for the fourth time.

'Don't give him any more,' she said. 'He's getting above himself.'

'Wadya mean?' Tino was red-eyed and hoarse.

'You know what I mean,' she said.

He stared at her, wondering how much she'd say in front of the Greek and deciding through an alcoholic haze not to take any chances with the boss who was a mean bastard if crossed.

The moment of tension passed Kyriakou by, and he continued his story of an art-forger friend and went on pouring the champagne as if nothing had happened.

The meal proceeded with Kyriakou doing the talking while Tino sulked. Manuela listened to the Greek with half attention, while she thought of other things. Towards the end of the meal he stood up. 'You two wait here.' He dabbed at his lips with a table napkin. 'I'm going down aft to see how Benny's getting on. Back soon.'

Manuela looked sad. 'Poor Benny,' she said.

Tino Costa snorted. 'How come a guy who claims he was an Olympic swimmer, pukes his heart out for a few waves?'

'A man can't help it if he's seasick,' said Kyriakou. 'He's not God.' The Greek took Manuela's hand and with an exaggerated bow kissed it before making an exit which included handwaves, smiles and shouted 'Allo's' in several directions. Black noticed that he himself was not among the recipients. Not long afterwards Tino Costa took over the Greek's empty chair and Black saw him slant towards the girl like a toppled sack of potatoes, sliding an arm along the back of her chair and whispering hoarsely.

She drew away, but a large hand pulled her back and the whisper continued. Whatever it was he was saying, the Puerto Rican girl didn't like it. She tried to get up but he pulled her back. This time she let fly and the noise as she slapped his face was like the muted crack of a whip. Tino's mouth fell open with surprise. He swore at the girl as she pulled free and moved away from the table.

As she came abreast of where Black was sitting the Cypriot caught up with her, grabbed her arm and said, 'You goddam bitch. You don't get away with that . . .'

Black had no intention of intervening. There were good reasons why he shouldn't mix in a brawl, but when she turned to him, eyes bright with fear, and whispered, 'Please help me,' her appeal was so urgent that he got up awkwardly, hating the involvement, and said to the Cypriot: 'Cut it out, chum.' He tried to sound friendly, to keep his voice free of animus, but Costa had drunk a lot of wine and was in no mood to let this Englishman stop him dealing with a woman who had publicly insulted him.

He put his free hand on Black's shoulder and pushed him away ,and only the roll of the ship saved the Englishman from the table behind him. 'Keep outa this,' the Cypriot warned hoarsely.

Conversation in the saloon stopped, all eyes on the two men while stewards hovered nearby. But even they did not see what Black did. In a quick movement he slipped between the Cypriot and the girl and the next moment Costa let go his hold, staggered back and clapped a hand to his arm, grimacing with pain. Recovering, he moved forward and squared up to Black just as a voice from the saloon door shouted, 'Quit that, Tino!' The big man dropped his arms, looking like a dog called to heel. Kyriakou pushed into the small group, jaw out-thrust, and glowered from Manuela to Black to Tino.

The girl said, 'He tried to get fresh, Kirry. I slapped his face. Then he wanted to hit me.'

Kyriakou turned on Tino. 'You goddam sonofabitch. Put one hand on that girl and I break you in leetle pieces. Understand?'

The Cypriot shook his head. 'I didn't get fresh, boss. She got me wrong.'

'Like hell she got you wrong,' Kyriakou's eyes dilated. 'You're drunk. Get to hell out of it.' He pointed imperiously at the door.

Tino Costa's perspiring face was agitated. Kyriakou had cracked the whip, and, befuddled though he was, Tino knew he had to obey. Shaking his head, muttering, he lumbered out of the saloon. At an adjoining table a thin man with dark glasses and a christ-beard got up and followed,

Manuela looked at Charles Black and then away. 'Thank you,' she said, her breath coming in small gasps. 'You stopped him. He's crazy.' Black liked her soft foreign accent, the inflections of Caribbean Spanish with North American undertones. Somehow the way she said them, expressed more than the words she used.

He hitched his shoulders. 'It was nothing.'

But he was thinking that it might have been if Kyriakou hadn't turned up. The Cypriot wasn't all that drunk. It would have been a brawl by any standards. He didn't really doubt his ability to deal with Tino, but these things couldn't be done neatly among the tables and chairs of a swaying dining-saloon.

Kyriakou turned off his rage like a tap, and became in an instant all smiles and geniality. 'Fine, fine, old chap,' he beamed, rubbing his hands and looking round to see who was in the audience. 'So you protect my leetle Manuela. Ah. Very nice. I am so much grateful.'

'I'm not *your* Manuela,' said the girl. 'And I wish you'd keep your *friend* Costa on a leash.'

The Greek's eyes flickered but he laughed as he took Black's arm. 'Ah. She make leetle joke, hey? Come along. Join us for a dreenk. We soon forget Tino's nonsense. He take too much vodka. Make him angry.'

Black hesitated, was about to refuse, when he remembered the dingy cabin. He wasn't tired enough for that. Besides these two might have some information, however little, that could help him. The girl saw his hesitation. 'Please,' she said. 'We would like you to.'

So he accepted, saying that he would join them when he'd settled his account with the chief steward.

After that he went across. Kyriakou had unbuttoned his coat and was sitting back smoking a cigar, shirt buttons straining across the round of his stomach.

'Aha! Sit down Mister . . . ? Forgeev me. I forget.'

'Charles Black,' said the Englishman.

Kyriakou's white teeth flashed under the black moustache. 'Of course, of course. The art critic. Yes?'

Black nodded and sat down. Kyriakou beckoned to a waiter. Black ordered a *coñac*. Manuela wouldn't drink, and the Greek ordered an *Oso*.

'You know Manuela Valez?' he asked, knowing perfectly well that Black didn't.

Black smiled at her. 'Hallo,' he said.

'Hi,' she replied and her dark eyes seemed to be trying to read his mind.

The Greek was preoccupied, and Black and the girl did most of the talking. The tables emptied and the stewards hovered, until Kyriakou lifted himself out of his thoughts and said: 'What say we go to the bar?'

Black was enjoying himself. Manuela Valez was not the person he had imagined her to be. She was intelligent and sympathetic. Most of the time they discussed Ibiza and he was amused by her gossip about the Ibizencan painters and writers, and though he'd not gleaned anything new he wasn't anxious to face the disenchanting cabin. It was not long after ten, so he said, 'Yes. Good idea.'

For the next hour or so they sat at the bar. She didn't drink, but somehow they laughed a lot, and Black wasn't sorry when on two occasions Kyriakou left them for one reason or another.

It was close to midnight when the party broke up, and by then they were all on first name terms. Black looked at Manuela. 'See you to-morrow.'

'Surely,' she said, and he wondered if she meant it and found to his concern that he hoped she did.

His last thought before going to sleep was to regret the fracas in the dining-saloon. It had been stupid and undignified, and it had made him conspicuous.

Chapter Four

Soon after daybreak the ferry steamer passed Tagomago Island and started down the coast of Ibiza. Wind and sea had dropped and the sound of the bow-wave reflecting back from the calm surface of the water was like rustling paper.

Black went up on deck as they passed Santa Eulalia. It was the cold of early morning and he kept moving to warm his body, his mind occupied with what lay ahead. At first he had the deck to himself but soon other passengers appeared, among them Kyriakou and Tino Costa who went by absorbed in conversation. Kyriakou gave him a preoccupied smile and waved, but the Cypriot looked away. After that, though he hesitated to admit it, Black was looking for the girl and that this should be so annoyed him. He regretted the party of the night before. If he'd refused the Greek's invitation she would have remained no more than a name and a face. It would have been better that way, he thought, but his eyes continued to search.

The sun rose as the ship rounded Isla Grossa and headed in between the Botafoc lighthouse and the breakwater running out from La Bomba. He looked across the harbour to the waterfront where the buildings of Ibiza crowded upon each other, rising until they reached the walls of the old town. There they halted, to emerge again on the terraces of D'Alt Vila, the white of tall Moorish houses emphasising the browns and terra cottas of buildings of medieval formality. Dominating them, tall and ecclesiastical, the cathedral of Santa Maria seemed to proclaim the truth that man cannot live by bread alone. The jumble of architecture with its Moorish, Carthaginian, Gothic, Castilian, Ibizencan reminiscences, was like pages torn at random from a history book. He tried to picture the pageantry, the splendour, the savagery, the battles fought beneath the citadel walls, the Moorish raids to rape and pillage, and his thoughts became sombre—man had not changed: the obscenities of Auschwitz, Buchenwald and Theresienstadt—worse probably than anything in Ibiza's long history—the brutality of Vietnam. Was there no end to it? Was the only lesson of history that nothing was learnt from it?

Manuela's voice broke into his thoughts. 'It is beautiful, is it not?' She pointed across the water.

'Hallo. Yes. It is.' He felt an inner excitement he would have liked to repudiate, and fought it by concentrating on what she'd said. *Beautiful*. But *beautiful* is not a good word, he thought. The harbour this morning with the town above it bathed in early morning sunlight, the sky opalescent, the whole thing looking like an illustration from Hans Andersen, requires something more definitive. Just as she does. One can say *Manuela is beautiful* but it does not describe her. What does? Idiom? *Fabulous*, for example? No. Overworked superlatives lose their meaning. So what?

She saw him smile. 'Why do you smile?'

'Nothing,' he said.

'You smile for nothing?'

'Sometimes. When I feel good.'

'Have you seen them?' she asked.

'Kyriakou and Costa?'

'Yes.'

'They were on deck a few minutes ago. They went down aft.'

She touched his arm. 'I am grateful to you for last night.'

'Forget it.'

'You have made an enemy.' She said it gravely.

'Tino?'

She nodded.

'Forget him, too,' he said.

'For me that is not possible.'

He thought he knew why.

She looked uncertain. 'I think I must go to find them.'

'They'll find you.' He knew he couldn't stop himself saying it. 'Hold on for a minute.'

'You think so?'

'Sure of it. How's your friend Benny?'

'Oh, still very sick, poor chap. They say he will rest for a while before going ashore.'

'Who is he?'

'A business friend of Kyriakou's,' she said casually. 'From Beirut.'

The telegraph bells rang and the ship's engines stopped. The bow swung in towards the cross berth and a motorboat with a one man crew chugged off towing a hawser. On the quay a longshoreman threw a heaving line. The man in the motorboat caught it and secured it to the eye of the hawser, and the longshoreman hauled it up and slipped it over a bollard.

As the steamer warped in, her passengers exchanged shouted greetings with those who had come to meet them; there were waves and grimaces, gestures of pleasure, of embarrassed recognition, while the distance between ship and shore was still too great for conversation.

Manuela and Black leant on the rail watching the upturned faces, the small unfolding drama of arrival.

'Anyone meeting you?' Why, he thought, do I feel this girl's proximity so acutely?

'No. And you?'

He shook his head. 'How do you get to where you're going?'

'It is not far. Kyriakou will take me.' She looked along the deck as if expecting him.

'I see,' said Black. He'd forgotten that tie up. The night before she'd said to the Greek, 'I'm not *your* Manuela.' With surprise he acknowledged that it pleased him to remember that. While he was thinking about it, a voice inside him said, snap out of it, man, remember what you're here for. He stretched his arms and stifled a yawn. 'Well,' he said. 'So long. Be seeing you.'

As he walked away he knew that his abrupt change of manner would be inexplicable and she would be hurt. Just as well, he thought, wondering how a certain synthesis of voice and manner, of face and figure, could affect a man's judgment. And for *this* girl. A pseudo abstract painter, a Puerto Rican drop-out, tied up in some way with Kyriakou who was said to be in the drug racket. She was probably a junkie, maybe a pusher, and—he shied away from the thought but came back to it—maybe the Greek's mistress. Christ, he thought, I must be going round the bend.

Down in the cabin he collected his suitcase and raincoat and went up on deck. Stevedores were running the gangway across into the hull where water-tight doors had opened to receive it. He walked to the after end of the boat-deck and looked down at the sailors taking lashings off the cars brought from Barcelona.

Kyriakou was there with Tino. They were fussing round the

Greek's powder-blue Buick which dwarfed the small Continental and British cars around it.

There was a smell of tarred rope, of fishing nets, of oil fuel and old drains, and the noise of steam winches, of men shouting, of cars and trucks revving on the quays, the barking of a dog and, above it all, the shrill cry of seabirds fighting for offal.

Black looked up towards D'Alt Vila to see if he could identify his room. He found the El Corsario and then, below it, he thought he could make out the Massa house, and high up in it the window of his own room. Maria Massa, his landlady, would be there, misshapen by work and poverty, industrious, honest, proud. She would be swabbing the floor, the terra-cotta tiles glistening with moisture, the rooms smelling of old age and stale cooking. She would be singing sad little Spanish folk songs about work and love and childbirth and death.

He went down a companion ladder and joined the stream of passengers making for the gangway. Once ashore, he set off along the quay carrying the suitcase and raincoat. It was not far to D'Alt Vila and he felt good. The sun was warm and the smell of coffee and freshly baked bread from the cafés made him hungry. He passed the Plaza Marino Riquer, the Bar Balear, Les Caracoles and went into Can Garroves. The tables were full so he stood at the counter and ordered coffee and *ensaimadas*. While he waited a couple left a table in the window, and he went over and put his suitcase and raincoat on it. When he returned with the coffee and *ensaimadas* a woman was sitting at the table. Her back was to him but he knew it was Manuela.

For a moment he thought of going back to the counter, but she turned and saw him and it was too late. He said, 'Hallo,' and sat down.

Her 'Hi,' was subdued and the way she looked at him he knew she was thinking of his earlier abruptness.

He stirred the coffee vigorously. 'Smells good.'

'I guess so.'

'Aren't you having anything?' he said.

'The waiter has not come.'

He took a mouth of *ensaimada*. 'He's busy. What d'you want?'

'Just coffee,' she said. 'Don't worry. I can wait.'

'No,' he said. 'I'll get it.'

When he came back she thanked him and for a moment they sat in silence. Then he said, 'Waiting for Kyriakou?'

She nodded. 'You don't like him?' It was more a statement than a question. He took another mouthful of *ensaimada* and when he'd dealt with that, and the crumbs, he said, 'I haven't really thought about it.'

A small procession came down the road from the town led by a priest with a crucifix. He was followed by acolytes carrying candles. Behind them about twenty men straggled in an untidy line. The procession passed the Can Garroves and turned right, going on in the direction of the ferry steamer. To Black there was a picturesque solemnity about the cortège, a pious, infinitely patient futility.

'Wonder what all that's in aid of?' he said.

'It's a kind of funeral. They go to the ship. You will see.'

The procession halted when it reached the ferry and its members stood in a semi-circle behind the priest.

Manuela pointed. 'You see. Now they will wait for the coffin from the ship. It must be an Ibizencan coming home to be buried. It is not unusual if they die on the mainland. They are superstitious.'

Black munched away at the *ensaimada*, stopping now and then to wash it down with coffee.

The train of thought which the funeral cortège had started was interrupted by a yellow Land-Rover which drew up in front of the café. The driver wore a blue and white striped sailor's vest, blue bell-bottoms and a beret with a red pom-pom. His arms were tattooed. Next to him sat a tall thin man with white hair and dark glasses. Even from the fifty feet which separated them, Black could see the scarred face and taut unsmiling features. The driver came into the café and bought a packet of cigarettes. He went out, said something to the tall man, then climbed into the Land-Rover and they drove off.

Black looked at Manuela. 'Know who that is?'

'Of course,' said the girl. 'Van Biljon.'

'Don't often see him around.'

She nodded. 'A strange man. They say he feels rejected socially because of his face. I think he is very unhappy.'

'Burns from an air crash when he was young,' said Black.

'It must be terrible to have your face destroyed.' She shuddered. 'Poor man.'

'Poor! He's stinking rich. At least he can be miserable in comfort.'

'Do you think that is a compensation?'

'Of course. He lives in a marvellous house in the hills near San José. He's reputed to have a fabulous collection of pictures. And that boat *Nordwind*, the fastest, most comfortable thing in harbour. That's his life. Collecting pictures, fishing when he wants to. What more could a man want?'

Manuela shook her head slowly. 'Do you think that is all a man wants out of life? He lives alone. No wife. No children. Not even friends.'

'Not quite alone.' Black poured himself another cup of coffee. 'They say he has a Spanish housekeeper, her husband, and two sailors living at Altomonte. And some Alsatians. That's hardly alone.'

'What sort of company is that for a cultured man?'

'I wouldn't know,' said the Englishman. 'I've never been invited.'

'Who has? They say he never allows visitors, except an occasional government official.'

Black exhaled loudly through his nose. 'I would love to see those pictures.'

She smiled sympathetically. 'What are they?'

'No one absolutely knows. They say mostly Impressionists and post-Impressionists. Collecting them is said to have been his life's work.'

She opened her bag, took out a compact and fussed with her hair, looking critically in the small mirror. When she'd finished she drew her lips in tightly and put away the compact. She looked up and saw that he was watching her in a strange way, so she turned her head towards the harbour. His stare embarrassed her. She felt he was looking at her without seeing her. An empty strained look as if he were searching *inside* her mind rather than outside it.

Something caught her eye. 'See,' she said. 'There is the coffin.'

He looked over to the ferry steamer. A derrick had swung over the ship's side and a coffin was being lowered. On the quay waiting hands steadied it, the rope sling was removed, and the priest began his benedictions.

A few minutes later the coffin was hoisted on to the shoulders of the pallbearers. The mourners and acolytes re-formed behind the priest and the procession left the quay and made off down the road.

Manuela looked at him. 'Do you believe in an after life?'

'No,' he shook his head. 'I do not.'

'I do,' she said with an assurance he envied.

He shook his head. 'Isn't it—a monumental conceit? To believe that.'

'No,' she said. 'You see I believe that people are reincarnated in their children.'

'That's another kettle of fish,' Black said. He was thinking what a strange person she was, how different from what he'd imagined and heard. Was she a junkie? Perhaps. She was fragile. Misty eyes with heavy rings under them. At dinner in the ship she'd eaten little and only played with her champagne: discreet sips, an upset glass, and at the end a full one untouched. After dinner she'd drunk nothing but coffee.

In front of the café a car hooted stridently. It was the powder-blue Buick, with Kyriakou and Tino Costa in the front seat. The Greek waved.

'Better hurry,' said Black dryly.

She gathered up her things and went out, calling over her shoulder, 'Thanks for the coffee.' But she didn't look back, and he felt as if a thread had broken.

For some time he sat thinking about her and what they had discussed. He hadn't learnt anything. His thoughts went back to the scarred face in the Land-Rover and he recalled the local gossip about Wilhelm van Biljon: born and bred in South America where his family had gone with other refugees from the Transvaal after the Boer War; a much respected figure on the island where he had lived for many years; rich, with investments in South America and South Africa; a recluse, known for his generosity to Ibizencan causes, particularly those associated with children for whom he did much.

Looking out from the window of his room in the late afternoon of that day, Black saw a white staysail schooner coming in to Ibiza Bay. When she was opposite Talamanca her sails were lowered and she moved slowly up the harbour, a wisp of diesel smoke trailing astern. She passed behind the customs shed and when she emerged again she was nosing in towards the quay where the inter-island schooners lay. Black took the binoculars from the corner table. When she turned to come alongside he was able to read her name and port of registration. She was the *Snowgoose* of *Piraeus*.

Chapter Five

Shafts of sunlight slanted across the big office, fine particles of dust curling and turning in them like bacteria on a microscope slide.

Outside the windows, the noise of traffic along the Avenida Ignacio Wallis rose and fell and in the room the smell of exhaust gases mingled with the mustiness of dusty files and cigar smoke.

A sallow man with sharp features and iron grey hair sat behind the desk, a splash of medal ribbons relieving the severity of his dark uniform.

He contemplated the end of a cigar, turning it slowly, checking the circle of burning ash, the hard lines of his face so immobile that it seemed made of wax. The three men opposite were silent, waiting for the Comisario de Policia to speak. Two of them knew him well enough to know that he was not in a good mood.

'This morning,' he said, 'the *Jefe* sent for me. He was not pleased.' The Comisario's deepset eyes moved from one face to the other and then back to the cigar. 'He tells me that Palma and Madrid are impatient. The reputation of the island may suffer.'

He pointed to a number of clippings on his desk. 'These are articles from the foreign press which Madrid has sent him. They are about Ibiza and each tells the same story. That there is trafficking in drugs here. That it flourishes. You will say they exaggerate grossly. They do. Journalists are sensation mongers and this sort of thing,' he flicked at the clippings contemptuously, 'is news. They blow it up.'

He drew on the cigar. 'But we know, gentlemen, that there is some truth behind this news. There is *some* drug trafficking. Unless it is stopped there will be more press reports. The island will get a bad name. You know what that means?'

There were murmurs of assent but he went on, determined to answer his rhetorical question. 'It means that the tourist industry will suffer. And it is vital to our economy. It means also that we shall attract here the sort of riff-raff we do not

35

want.' He paused. 'We have enough of them already.'

He stood up and moved to the window, looking down on the street. 'The *Jefe* wants results and,' his voice rose. 'I want results, gentlemen. And I want them quickly.'

With slow deliberation he went back to the desk and lowered himself into the swivel chair. 'And now,' he said, 'your report.'

He looked towards the thin man with dark glasses and a christ-beard who was sorting through a file.

'We are making progress, señor Comisario,' he said. 'I came from Barcelona this morning. Torreta is in charge of investigations at that end. We had lengthy discussions, compared our results so far, and came to certain conclusions——'

'Such as?' interrupted the Comisario.

'The main source of supply is Beirut. The drugs are reaching Barcelona by sea. From there they come here by sea.'

'Are you sure of all this?'

'Fairly certain. We are watching a man who came over on the steamer from Barcelona last night. He travelled tourist, but he was in touch with Kyriakou and Costa during the journey. Ahmed ben Hassan is his name. He is from Beirut. The U.S. Narcotics Bureau list him as a known dealer. Also it is easier for us to check on aircraft than ships, and we have checked the aircraft thoroughly. They are not being used.'

The telephone on the Comisario's desk rang. He picked it up. 'What is it?'

In the room they could hear the distant blur of the caller's voice.

'No. No,' said the Comisario. 'Not now. I am busy.' He put the phone down and waved a hand at the thin man. 'Go on.'

'We believe that this traffic is organised here. Our difficulty is to collect hard evidence. Of the method of importing, of storing and distribution.' He inclined his head towards the two uniformed men. 'Capitan Sura and Teniente Lorenzo have identified two pushers. They are being watched and we hope they will provide leads.'

The Comisario looked up suddenly. 'Do they deal directly with Kyriakou?'

'No, señor Comisario. Not directly.'

'Indirectly then?'

'Yes.'

'You're certain that Kyriakou is at the centre?'

'Almost certain. I prefer at this moment not to be specific. But there are good indications. For example,' he hesitated. 'Banking accounts. They tell a story . . .'

The thin man seemed anxious to change the subject. He rustled the papers in his file. 'There has been,' he said, 'a new development. It concerns Kyriakou. On Friday he visited van Biljon at Altomonte.'

There was a murmur of surprise, and the Comisario abandoned for a moment his official mask of impassivity. 'Van Biljon! You suspect him?'

'Not yet,' the thin man said. 'The visit by Kyriakou stands only as a fact. Something we have observed. It is too early to draw conclusions. But it is an unusual fact. Señor van Biljon does not have visitors at Altomonte. Except occasionally,' he hesitated, 'government officials.'

The Comisario's smile was arid. 'Like me. I have been to Altomonte. I trust I am not on your list of suspects.'

The thin man's manner was deprecatory. 'Indeed, not, señor.'

'What are you doing about this. The possible relationship between Kyriakou and van Biljon?'

'Nothing at the moment. But inquiries will be made.'

The older man leant back in his chair and watched a ring of grey smoke climb towards the ceiling. 'You are circumspect in what you say.'

The thin man propped his elbows on the desk, his hands together as if he were about to pray. 'It is necessary to be discreet, señor. Our work is hampered by leakages.'

The Comisario watched him speculatively. The thin man was on loan from Madrid. 'What leakages?'

'I would prefer not to go into details.' He looked out of the window.

The moment of embarrassment was broken by the Comisario's sigh. 'I see. Very well. How long will it be before you have the hard evidence you spoke of?'

The thin man took off his glasses and wiped them. His eyes could be seen to be small and red rimmed. 'Soon, I hope. We have the problem that people who could give us information will not come forward because they are afraid.'

The Comisario picked up a brass paperweight and balanced it on the back of his left hand. 'But nevertheless you say soon.'

'Yes. There has been an important breakthrough.'

'Perhaps you will tell us about it?' The Comisario watched him through a screen of smoke.

The Capitan shrugged his shoulders and fidgeted with his beard. 'Later, if you please, señor.'

The grey-headed man turned to the two uniformed officers. They were members of his own staff. 'Well, gentlemen,' he said. 'Thank you. That will be all for the present.'

There was a scraping of chairs as they got up to go. 'Not you, Capitan.' He held up his hand, his eyes on the thin man. 'There is another matter I would like to discuss with you.'

When the others had left the room the Comisario turned to him. 'Well, Capitan. Can you tell me now?'

The Capitan placed his fingertips together gently, as if they were fragile, looking towards the door through which the others had gone. 'I am certain Sura and Lorenzo are reliable. It is, however, a condition of the co-operation we receive from the U.S. Narcotics Bureau that I do not divulge information concerning their agents' identity or activities.'

He paused and cleared his throat. 'But I can say for your confidential information, señor, that the agent here has had much difficulty in penetrating the organisation, in becoming accepted. But progress is being made. It is for this reason we hope soon to have hard evidence.'

The Comisario stared at the thin man as if he were trying to read his mind. Then he drew on his cigar. 'Thank you. I hope you will not be disappointed.' He looked at his watch. 'Is there anything else you can tell me? I have to report to the *Jefe*.'

'Yes,' said the thin man. 'We are watching a woman, Manuela Valez, and a man, Charles Black. She is a Puerto Rican artist and has been much in Kyriakou's company lately. The other is an Englishman. An art critic of sorts. His movements have . . . well, how shall I say . . . made us feel we should know more about him.'

'Do these two know each other?'

The thin man stroked his beard. 'They have either just met —last night on the ferry steamer to be exact—or they are good actors. It is not yet possible to say.'

It was a fine day, the air still cold, the sun shining from a clear sky. It is a pity, he thought, that the drains smell so foul. And it is probably unnecessary. Somewhere they are blocked and it should not be impossible to clear them. The Spaniards are a fine people, a proud, intensely human race, but why do they accept foul smelling drains and rancid butter and bacon with such unnecessary stoicism. He turned into Calle Abel Matutes and went into the Spar where he bought sardines, butter, eggs, cheese and spaghetti and put them in the basket which hung from his shoulder.

The olives and tunny he would get at the market, the wine at Anselmo's, the bread at the *pasteleria*, but first he would see Haupt. He joined the queue by the cashier. His turn came. She checked his purchases, tapping the amounts on to the cash register, gave him the slip and he paid. Outside he turned right and then left and went down the pavement past the travel agency where he turned into a narrow lane. Half-way along it he stopped before a door which had on it a board inscribed 'Haupt & Diene, Architects.' He went up the stairs to a small general office where he spoke in Spanish to a thin red-eyed girl who took his name and asked him to wait.

A few minutes later she came back and beckoned him to follow. At the end of a short passage she knocked, opened a door and said, 'Señor Charles Black,' before ushering him in and closing the door behind him.

A pallid man of middle age with tired friendly eyes left the drawing board where he'd been working, came across and held out his hand.

'*Buenos dias, señor*,' he said, and Black realised that the man's Spanish was poor.

'Mr. Haupt?' he inquired in English.

'Yes. Can I help you?' Haupt spoke with a Dutch accent.

'I hope so. It is a professional matter.'

Haupt looked at him uncertainly, then smiled and pointed to the desk. 'Please.' He pulled out a chair. Black sat down and Haupt took the chair on the other side of the desk.

'Are you a visitor, Mr. Black?'

'I've been here nearly two months.'

'On holiday?'

'No. I write.'

'Oh. Very interesting. There are many writers here.'

'So I believe.'

Haupt searched a drawer and found a crumpled packet of cigarettes. He held it out to Black. 'Smoke?'

'No, thanks. I don't.'

Haupt laughed. 'Me, neither.' He put the packet back into the drawer.

'I've had a letter from an old friend—a close friend,' Black corrected himself. 'He is in England. Likes Ibiza. Wants to retire here. He has asked me to make inquiries about a house.'

Haupt showed interest. 'I see. What sort of house? I mean, big or small?' With his hands he illustrated the alternatives of size.

'Big. He's a rich man.'

'He wishes to build,' Haupt suggested.

'In a way. He's keen on buying a *finca* and converting. A large one. He'll want a lot put into it. Several bathrooms, central heating, guest suites, big reception rooms. That sort of thing.'

Haupt frowned. 'Has he seen an estate agent? Is it a particular *finca* he has in mind?'

'No. He wants to be outside Ibiza, but within ten kilometres of the town. He's left it to me to find out what's available and what conversion costs are likely to be. He's coming here in June. Wants me to do the spade work before he arrives.'

'And you wish me to . . . ?' Haupt paused.

'Give me an idea of what conversion might cost.'

Haupt held out his hands in a gesture of futility. 'Impossible! I must know the *finca* and what has to be done. It could be anything. Half a million pesetas. A million. Two million, anything.'

'I'm told you've already done the conversion of a big *finca* on a . . .' Black sought for words. 'A very generous scale.'

'You mean Altomonte?'

'I am not sure of the name. Does it belong to a man called van Biljon.'

Haupt nodded. 'That is Altomonte.'

'I am told it is a magnificent conversion.'

Haupt gave a little bow. 'Thank you.'

'I gather,' said Black, 'that van Biljon doesn't permit visitors. No chance of my getting to see it, I suppose?'

'None at all,' said Haupt. 'If there was I would offer to arrange it for you.'

Black came straight to the point. 'What did that conversion cost?'

Haupt thought for a moment. 'That was more than ten years ago. To-day it would cost—let me see,' he pencilled figures on a note pad. 'About four million pesetas.'

Black did some mental arithmetic. 'Nearly twenty-four thousand pounds. That's a lot of money.'

'A lot of work was done. It was exceptional.'

'It must have been an interesting job.'

'Marvellous.' Haupt's tired eyes shone momentarily. 'Expense was no object. Van Biljon was the perfect client. He knew basically what he wanted, but left the interpretation to me. Gave me a free hand. It was fabulous.'

'This could be, too,' said Black. 'My friend in England is like that. He knows what he wants. Is prepared to pay for it and wouldn't interfere. Anyway, he's far too busy. He might fly out occasionally to see how things are going, but you'd have a free hand if you got the job.' Black took out his notebook and pencil and wrote, *Altomonte, conversion, 4,000,000 pesetas*. He left the notebook open and laid the pencil on it.

'I think,' he said, 'it would help if we took Altomonte as an example.'

Haupt hesitated. 'I don't follow.'

'Well, if I could see the plans and discuss them with you. Get some idea of what the *finca* was like originally, and what you made it into. And perhaps some of the main items of cost. That will give me something definite to work on.'

Haupt's first reaction was to refuse firmly but courteously to produce the plans. He explained that it would be unprofessional, that van Biljon would never forgive him if he knew that they had been used to do business with a third party. Van Biljon, he said, owned a good deal of property in Ibiza, and apart from any other consideration Haupt could not afford to fall out with him.

Black pointed out that there was no question of copying the Altomonte design, that it was to be used only for purposes of discussion, and that he would under no circumstances reveal that he had seen the plans, not even to his friend in England.

He appealed to Haupt to help him settle the matter in such a way that he would not be obliged to go to another architect. 'You know, having heard what a marvellous job you did on Altomonte, I'm particularly anxious to see you get this.'

Slowly Haupt gave ground and before long locked the door to his office, produced the plans and spread them on a table by the window. For the next hour the two men sat over them, Black making rough notes of layout and cost. By the time he was ready to leave they were on good terms, and they had agreed to treat the matter as strictly confidential.

'I'll write off to him in the next day or so. Then it's over to him,' said Black. 'Shouldn't be surprised if he flies out by way of reply. That's if he's not in New York or Tokyo or somewhere. He's always on the move.'

Haupt expressed his thanks and showed him to the top of the stairs.

Black went down the lane whistling, pleased with the morning's work. As he reached the square and turned right to cross to Anselmo's he saw a big man with a deeply tanned face come up from the opposite pavement and stop outside the entrance. The moment he saw the face, Black's nerves reacted like a triggered electronic alarm. Stepping behind a Volkswagen, he bent down, put his foot on the rear bumper and fussed with his shoelaces. Through the rear window he watched the man opposite, saw him stand in the doorway, hesitate for a moment, then go into Anselmo's.

The Englishman was trembling and it was, he knew, the response to both shock and relief: shock that Ahmed ben Hassan of all people in the world should be on Ibiza at that moment, and relief that the Arab had not seen him. Standing behind the Volkswagen, his mind spewed out thoughts with the speed of a computer: if Hassan recognised him it would soon be known in Ibiza who he really was. In no time the information would reach van Biljon and then all ZID's carefully laid plans, all the work of past years—particularly of the last eight months—would lie in ruins.

There were, he knew, two alternatives, but each was equally difficult to contemplate. Either the operation must be called off or Hassan removed—from Ibiza at any rate. How that could be done he hadn't the vaguest idea. But if there was one imperative it was that he should know where Hassan was staying. Translating the thought into action, he moved from the Volkswagen and took up a position on a side street pavement from which he could watch the entrance to Anselmo's. He leant against the wall, shielded by a truck, pretending to read the newspaper he'd taken from the shopping basket, and while he waited his mind went back to the night in Rafah. His company had been parachuted in at dusk with orders to cut off any motorised elements which tried to escape along the coast road. After the drop there had been virtually no opposition. Some of his men had rounded up gangs of demoralised prisoners who threw away their weapons, while others prepared fighting positions. Then they had sat down to wait for an enemy who failed to materialise, and for their own tanks and infantry which were expected some time after midnight. At about ten o'clock, two of his men had brought in a big, handsome, but very frightened Arab. He'd been found in civilian clothes, hiding in a deserted house. He had denied that he was an Egyptian or indeed any sort of fighting man, but in view of his lack of papers and evasive answers he'd been brought in for interrogation. 'Terrorist or political agent,' the young Israeli sergeant had said with withering finality.

You did not, reflected Black, forget the face of a frightened man you'd been watching at close range under a bright light for over an hour. He could recall every moment of that torrid interrogation in the hot stuffy room which had smelt so overpoweringly of stale sweat. He himself tired, suffering from nervous exhaustion, frustrated and worried because he'd damaged his ankle in the drop—and the big Arab, older than he, frightened, even terrified at times, pleading that he was a civilian caught by chance in Rafah through the fortunes of war which had started only the day before. He was, he claimed, Ahmed ben Hassan, a merchant from Beirut, but he had no papers of any sort to support this. The Egyptian soldiers he said, had beaten him up and taken his wallet—in it all his papers—before they cleared out of Rafah. With pathetic dignity he had showed them his bruises. He had, he said, come to Rafah by way of Cyprus and Port Said, and had only been in Port Said because business had taken him there, not for any love of the Egyptians. As to the precise nature of that business he had been equivocal, until Black had worn him down with threats of violence. Threats of which, in normal times, the Englishman would have been ashamed but which, in those circumstances, at that time, in the heat and clamour of war, he supposed he might well have carried out. One never knew. But Hassan had broken then, admitted that he was a dealer in currency and hasheesh—a spiv to be explicit—and it was that which had brought him there, and taken him to Cyprus and Port Said.

In that long hot hour of interrogation Black had become almost resentfully aware of a growing pity for the man who stood before him, frightened, helpless, and alone. Indeed, towards the end, he had even been conscious of a sort of kinship, as if each was wistfully aware that in other circumstances they might have been friends, that the confrontation was a product of forces which had not been of their seeking. But he had fought down these feelings and when soon after midnight forward elements of the infantry had driven into Rafah with the tanks, Black had handed the Arab over to an officer in military intelligence—and that was the last he had seen of him, or indeed even thought of him, until a few minutes ago outside Anselmo's.

And so his thoughts came back to the present—Ahmed ben Hassan in Ibiza. For Christ's sake! Just as he could never forget the man's face, he had no doubt Hassan could never forget his. He thanked his stars that he now wore a beard and decided that as from that moment he would never fail to wear his dark glasses. But if he were to meet Hassan face to face, to be in his company for even a few minutes, he had no doubt he would be recognised—a voice was something which could not be disguised, and a voice that had for more than an hour interrogated you, threatened you with torture and death—and all less than twelve months before—was not one that was likely to be forgotten.

Black got back to his room that night in a state of exhaustion brought on by the physical energy he'd expended in shadowing Ahmed ben Hassan through most of the day, and the nervous strain which this new and unexpected complication had engendered. But at least the shadowing had paid useful dividends.

He had followed him down to a pension, Vista Mari, on the Figueretes side of Los Molinos and then, after a long afternoon during which the Lebanese had not emerged—and when Black was about to leave in the belief that his quarry must have gone out through a back door—he had seen Hassan come out. He had changed into blue cotton slacks and a T-shirt, and a bathing towel hung round his neck. Keeping well behind, Black had followed him up over Los Molinos and down past the military hospital. From a safe distance he had watched Hassan go to the end of the rocks where he had divested himself of the T-shirt and slacks, to reveal a powerful

44

muscular body clad in bathing trunks. The Arab had then pulled on a white rubber skullcap and dived into the sea.

He was a strong swimmer and with long powerful strokes and rhythmically beating feet, he had set out for the big rock which stood out massively several hundred yards from the shore. There was a strongish breeze from the north-east and Black could not help admiring how Hassan headed boldly into wind and sea with what seemed little effort.

The Englishman shivered. The sun was low in the sky and the wind cold. There were no other swimmers and he was not surprised, it was too late in the afternoon and too early in the year. When he judged that Hassan was half-way towards the big rock, Black went on down the slope to the kiosk. He greeted the Ibizencan bar-tender, who was packing up for the night, and ordered a *coñac*.

'He must be tough,' he said to the Ibizencan, gesturing with his head in the direction where Hassan could be seen swimming out to the rock. 'It is cold.'

'*Si, señor*. But he swims at this time every evening.'

'Every evening?' said Black doubtfully.

'*Si, señor*. Around that big rock. At least for the last few days. He is a visitor from the Lebanon. Sometimes he talks to me. A strong man with a fine body. Says he swims every day of his life when he is home. A friendly fellow, but he does not drink because he is a Moslem.' The bar-tender shook his head sorrowfully.

'Well,' said Black. 'It is cold. I must be moving. *Adiós*.'

'*Adiós, señor*,' said the barman as Black moved away and started up the path away from the kiosk. He had not gone far when he turned and looked back. Hassan was no longer in sight and Black realised that he must be on the seaward side of the big rock.

It was only then, while he waited for him to re-emerge, that Black realised—suddenly and with terrifying certainty—that Kyriakou and Manuela's friend 'Benny' in the ferry steamer, the Olympic swimmer who suffered from seasickness, was Ahmed ben Hassan. Hassan a colleague of Kyriakou's! Black felt a tightening of his stomach muscles and then, while he was still tussling with the implications of this discovery, he saw the white rubber skullcap round the eastern corner of the rock and Hassan, wind and sea now behind him, came swimming shorewards. Deciding that he had seen enough for

45

the day, Black set off up the steep path, making for the tunnel in the Citadel walls through which he could reach D'Alt Vila.

In his room that night he sat grappling with the new and potentially disastrous complication. At nine o'clock Maria Massa knocked on the door and inquired if he was not going down to the town to have something to eat, as was his custom. He told her he had a headache, and refused her offer to prepare something. 'All I need,' he said, 'is a cup of tea and I'll make that myself. *Muchas gracias, señora.*'

And she had gone away querulous and dissatisfied, to leave him alone with his problem.

In the end he came to the conclusion he'd known he'd have to in the beginning: that this was essentially a task for Werner Zolde and André Lejeune. He was too well known in Ibiza, in too exposed a position—and entirely without the facilities *they* had—to deal with Hassan. It was for them. He would make suggestions, and if these were not practical—well, it was up to them. With the means at their disposal there were various alternatives. But there were two imperatives now— Hassan had to be removed from the scene, and it had to be done quickly and with discretion.

He took up a pen and paper and wrote the letter to Werner Zolde, telling him that Hassan was on the island, explaining who he was and the threat he represented. He was, wrote Black, to be removed and kept out of Ibiza, at least until the project had been accomplished. He mentioned that Hassan was staying at Vista Mari, the pension at Figueretes, that he apparently swam from the rocks below the military hospital every evening about six, swimming round the big rock. Black suggested the scheme he had in mind, but stressed that what was done finally was for Werner Zolde to decide and that in any event the utmost discretion was necessary.

I will, wrote Black, *call at the post office each day. If you have any message for me post it c/o Lista de Correos. I must know as soon as you have completed your task, for until then I cannot continue with the project.* He folded the letter, which was without the sender's address or signature, and placed it in an envelope. He had written *Werner H. Zolde* on it, when he stopped and frowned. 'Christ,' he muttered desperately. 'What a silly bloody mistake. I must be crazy.' He tore the envelope into small pieces, took a fresh one and wrote on it *H. W. Liebson, Lista de Correos, Ibiza.* Then he took a stamp from his wallet and stuck it on the envelope. Soon after ten o'clock he went down to the post office and dropped the letter into the box.

When he got back to his room, tired as he was, he studied the plan of Altomonte which he'd made from the notes taken in Haupt's office.

Chapter Six

The light from the shaded lamp spilled across the desk, throwing into relief the bony white hands holding the letter. They were ghostlike, their roots lost in the cuffs of the black velvet smoking jacket.

The hands folded the letter slowly, began replacing it in the envelope, hesitated, and then carefully, methodically, tore it into small pieces, dropping them into the wastepaper basket.

In one movement the hands clicked off the desk light and switched on wall lights which brought their owner to life, as when a dark scene on a stage is suddenly illuminated. The man stood up, tall and straight, his hair silken white, the weathered face sun-tanned, the folds of the scars exaggerated by the shadows, the dark glasses reflecting the lights on the walls. He walked stiffly, age inhibiting movement, making for the chair in the corner. Before he reached it there was a knock on the door. He stopped, turned, and called, '*Adelante!*' The door opened and a man came in carrying a tray, the silver coffee set and crystal glass and decanters throwing back the lights of the room in kaleidoscopic patterns.

'*Son las diez, señor,*' said the servant. 'It is ten o'clock.'

The old man looked at his watch and a moment later the clock on the desk chimed ten. '*Bueno, Juan,*' he said.

The ritual never changed. He dined at nine, alone, after which he came to the study. At ten o'clock, Juan would knock on the door and enter with the coffee and liqueurs. Always he would announce, '*Son las diez, señor,*' always van Biljon would look at his watch and say, '*Bueno,*' always the desk clock would chime the hour. But the ritual never palled. It was the moment of the day to which he looked forward most, the one he enjoyed above all others.

Juan stood inside the door, immobile, impassive, holding the tray. The old man paused, looked round the study and then, lifting his head and jerking his chin forward, he walked stiffly from the room, along the passage, down through the sitting-room to the hall and up stone steps to the patio. At its centre a swimming pool shimmered with reflected light and along three sides vines climbed and twisted on pergolas.

Followed by his servant, he started across the patio keeping to the left of the pool which was flanked by the two wings of the house, their white sides studded with windows.

The old man stopped before a wrought-iron door, drew keys from his pocket, unlocked first the iron door, then the heavy wooden one behind it, and stepped inside. As he turned on the switches the dark abyss of the gallery glowed into life. For a moment he stood still, accustoming his eyes to the light, then went in, closing the doors behind him. Juan followed, carrying the tray.

At the far end of the long room a leather settee and armchairs stood in a recess furnished with low tables, a tall glass-fronted bookcase, a writing-desk, and two cabinets on elegant brass-shod legs.

The tall man stood watching while the servant placed the tray on a table before the settee, lit the lamp under the coffee percolator, and transferred the decanter and liqueur glass to the table. With an almost imperceptible bow, he withdrew from the recess and went up the gallery, closing the double doors as he left.

The old man walked over to the bookcase, opened a drawer and took from it a cedarwood cabinet. He spent some time choosing a cigar, preparing and lighting it. After drawing on it he examined the line of burning ash and, satisfied, stood for some time, legs apart, arms folded across his chest, head sunk, deep in thought until the cough and splutter of the percolator alerted him.

He sighed, shook his head as if in disagreement with his thoughts, and moved to one of the cabinets. Opening it, he selected a record, drew it from its sleeve and, sliding aside the lid of the second cabinet, placed the record on the turntable. He started the player, adjusted it for tone and volume, and returned to the armchair. Then he held a coffee cup under the tap of the percolator, filled it, and drew the stopper from the decanter, holding it beneath his nose for a moment before pouring the brandy in a thin translucent stream.

The room filled with the mosaic of a Debussy prelude, and the old man leant back in the chair, legs outstretched, his head resting on its back, his arms upon its sides. As his muscles relaxed, he felt the tiredness leave his body and his mind emptied. For several minutes he lay still, sublimated, before leaning forward to taste the coffee and liqueur.

The clock on the desk marked the quarter hour with a single chime. It was the signal to begin the tour of the gallery. He followed always an unchanging route, stopping to admire one picture, examining closely another.

At times he would stand before a picture, arms folded across his chest, cigar smoke gathering about his head, lost in the thoughts it evoked.

The clock on the desk chimed eleven soon after he'd left the last picture and gone back to the recess. From the bookcase he took an art catalogue and from the table a copy of *The Connoisseur*. He switched on a reading lamp, the red shade gleamed and its light suffused the armchair into which he dropped.

At eleven-thirty there was a knock on the door. It was Juan to announce the time, replace the coffee cup, decanter and liqueur glass on the tray and lift it from the table.

His master sighed, struggled out of the chair, returned the catalogue to the bookcase, the magazine to the table, and began a stiff-legged walk to the gallery doors. The servant went out first, the old man switched off the lights, closed the doors, locked them and pocketed the keys.

Then, with Juan following, he crossed the patio, keeping to the left of the pool, and descended the long flight of steps to the main house. Inside, Juan placed the tray on a side table and followed his master across the hall to the sitting-room in the west wing; there he stood at the foot of the stairs, impassive and sentry-like, as the old man went up them. Juan followed, closing the heavy iron gates on the landing against his master who locked them on the inside, their trellised patterns casting weird shadows on his scarred face.

'*Buenas noches, Juan*,' he called through the gates, and the servant answered, '*Buenas noches, señor*.'

So ended, as always, the ritual of Hendrik Wilhelm van Biljon's after-dinner visit to the gallery at Altomonte.

Chapter Seven

It was a grey day and from his room in the old town Black looked down on the harbour and saw the wind whip the smoke from the funnels of the steamers at the quays and blow it in rippling swathes across the water to Talamanca, the sea beyond the breakwater tumbling and boiling in distant turmoil.

He grumbled as he put on his socks. His mood needed a fine day, calm with warm sun and blue sea and sky. He pulled on slacks and a heavy woollen jersey, hung a basket over his shoulder, locked the door and went down the stairs. Maria Massa was singing in the kitchen. He stopped and they talked in Spanish. He asked after the children and told her it was time she found a husband, and she laughed toothlessly and said she'd had one and that was enough and a new one would only give her more babies to struggle for and worry about. Silently reproaching the Pope, he reached the lane.

He went along it, turned into Calle Pedro de Tur and carried on past the Plaza de España, the school and seminary, following the sharp turns of Calle General Balanzat into the Avenida del General Franco.

As he passed the glass and picture shop he looked in to see if the dark girl was there. She was. He waved and saw her laugh, but she didn't wave back.

He felt more cheerful and when he reached the *pavé* and the descent became steeper he began to whistle *Colonel Bogey*. His stride lengthened and in his mind he saw Alec Guinness at the head of the tattered battalion.

A group of children playing in the street called to him and he answered and told them to be good and obey their mothers, and when he'd passed they turned to watch him go and then, with a burst of laughter, went on with their games. He followed the cobbled road where it wound through one hundred and eighty degrees towards El Portal de Las Tablas, past La Carbonera, the Bodega D'Alt Vila, the Vitoria Bar, and the Sandal Shop. Each reminded him of something or someone. There were few bars in Ibiza he'd not visited. He turned right, passed through the gate and went down the ramp, turning into Calle Antonio Palau when he reached the market.

There was in the air that smell of recently baked bread and freshly ground coffee beans which he could never resist, so he stopped on the corner at the Bar Maravilla and drank coffee and ate *ensaimadas* and felt refreshed. It was after ten when he reached the post office and joined the *lista de correos* queue. Two American girls ahead of him talked incessantly and he listened in a casual offhand way, wondering who and what they were. In front of him a young German, tall with flaxen hair and broad leather-jacketed shoulders, shook his head in disbelief when the clerk said there was nothing for him. What was he expecting, wondered Black. Love letter, editorial slip, remittance? That was the most important mail for many on the island. It was difficult to be a drop-out for long if there wasn't a patron somewhere in the background: a parent, a lover, a mistress, a family firm. It didn't matter so long as the remittance came. There was no mail for him, so Black went out into the Paseo Vara de Rey, looking uncertainly up and down the street and then set off towards the telegraph office. Beyond it, outside the curio shop, he saw Werner Zolde leaning against the wall reading a letter. As he passed him, the German gave an affirmative nod. Black did not stop, nor did he acknowledge the other man, but he knew his letter had been received, its contents understood, that it would be acted upon expeditiously.

While he shopped he thought about the time-table. It was the twenty-seventh—three more weeks. Now that the time for action was approaching he felt a keying up, an apprehension, heightened by the unexpected presence of Hassan on Ibiza, which he'd not experienced for a long time. He was tired of acting a part and feared that somehow both his health and resolve might weaken if he played it too long. Not only had he to remain physically fit for what lay ahead, but he had to be psychologically tough. And that sort of fitness and toughness was difficult in a soft environment.

After posting the letter to Werner Zolde he had spent a good deal of the previous night studying the plan of Altomonte made from the notes taken in Haupt's office. The gallery *was* in the west wing. The lights there had gone on at ten o'clock. Was that a pattern or was it variable? Better to assume it was variable. The thing was to get into the house. It was difficult, probably impossible, to do it alone. He would need assistance. He thought of Manuela. He knew she liked him. Why, he couldn't imagine. Perhaps she just liked people. She liked Kyriakou and he was a creep if ever there was one. But he was rich, and there were the drugs. If she were hooked, there was the explanation, ugly and uncomplicated. He couldn't imagine why he felt bitter about that. He tried to laugh it off and knew he wasn't succeeding and felt diminished. Surely to God he couldn't allow himself to be influenced by this girl he didn't know, whose only claim on him was that he had responded reluctantly to a cry for help because a drunken Cypriot had made a pass at her.

But since there was not much time left he would have to see something of her in the next few weeks if he was going to use her. He realised that this was in a sense special pleading, but he intended to be objective and methodical about what had to be done and, as to her, he had no conscience. The means would justify the end. That covered a multitude of sins.

Towards noon he made for the Montesol. As he crossed the *paseo* he saw her at a table with Kyriakou, Ilse Berch—a young Norwegian artist he'd met before—and a young man, bearded and scruffy, whom he didn't know. He left the *paseo*, crossed over by the Cine Serra and turned back along the pavement. When he reached the tables outside the Cristal and the Alhambra he slowed down and stopped once or twice to greet people, his senses keyed and alert, his eyes searching ceaselessly for Hassan.

He had chosen a route which would ensure that Manuela saw him as he neared her table. The strategy succeeded. She smiled and when he waved a hand in acknowledgement she called 'Hi.' Kyriakou turned, switched on a big smile and said, ' 'Allo there, Charles.'

Nodding to the Greek, Black stopped at the table. 'Hallo, Ilse. Hallo, Manuela,' he said.

'You busy?' asked Ilse Berch. 'Writing?'

He patted his bulging basket. 'Shopping.'

'You should have a wife.' Kyriakou winked at the Norwegian girl.

Manuela pointed to the empty chair next to her. 'Sit down.'

Black looked at her, thought how handsome she was, and

smiled with a pleasure he made no effort to conceal. Kyriakou pushed himself back in his chair and aimed his cigar at the untidy young man. 'You know George?'

Black shook his head.

'George Madden,' said Kyriakou describing a figure of eight with the cigar. 'Charles Black.'

Madden said 'Hi,' and Black nodded a response, wondering if this pallid-faced, pouchy-eyed young American was one of the Greek's pushers.

A waiter came to the table.

'What you like?' asked Kyriakou.

Black had been long enough on Ibiza to know that one paid for one's own drinks under these circumstances. He shook his head. 'Thanks. But I'll buy my own.'

Kyriakou shrugged his shoulders and with his teeth tilted the cigar. Black ordered a *coñac*. Manuela was drinking orange juice. Junkies drink soft, a part of his mind nagged. Why the hell shouldn't she, the other replied.

The conversation became general. Ilse Berch wanted to know how things were in Madrid, and what de Salla's *vernissage* had been like. She'd just got back from seeing her parents in Bergen. They still didn't approve of her way of life.

'Why worry,' said Kyriakou. 'As long as you approve, what the hell.'

Black saw him nudge Manuela. 'What you say, leetle one?'

'I don't say,' said Manuela.

Kyriakou slapped his thigh. 'Ha, aha, ha.'

'Very funny,' said Black.

The Greek saw that the Englishman was not amused. 'What's that?' he said leaning forward, his white teeth gleaming. 'You no like, hey?'

Black shook his head. 'On the contrary. I think you're very funny.' He saw Manuela's eyes signalling him to be careful. When he winked back he realised that the Greek had seen the private exchange and wasn't pleased.

Adroitly Manuela changed the subject to de Salla's painting, and that led to a general discussion on art. Black steered it round to the Impressionists and the post- and neo-Impressionists, and the level of discussion rose over the heads of George and the Greek. It was left to Black and the two girls to fight out his thesis that contemporary art owed its greatest debt to those who had first departed from solid form and the subservience of the eye. Then, when the argument was at its height, it shifted suddenly to hilarity and Kyriakou and George Madden came into their own again.

But Black had introduced the subject with a purpose he'd no intention of abandoning. 'You know,' he said, frowning as he thought about how to get the thing going. 'We sit here and talk about these things. Yet I'm prepared to bet that not one of us has seen what is—' he looked round, pausing for effect. 'What's believed to be one of the finest private collections of Impressionists and post-Impressionists in Europe. And it's here. On Ibiza.' He thumped the table for emphasis.

'You mean van Biljon's?' said Ilse Berch.

'Yes.' He leant forward, challenging one face after another. 'Have any of you seen it? Any of you?'

None of them had.

'Nor has anyone else,' he said.

Manuela watched him curiously over the rim of her glass.

'Perhaps the pictures don't exist.'

He shook his head. 'They exist all right. Most of them are internationally catalogued. In the dealer world they've a pretty shrewd idea what he's got.'

'Why d'you get so—so, what can I say, *hit up*?' Ilse Berch arched her eyebrows.

Black realised that he'd raised his voice and was using his hands. 'I'm not hit up. I'm . . .' he laughed with embarrassment. 'I'm indignant. I'd give anything to see that collection but I haven't a hope. Not only does he not show it to anyone, but he hates the guts of art critics. Journalistic or otherwise.'

'Maybe he's got something there,' said Kyriakou.

Black looked at him for a moment, was about to be rude, but changed his mind. 'There are two art journals badgering me for articles on that collection. They'd pay me a packet if I could send them what they want. Photos, interviews with van Biljon, the lot.'

'Aha. So that's it,' said Kyriakou waving his cigar. 'Our old friend lolly. So you are a materialist after all. Not an artist.'

'He's got to live,' said George Madden lugubriously. It was his first constructive contribution.

'Why?' said Kyriakou. 'It's not compulsory.'

'It's more than money,' said Black. 'No man should keep a collection like that to himself. Those pictures belong to everyone. Just as much as great music and literature. Van

Biljon is their temporary custodian. Nothing more. Unless they're seen by others their existence is meaningless. I don't know van Biljon, but he must be pathologically selfish.' He realised that he had raised his voice again, for at the next table the thin man with dark glasses and a christ-beard looked up from the crossword puzzle he was doing. The Englishman remembered having seen him in the ferry steamer a few days before.

Manuela put down her glass with a clatter. 'I don't really know van Biljon either, but I think you misunderstand his motives. It is his face. He's scared of people. He's a recluse.'

Black waved away her statement with his hands.

'He could open the gallery to the public occasionally. Hide himself away? They tell me it's a big house.'

'All right,' said Manuela. 'So he's a crank. He doesn't want to meet people. He doesn't want them at Altomonte. Maybe he values his privacy above everything. Why not if he wants it that way? It's his life. His house. His pictures.'

Black looked at her in genuine surprise. 'Don't you see it as an almost criminal act of selfishness?'

'No. Not at all.' She leant forward, stabbing in his direction with her comb. 'He's not selfish. They say he is fabulously generous. Especially for anything to do with children. They say he is wonderful with them. You know why?'

Black shook his head, half smiling at her earnestness.

'Because,' she went on, 'children like a person for what he is. They see the scars but they don't mind. They know what's behind them. Children and dogs. They can always tell.'

'Manuela,' Black said it slowly, breaking the name into syllables, shaking his head in good natured disbelief. 'You don't really believe that, do you?'

'About dogs and children?'

'Yes.'

'Of course I do.'

'Amazing,' he said.

'Not at all.' She wiggled her eyebrows. 'And anyway you're not listening to me,' she added indignantly.

'How can you say that?'

'Because you keep looking round as if you're expecting somebody. Are you?' she challenged.

'No,' he said. 'I'm just curious. Half the fun of sitting in front of the Montesol is to watch the characters go by.' But she was right, and he resolved to be more careful.

Kyriakou jiggled his cigar about in his mouth, hooked his thumbs in his braces, and leant back in his chair.

Ilse Berch said: 'You've met van Biljon haven't you, Manuela?'

'Once,' she said. 'For about two minutes. At the airport. He dropped his ticket and I picked it up. We spoke a little. He was shy, but he was sweet to me. I think he's a sad man.'

'For Chrissake!' Kyriakou pushed his feet forward and tipped the straw hat over his eyes. 'You'll make me cry. Let's talk about something different.'

Manuela said, 'Like what?' Black sensed her irritation.

'Anything,' said Kyriakou. 'Wine. Women . . . or whatever.'

'Drugs,' suggested Black. For an instant the Greek's facial muscles contracted but he gave no other indication of having heard the remark.

'There's only one subject which interests him,' said Manuela.

'What's that?' Ilse Berch rattled the ice cubes in her empty glass.

'*Mister* Kyriakou,' said Manuela.

The Greek jerked himself and the chair back into an upright position and took the cigar out of his mouth. 'You wanna be careful what you say, baby.' The way he looked at her, the menacing voice, made Black believe all he'd heard of him.

Manuela must have realised she'd gone too far. 'I'm sorry, Kirry,' she touched his arm. 'I didn't mean it. But you were being lousy. I said it to hurt. I'm sorry.'

'Okay,' said the Greek giving her a long hard look. 'I'm glad . . . for your sake.'

Ilse Berch tried to gloss things over with a change of subject but it didn't work. The tension between Manuela and Kyriakou, blown up so suddenly, hung in the air like a bad smell. Black decided it was time to leave. He didn't want to get involved in another fracas like that in the ferry, and he realised that to sit there much longer was tempting fate for it was a high probability that sooner or later Hassan would appear. It was said on Ibiza that if you sat in front of the Montesol long enough you saw everybody you knew go by, and he had every reason to believe it was true. As he walked away he thought of Manuela, and because he was beginning to like her he worried.

Why was she mixed up with the Greek? They weren't

remotely the same type. What could they have in common? Was it just that he represented a meal ticket, that she liked life on Ibiza, playing at painting, loafing around? And the Greek made it possible?

She was afraid of Kyriakou, he could see that, so why didn't she go? Reluctantly he accepted that there was only one rational explanation: she couldn't break away because she was under some sort of obligation. And it wasn't too difficult to imagine what that was. She was hooked. Maybe she was one of the Greek's pushers, just as George Madden was likely to be another.

And if that was her position, what would happen to her? Life itself didn't last very long for a junkie. The only comfort he could find in these rhetorical questions was her appearance. Although there were heavy shadows under her eyes and she looked fragile, she didn't appear to be on the point of collapse, she was not withdrawn, and her morale was good. Maybe it was still only hash and LSD. But if so it wouldn't be long before it was the amphetamines and heroin. Not if she hung around Kyriakou much longer. Vague notions of rescuing her, of some absurdly quixotic act, floated through his mind until he thought of Kagan and jerked back to reality. He wasn't on Ibiza to solve the problems of feckless young women, however attractive. He sighed. He hadn't learnt much about life in his thirty-five years. Least of all where women were concerned.

Soon after Black had gone Kyriakou suggested to George Madden that it would be a good idea if he made himself scarce, and the young man, looking mildly surprised, dragged himself from his chair, said, 'Be seeing you,' and shuffled off.

Kyriakou watched him go and then turned on Manuela. 'Why the hell you ask Black to sit here?'

'Why not? I couldn't leave him standing there, gaping at me. It was what I'd do for anybody. Anyway, who asked him to join us in the steamer the other night? *You*. That's how I got to know him.'

The Greek chewed on his cigar, frowning. 'That's different. Then you had trouble with Tino Costa and the Englishman helped you. I wanted to teach Tino a lesson.' Almost as an afterthought he added, 'I wanted also to find out more about Black.'

'Why?' She opened her handbag, took out a comb and used it on her hair.

'This is my business.'

'And did you?'

'Enough. Enough that I know it's not good for you to be too friendly with him.' He disgorged an olive pip, took a toothpick from the glass on the table and began picking his teeth.

Manuela looked at herself in the compact mirror, moving her head from side to side. 'I'm not getting too friendly with anyone.'

'I see how you and Black look at each other and talk. He likes you. You like him. First many hours' talk with him in the steamer. Then long talk next morning at Garroves. Now . . .' He threw up a hand as if he were getting rid of it. 'This morning, you sit here and talk cock with him about art. You don't talk with me like that.'

'Charming, aren't you?' she said. 'So. What's your complaint?'

The Greek's eyes gleamed. 'Don't forget. You need me, my leetle one. You *need* me.'

'Maybe. But maybe not all that much.'

Kyriakou held out his hands in a gesture of appeal, the toothpick in one of them. 'Look, baby. What we fighting for? You know I go for you in a big way. Why you want to crucify me? Why you cheek me in front of heem?'

'I'm not crucifying you, Kirry.' Her manner changed and she spoke gently. 'But you're being silly about a guy I've just met who means nothing to me.'

Kyriakou looked round at the adjoining table to make sure he was not being overheard. He lowered his voice. 'Manuela. I don't trust Black. That ees why I'm worried. I getta tip from—' he paused, rolling his eyes, 'a *friend*. Now they begin to step up drug law enforcement. Plant *informadores*. I know.' He tapped his forehead. 'I'm wise guy, baby. Black could be a plant. Nobody here knows about him. He never give information about himself. What he's doing for the rest of life? I mean before he comes here coupla months ago?'

Manuela put the comb and compact back into her bag and snapped it shut. 'You think I haven't noticed that?' She glanced quickly at the Greek. 'Don't act so dumb, Kirry. Why d'you think I've been nice to him? The better I know him, the better my chance of finding out if he's working for the police. I want to get to know him a *lot* better.' She smiled coquettishly.

Kyriakou looked at her with a mixture of admiration and suspicion. 'Okay. But don't make too much with the act. If you want to give favours, remember Kirry is top of the list.'

'I'm not handing out those sort of favours,' she said. 'Not yet anyway. You should know that.'

He put his hand to his forehead and grimaced with imaginary pain. '*You* tell *me*! You driving me crazy. *Not now Kirry. You must wait. Another time, Kirry.* What's wrong with you? It's not the crown jewels you know.'

'Why bother about me, then?'

'You know why?' He banged the table and the glasses shook. 'Because I'm crazy about you. That's why. I say to myself every morning when I wake up. I say. Be a man, Kirry. Forget this bloody girl. Always plenty nice girls waiting for you. But I can't forget Manuela. Every time you come to me and say, "*Give me some hash, Kirry. I want to make a trip. Give me some acid, Kirry. I want to get high.*" I give it to you. And you? You give me *nothing*. Not right like thees.' He shook his head. 'Not right.'

'You've got other girls.'

'They're nothing. *Nothing.* Not same like you. I want you.'

The thin man with the dark glasses and the christ-beard got up from his table, walked down to the corner and turned into Avenida Ramon y Tur. A few feet down it, leaning against the wall of the Montesol, was a man with a black beret and a mournful face. The thin man gave him the newspaper as he went by but no word was spoken, nor did they look at each other.

A few moments later the man with the beret read the pencilled message on the newspaper and moved round the corner of the building. He leant against the wall where he could see the tables on the pavement in front of the Montesol. Later, when Kyriakou and Manuela Valez got up to go, he followed them.

Chapter Eight

The yellow Land-Rover came in along the Figuretes road, turned left at the end and made for the harbour, keeping north of the *paseo*.

'Not so fast, Juan.' The tall man looked straight ahead, his lips barely moving, his thin body rigid.

The driver mumbled, '*Si, señor*,' and slowed down. He was wearing the striped vest and bell-bottoms of a sailor.

When the Land-Rover reached the harbour it swung round opposite the customs shed and made up the quay, stopping close to where the *Snowgoose* was berthed. Astern of her lay the inter-island schooners, rust-streaked white hulls contrasting with red upperworks, yellow bowsprits and green sails. Farther up the quay, the fishing boats had hoisted nets to their mastheads to dry.

There was an odour of fish, of tar and paint and fuel oil in the air; and the noise of winches, of shouting stevedores, of chipping hammers, of throbbing diesels, and the cry of sea-birds.

The Land-Rover stopped and the men in her looked over the water to the motor-cruiser coming across from the yacht moorings in front of the Nautico clubhouse. Van Biljon tapped his watch. 'Pedro is five minutes late.'

Juan nodded. '*Si, señor*. I expect he had trouble starting the engines.'

'He should have been alongside when we arrived. The children will be here soon.'

'*Si, señor*. Do not worry.'

The motor-cruiser turned in towards the quay and the note of her engines fell. Van Biljon sat motionless, watching the manœuvre, giving no sign to the man next to him of his elation, of the sensual pleasure he derived from the *Nordwind*'s fine lines, the gleam of her enamelled hull as it reflected the light from the water, and the sparkle of sunlight from the windows of the deck-house. Built by Vospers, she had cost him thirty-five thousand pounds, but she had been worth every pound of it for she gave him many things: the thrill of high speed over water; the satisfaction—to him almost a sublimation—of catching fish (Juan and Pedro had been fishermen before they came to him, and they knew the fishing banks as they knew the streets and alleys of the *barrio* sa Peña); the means to give pleasure to children; to get away from the island at any time he chose and to have privacy outside Altomonte. Above all, the boat satisfied his insatiable desire to possess fine things.

Juan got out of the Land-Rover. The motor cruiser was almost alongside now, fenders over the side, her bows coming up so fast on the stern of the *Snowgoose* that collision seemed inevitable. Then a deep throb reverberated over the water as her engines were reversed, water cascaded from her stern and she lay parallel to the quay, a few feet from it. Juan took a bow-line from Pedro and slipped it over a bollard, then a stern-line, and the boat was warped alongside. The two men called to each other, laughing at something in a ribald way. Juan went back to the Land-Rover. He opened a door and van Biljon passed him his duffel coat, binoculars and camera. Stiffly, awkwardly, the old man got out of the car and, helped by his servants, climbed aboard the motor-cruiser. He went at once to the after cabin, where the curtains were drawn.

The two sailors stayed on the quay, enjoying the warm sunshine. They talked about the *Snowgoose*, admiring with the professional eyes of seamen her fine lines and high masts and rigging. In the bows of the schooner Dimitri was sewing canvas. Kamros sat on a box beside him, legs crossed, smoking a pipe.

'She must have big engines,' said Juan. 'See the size of the exhaust outlets.'

Pedro grunted. 'She is the boat of rich people. They always have the best.'

'*Nordwind* is a fine boat,' said Juan. 'But I wish she also had sails. Such are more of the sea.'

'*Nordwind* has mighty engines. Great speed. Radar. A boat cannot have everything.'

From behind them came the sound of children singing. A bus drew up and the singers swarmed out. The driver, a gnarled bent man, called to Pedro and Juan. They went over and he handed down baskets of food. Having undertaken to be back on the quay at five, he drove off.

A teenage boy and girl were in charge of the children from whom came a happy clamour. The teenagers marshalled them into some sort of order and Juan addressed them, outlining the plans for the day and the disciplines which had to be observed: no climbing on to bulwarks or guard-rails, and no visits to engine-room or wheelhouse unless by invitation. When he'd finished, the teenagers led their charges across to the *Nordwind* and helped them aboard. Soon the motor-cruiser was overrun with children and their shouts and laughter drowned most other sounds.

Juan and Pedro carried the lunch baskets on board. After reporting to van Biljon, Juan went to the wheelhouse. Pedro cast off the bow and stern ropes, and bore off the bows with a boat-hook. Slowly *Nordwind* drifted clear of the quay, the note of her engines rose and a bow-wave formed as she gathered speed and made for the sea. Only when they had passed Botofoc lighthouse and altered course to the south-east, did van Biljon come out of the owner's suite and join the children.

Many of them knew him, some well enough to run to him and hold their arms round his legs, reaching as high as they could, and since he could not smile he would touch their heads with the only gesture of affection left to him. He spoke to them in Spanish, asking what they had been doing at home and school and how their parents were. If they were new to him he would ask their names and question them about their families, and they would look at him with wide eyes, uncertain as yet of this old man with the scarred face whose eyes they could not see behind the dark glasses. But there was something in his voice which reassured them and soon they would forget their shyness and call him *tio*, uncle, and run off shouting to their friends.

It was a fine day, the sea calm under an almost cloudless sky. For these trips the weather was chosen with care, and the disciplines explained by Juan were strictly enforced.

When van Biljon reached the wheelhouse he ordered speed to be increased to twenty knots. Juan advanced the throttle and the *Nordwind*'s stern settled more deeply in the water, the hull vibrations increased and the deep note of the diesels rose.

They overtook the small ferry making for Formentera, and Punta Tramontana lighthouse on Espardell island grew taller as they approached, and soon fell astern. Fifteen minutes later they passed down the eastern side of Formentera, keeping a few miles offshore. Punta la Creu came out to meet them, and they passed El Pilar and followed round the heel of the island. When the high lighthouse at Mola was abeam, they altered course to the south.

It was midday when they closed Abago, a small uninhabited island to the south of Formentera, and there were shouts of recognition from the children who had done the journey before.

Speed was reduced and they rounded the island and nosed into a bay on its south-western side. The anchor was dropped about fifty yards offshore, and the *Nordwind* swung head-on to a light breeze from the sea. The motor dinghy was lowered and after several journeys, Juan and Pedro had ferried van Biljon and the children ashore.

On the warm sand strewn with sea-weed, the children made stacks of shoes and socks and discarded items of clothing before splitting up into groups. Some went digging in the sand, others explored the rocky pools, and some played tag or rounders. The two teenagers were everywhere at once, enjoying their authority, encouraging, suggesting, cajoling and scolding. Van Biljon took no part in this but moved among them, saying little, a gaunt figure walking with a stick, the masklike face giving no indication of its owner's emotions.

Juan and Pedro unpacked the baskets and prepared the lunch: water boiled in pots hung from iron tripods over a driftwood fire, and sausages spluttered and sizzled in big saucepans.

When all was ready Juan reported to van Biljon, then sounded a blast on a whistle. The games petered out and from the rocks and beaches the children came running. Lunch was soon in full swing, with much laughter and chatter and, occasionally, tears. Van Biljon sat on a rock outside the main group, a small boy and girl keeping him company. While they ate from heaped plates he spoke to them, but had no food himself. Juan and Pedro, busy handing out the meal, making coffee, tending the fire, exchanged odd snatches of conversation.

'He is a strange one,' said Juan. 'So stern with men and women. So gentle with children.'

'It is a madness,' grumbled Pedro. 'To spend all this money, to make all this work, for these ungrateful little wretches.'

Juan shook his head. 'You have no children of your own. You do not understand.'

The other man chuckled. 'None that know me.'

'These children are poor. Imagine the joy this gives them.'

'I imagine only the work it gives me, Juan.' With a hairy forearm he wiped the sweat from his forehead.

When the last of lunch had been eaten, van Biljon told the children that he would take them inland to explore. There were excited shouts and they gathered about him in groups, asking questions. When they had put on their socks and shoes, he took up his stick and started stiffly up the sandy incline, plodding through the carpet of succulents and grass which bordered the beach. The children followed, crowding behind him at first, but dropping back until a long line had formed, the teenagers at its end rounding up stragglers, the older children close on the old man's heels.

He would stop at times to point to a shrub or wild flower, telling them its name in Castilian Spanish and then its often different Ibizencan name. He would pick up a stone or touch a rock with his stick, tell them its geological significance and point to the ravages of wind and weather. Switching to the history of Ibiza and the other islands in the group, he would explain that the Greeks had given them the name *Pityusas* because of the pines which covered them. He recalled the original names of the islands: *Augusta, Ibosim, Ebysos, Insula* and many others, how their history was made, the comings and goings of sailors and merchants and warriors, the Chaldeans, Phoenicians, Egyptians, Carthaginians, Romans, Vandals, Byzantines, Moors, Turks, and in the end the Spaniards.

Somehow this elderly childless man, stern and remote, was transformed by the children. He seemed so well to understand them, what interested them, and how to communicate it.

The island was small and soon they reached the beach on its far side. There the children paddled and played on the sand while Arturo, the teenage boy, was sent off by van Biljon to lay a paper trail back to the beach where they had landed. While he was away the children gathered round the old man who explained a paper chase. Some had played it before, but to many of the smaller ones the game was new. Presently he sent them off in groups, the youngest first, and soon the chase was on, the children spread out in a long sinuous line, their cries carrying back in the wind. Van Biljon came up behind, two small children with him.

At first they walked in silence, then the little girl said, 'Why is it called a *chase*?'

'Because Arturo is trying to escape and the others are *chasing* him,' said van Biljon.

'Then why does he leave little bits of paper to guide them?'

'Those who are chased always leave things to guide their pursuers,' said the old man. 'Like the fox who leaves his scent.'

The little boy said, 'Is the fox frightened?'

'Very,' said the old man.

'Why?'

'He knows if the hounds catch him they will kill him.'

'Will Arturo be killed?' said the little girl.

Van Biljon looked at the dark upturned eyes and patted her head. 'No. It is just a game. They will not harm Arturo.'

'Why do they kill the fox?'

'Because they think he has done wrong. Stolen their fowls and ducks perhaps, and sometimes lambs.'

'Why does he?'

'For food. He has to live.'

They walked on in silence, the old man's stiff gait somehow matching in pace the runs and jumps of the children. The little girl said, 'I don't think it is a nice game, *tio*. It is cruel.'

'The chase is part of life,' said the old man. 'Life is cruel. We are all pursued at times. In many different ways, by many different things. Sometimes it is only in our minds, but we are afraid, and like the fox we suffer.'

A big boy appeared suddenly over a sand dune, running back to them, breathless and excited. 'They caught Arturo,' he cried. 'They caught him. I saw it happen.' He pointed to the top of the sand dune.

'Poor Arturo.' The old man said it heavily, and the children tightened their mouths and were sad.

The *Nordwind* got back to Ibiza in the late afternoon and made slowly up the harbour, crowded with children who were tired but determined to miss nothing. Van Biljon was in the wheelhouse talking to Juan.

'When did she arrive?' He was examining the *Snowgoose* through binoculars.

'Three days ago, señor,' said Juan.

'To whom does she belong?'

Juan turned the wheel to port and closed both throttles. 'Two young men. One French, the other German. They are writing a book about the Mediterranean islands.'

'She is a fine schooner,' said van Biljon. 'They must have much money.'

Juan grunted, put his head out of the bridge window and shouted to Pedro who was talking to the children. Pedro left them and began putting fenders over the side. The *Nordwind*'s bows came round to port. Juan put the port engine half-astern and the starboard engine slow-ahead. The motor-cruiser trembled and the air vibrated with the noise of the exhausts. As the boat closed the quay astern of the *Snowgoose*, van Biljon looked through a wheelhouse window at the knot of people on the quay.

He muttered an oath. 'I'm going down to my suite, Juan. When the children have gone tell me.'

Juan replied, '*Si, señor,*' but his mind was on getting the boat alongside. The old man need not have told him. He always went to the cabin on arrival. So that he should not suffer the inquisitive stares of people who like to catch a glimpse of this rich but curious philanthropist.

Among those on the quay who had been watching the return of the *Nordwind* were Black and Kyriakou. They had not met by chance. Black had been sitting outside the Bar Pechet when he saw the *Nordwind* moving across the harbour towards her berth, and he had gone across to have a closer look. On nearing the quay he had seen Kyriakou, and while his first instinct had been to turn away it had occurred to him that it might be wise to make a friendly gesture to the Greek.

That morning Black had found a letter from Werner Zolde at the post office. It had been brief and to the point. *Your man went last night to Palma for three days. We will contact him on his return. Do not worry.* Black had experienced enormous relief on reading the letter, and now while they stood talking, watching the motor-cruiser manœuvre alongside, he felt relaxed, well-disposed even to the Greek.

The children came ashore and climbed into the waiting bus. The empty lunch baskets were handed up to the driver and the bus moved off. After they had gone, Juan went across to where the yellow Land-Rover was parked and drove it up the quay alongside *Nordwind*. He got out and went back on board. Presently van Biljon came on deck and walked up the small gangplank. With Pedro following, the old man went towards the Land-Rover. As he approached he nodded briefly

67

to Kyriakou.

Charles Black smiled. 'You had a lovely day for your outing, sir,' but van Biljon, looking straight ahead, gave no indication that he had heard.

'Not madly friendly, is he?' Black laughed drily.

Kyriakou adjusted the red silk handkerchief in the pocket of his striped coat. 'You think you make friends and see the pictures, hey?'

'The thought crossed my mind.'

'Aha, my friend. Not so easy?' The Greek seemed to relish the Englishman's frustration.

'He knows you?'

Kyriakou examined the end of his cigar. 'Everybody knows Kirry.' His complacent smile was boyish.

When Pedro had taken the *Nordwind* back to its moorings and the Greek had gone, Black walked up the quay past the white schooner and made his way to the Bar Pechet.

In a room above a shop, across the road, the thin man with dark glasses and a christ-beard put down the binoculars he'd been using to watch the arrival of the *Nordwind* and to check who'd been on the quay to meet her.

It was the hour after dinner at Altomonte. Van Biljon was in his gallery standing before a Renoir—a girl with a lace hat and a green parasol.

As always it evoked memories of a January night, frost on the ground, the smell of snow in the air, the sound of an engine across the lake, its note rising and then, when it seemed upon him, ceasing altogether; the lick and slap of disturbed water and from the darkness the low cry, 'Joachim, Joachim,' followed by his answering call, 'Therèse, Therèse.'

An owl had hooted and quite soon he'd heard the crunch of the boat on the shingles and dark shapes had come splashing through the shallows. First the little girls, then their mother, and finally Kauffman himself, pouring out thanks in a voice broken with emotion. They had gone to the van and it was there that Kauffman had shown him the Renoir. He could still feel the exultation of that moment.

He had disliked the Kauffmans. The man oozed obsequiousness and she kept whining her gratitude. And why did they have to bring the children? Was it to crucify him?

Chapter Nine

The noise which had seemed a part of Black's dream resolved itself into a car accelerating in the street below, and he turned over on his side and pulled the bedclothes up over his head to shut out the sound. Then he realised that it was daylight and he looked at his watch. Nearly eight o'clock. His head felt heavy and when he stood up nausea swept him. He touched the back of his neck and his hand came away moist with sweat.

On the bedside table there was a bottle of water and a thick glass. The water was tepid because the bottle had been standing in sunlight, but it took the dryness from his mouth. God, he thought, I shouldn't have drunk so much. He stretched and thought of the long night behind him: La Terra, Clive's Bar, the Delfin Verde, the Savoy Bar, Bud's Bar, the George and Dragon, Mariano . . . she'd not been in any of them but he'd filled in time drinking at most, hoping she'd turn up. Later he'd gone into the old town . . . to La Carbonera, but she wasn't there. He'd tried El Bistro, Antonio's, Los Pajaros . . . and still no luck and he was getting pretty high. He had a hunch and went down to The Paseo Vara de Rey and took a taxi out to the Mar-Blau. She wasn't there either but Ilse Berch was, and after she'd told him he wasn't walking too well and a few other things, she gave him Manuela's phone number. That hadn't helped. A woman had answered after a long wait, a Spanish woman, and she'd said Manuela was out and anyway what was he doing ringing a respectable house at such an hour. So he'd given up and gone back to his room.

It had been a crazy night anyway, but he'd known that it was in a sense his last chance for Hassan was returning from Palma the next day. Thus it was a night on which he'd been able to let his hair down without risk of encountering the Arab.

As for this day, he must spend it in the *campo*, both to be out of the way while Werner Zolde and Lejeune dealt with

Hassan, and because there was important work to be done in the hills round San José—and for that to-day would be as good as any, and better than most.

Now he filled the porcelain wash basin with cold water and bathed his face, spluttering and snorting, drying his head and face roughly as if to rub away the pain.

In his notebook he found the number Ilse had given him. He put on a dressing gown and went down to the landing where the phone was and dialled the number. The Spanish woman of the night before answered. He held his fingers against his mouth to distort his voice and asked for Señorita Valez. There was a long wait before Manuela came on the line.

'Hi,' she said. 'Who is it?'

'Charles Black.'

'Oh, Charles.' She sounded pleased. 'How did you know my number?'

'Ilse gave it to me.'

'How are you?'

'Terrible,' he said. 'I want your help.'

'Is there something wrong?'

'Yes. My head.'

'Your head? I don't understand.'

'I went looking for you last night. In just about every bar on the island. When I couldn't find you I drowned my sorrows.'

'Oh, nonsense,' she laughed. 'They all say you drink too much. I heard this before I met you.'

'They lie. Will you help me?'

'How can I help you?' There was laughter in her voice.

'Come and spend the day with me. In the *campo*.'

'In the *campo*? What for?'

'To clear my head. Get back to nature.'

She laughed again. 'You can do that without me.'

'Much nicer *with* you,' he said.

At first she refused, said she must paint, that she had many things to do. But he persisted and at last she gave in and they agreed to meet outside the tourist office at eleven.

'Wear heavy shoes,' he said. 'I'm going to make you walk and climb.'

'Oh. It will be an *awful* day, I'm sure.'

'No,' he said, 'it will be fabulous. But don't wear bright

colours. I want to show you some birds.'

Back in his room he made a syrup of sugar and water, smeared the bottom of an empty Kodak carton with it, and put the rest in a saucer which he placed on the window ledge facing the terrace. Then he opened the window and went to the bathroom.

After his bath he soaked a spill of cotton wool in ink and rubbed it on his left ankle. While it was drying he sat watching the bees at the saucer. Then he rubbed over the inked ankle with a wet handkerchief, leaving a blue stain.

When he crossed over to close the window, the bees buzzed angrily but stayed at the saucer. Using tissues, he caught four and transferred them to the empty carton, the lid of which he'd punctured with small holes. If that doesn't work, he thought, there's always the snake-bite serum.

She was wearing blue denim slacks and a shirt to match when he met her outside the tourist office on the Paseo Vara de Rey. He thought she'd never looked more attractive.

'Do you approve?' she asked. 'Not too bright?'

'Not bad. Got a jersey?'

She patted the straw bag hanging from her shoulder. 'Here.'

'Raincoat?'

'Also.' She touched the bag again.

'Good. I have the lunch.' He showed her the fisherman's bag. 'We'll take a bus to San José. Then walk.'

She touched his arm impulsively and her eyes shone. 'Oh. It will be fun. I haven't done anything like this for years.'

They had reached the end of the pavement and started across the *paseo* when she said in a low voice, 'I think we're being followed.'

Black felt an involuntary contraction of his muscles, a jangling of alarm bells in his ears, and in his mind's eye an image of Hassan loomed like a wide-screen close-up.

'By whom?' he said quietly.

'Man in a black beret. I saw him come down the road behind you when I was waiting. He sat on a bench on the *paseo* while we talked. Now he's behind us.'

'It may be coincidence. We'll soon see. In here.'

They stepped into a shop where Black bought a box of

matches. When they came out the man in the beret was looking in the window. With enormous relief he saw that it was not Hassan.

Black saw that she was worried. 'Right. Now for test number two.'

They turned left and started towards the hill, then left again into a dusty road which led to the fish market, then right until they had described a circle and come once again to the tourist office. Black looked back over his shoulder. The man in the beret was behind them, looking into the toyshop window.

'Clever girl. He's following us all right.'

'Why?' Her face screwed up with surprise.

'Haven't a clue. But let's give him a neurosis. You go into the Montesol. Spend five minutes in the loo. Then out through the back entrance and down to Aviaco's office. Near the bus stop. Know it?'

'Yes.'

He looked at his watch. 'I'll be there in ten minutes. In a taxi.'

'What will you do now?'

'See which of us he follows.'

She walked across the *paseo* towards the Montesol while Black watched the man in the black beret who was fidgeting with his hands and showing other signs of nervousness. There was a line of taxis opposite. Black took the head of the line. 'El Corsario,' he said. As they pulled away he saw the man in the beret move across towards the rank.

Black took two one-hundred peseta notes from his wallet and tapped the driver on the shoulder. 'At El Corsario,' he said in Spanish, 'ask for Señora Alba. Bring her to the Montesol. If she is not there, don't wait for more than five minutes.'

The taxi turned right into Conde Rosellon, then left along Calle Anibal. Two cars ahead slowed down for people on the corner who were waiting to cross.

Black looked through the rear window. There was no taxi following. He thrust the peseta notes into the driver's hand. 'Turn right and drop me,' he said. As the taxi turned into Calle Montgri, scraping by the people on the corner, he slipped out and joined them outside the shoe shop. He looked back to see a taxi begin its turn into Calle Anibal.

Before it had rounded the corner he went into the shoe shop. Through the glass of the shopfront he saw it go by, the man in the black beret leaning forward, engrossed in the pursuit. Funny, he thought, if there is a Señora Alba at El Corsario. He rejoined the shoppers on the pavement and made for the harbour. Minutes later he stopped a passing taxi and asked the driver to take him to Aviaco. On the way he thought of what had happened, and it left him worried. It was he and not Manuela who was being tailed. And then, as if one shock, one complication, were not enough, his thoughts went to Werner Zolde and he wondered how the German was dealing with Hassan: had he started yet, if not at what time would he, and how? And would he and Lejeune have followed up his suggestion?

They must be discreet, he thought, my God they must be discreet. Failure on their part could destroy the whole operation. He knew what Kagan would have done once Hassan's presence on the island had been known, and it was precisely for that reason that Black had not informed ZID. Kagan would have called the operation off at once rather than have it compromised. 'We can wait,' he would have said. 'Another month, another year, what difference? We can wait, so long as in the end we succeed.'

But Black knew that if the operation were to fail now he wouldn't get a second chance. If Hassan were here this time, he could be here next time. Kagan would choose someone else. Someone who could not be compromised in that way. No one knew better than Black himself the element of recklessness which was so much a part of his nature. Well, he thought, that's the way I am and that's the way I'll always be, and we are not going to call off this operation.

The bus put them down outside San José and they walked back along the road towards Ibiza until they reached the dirt road which would take them into the hills.

It was well past noon and sun from a cloudless sky had warmed the earth. The road led through terraces of almonds and caribs and as they walked the air vibrated with the hum of bees and the high note of cicadas.

The terraces were carpeted with marguerites and poppies, charlock and pea flowers, and their warm spring perfumes were overlaid by the aromatic scent of rosemary and sage. On the stone walls of the terraces little green lizards came suddenly into the sunlight to watch them, throats palpitating, before slipping back into crevices and shadows.

Later the road steepened and they took to the hillside, making their way through undergrowth which grew denser as they climbed.

At times he would stop and point to a bird, then watch it through binoculars, describe it to her and sometimes make an entry in the book he carried in the bag. It seemed to Manuela that he knew a great deal about these things.

Once he stopped and listened. 'Hear that?'

At first she could not, then beneath the complex hum of insects she heard a low 'tec, tec.' She nodded.

He whispered, 'Icterine Warbler, I think. Keep still. We may see it.'

She looked in the direction from which the noise came, saw movement in a shrub, and a bird appeared. Small and undistinguished, a pale earthy brown.

'No,' he said. 'It's the Olivaceous Warbler. *Hippolais pallida.* See the long bill and pale stripe above the eye.' He passed her the binoculars and while she was using them he was trying to free his mind of the nagging picture of the man in the black beret leaning forward as the taxi passed the shop window.

Farther up the hill she stopped, touched his arm and pointed to a small bird perched on a dried stem. It had a black crown, grey upperparts and white undersides. A distinctive white line, like a moustache, ran from the bill. Its eyes and legs were russet.

'My bird is prettier,' she whispered.

He nodded. 'Ruppell's Warbler. Handsome little chap.'

The bird made a diminutive rattling noise and whisked away. Black looked at Manuela's flushed face. Her eyes were brighter than he remembered them. 'Enjoying it?'

'Very much. It is for me something quite different.'

He said, 'I wonder how many men have told you you're beautiful?' She stopped and tossed her black hair back so that she could see him better. 'Why do you say that?'

'Because you are. And the thought just crossed my mind.'

She stared at him as if she were seeing him for the first time, then she looked up the hill towards the pines. 'Come on,' she said. 'You say we lunch in the woods. I am hungry.'

They sat under the trees on a carpet of pine needles to a late lunch of *bocadillos*, long crusty rolls filled with cheese and tunny, a bottle of red wine and some oranges. When the meal was finished, Black put the empty wine bottle and crumpled paper into the fishing bag. 'Had enough?' he said.

She was lying on the pine needles, her hands clasped behind her head. 'Yes. The *bocadillos* were marvellous. Where did you get them?'

'At the market.'

He lay on his side next to her, chin in hand, elbow on the ground, examining her face feature by feature, approving it. He put his little finger on her lips. They were soft and moist. He took the finger away and examined it.

'No lipstick,' he said.

She nodded, her eyes half closed. 'All my own work.'

'Nature's,' he said, and saw the dark hollows under her eyes and ran his finger gently over them and examined it. There was nothing on it. 'That nature too?' he asked and there was an edginess in his voice.

'My liver. That is nature.'

You're lying, he thought. It's those bloody drugs. He wanted to take her roughly and shake her as if he could physically empty out the nonsense.

He asked her about her life, her family, her hopes and fears. She told him of her childhood in Puerto Rico, of her schooldays there and her two years at a university in Southern California where she'd taken fine art.

Yes, there had been some men in her life. No, she had never married. She was twenty-five, she said. She had lived in Paris for three years, painting, then gone back to her family in Puerto Rico when her mother died. After some time in Seville where she'd joined an art colony, she'd come to Ibiza.

So he had to tell her about himself: his life as a boy in England; the death of his father, mother and sister in a car accident towards the end of his time at school. He'd stayed with an aunt after that, and his father had left enough money for him to study politics and philosophy at London University. But he'd not graduated because he'd found too late that his real interest was art. On the money left him he'd travelled and in later years his interest in art had led him into journalism, first on the staff of a provincial newspaper, then in London, and finally as art critic on a Montreal newspaper. Tiring of newspaper life he had free-lanced, travelling widely and making just enough money to raise his income to a level which supported his independence.

When he'd finished he thought, well a good deal of that's true though a lot's been omitted. I wonder how much of her story's true and how much she's omitted? That's life, isn't it? We're always putting on an act. There's always a hidden motive. And who can say which motive is good, and which is bad.

'Are you married?' Manuela watched him through half-closed eyes.

'No. Never.'

'No women in your life?'

'A few. Nothing remarkable.' That at least was true.

'That is strange for thirty-five.'

'By no means unique,' he said. 'I've never wanted to give up my independence. Besides, I've moved about a lot.'

'I can understand that. About independence.' After a while she said, 'Love is possible without marriage.'

He tickled her forehead with a spur of pine needles. 'Yes. For a time. But it never really endures, does it? I mean that is the sadness. Falling in love is sublime. The moment of truth, without cynicism. But it doesn't last.'

'The grand passion doesn't last,' she said. 'But there are other things. Children, companionship, affection, shared experience.'

He laughed. 'Manuela! You sound like Godfrey Winn.'

'Who is he?' she asked.

'A bachelor who writes about marriage.'

'You mustn't laugh at me when I am serious.' Her eyes were sad and reproachful.

He bent over her and she put her arms round him and held him tight.

She had finished doing her hair and repairing the damage. 'Really,' she said putting her comb and compact back into the grass basket. 'The things you men do to us girls.'

He was looking at his watch, worried and preoccupied, assuring himself that she really meant nothing to him. She was good to look at, sympathetic, intensely feminine. It was no more than that. Proximity. Physical. Ephemeral. She was essential to his plans and this was a means to an end. Besides she was Kyriakou's girl. Neat and rational as all this was, he knew he was not convinced. And so he frowned. 'It's nearly three,' he said. 'We're about half-way.'

She stood up, hanging the basket over her shoulder. 'Will we make San José before dark?'

'We'll make it all right,' he said. 'Come on, let's go.'

They set off through the wood, crossing obliquely from left to right, climbing steadily, the line of sunlight ahead widening as they approached the firebreak. He got there first and stood waiting for her. There was a ravine on the right and below them the dirt road snaked up the valley, crossing the ravine and losing itself in the folds of the hill. Above them, on the far side, the sun picked out the white walls of a *finca* set in the hillside.

Black pointed to it. 'Know that house?'

She shook her head. 'Fabulous site.'

'When we get higher you'll see more. It's *some* place. You can't see from here, but beneath it the ground falls away in terraces. The view is open to the sea beyond San José.'

'Whose is it?'

'It's Altomonte.'

She looked at him in surprise. 'Van Biljon's?'

'Yes.' He stopped to tie a shoelace.

'Have you been there?'

'No, never.'

'Then how do you know?'

He straightened up. 'It was pointed out to me some time ago when I was climbing here. With friends.'

'Friends?' she challenged. 'Which ones?'

He didn't answer, and she saw that he was looking down the valley with the binoculars.

'What is it?' she asked.

'Look.' He put a hand on her shoulder and pointed to where the road edged into the foothills. In the distance she saw a cloud of dust. Immediately ahead of it a car was coming up the valley.

He pulled her into the trees.

'What's wrong?' she said.

'Look at the car now.' He passed her the binoculars. 'We

can't be seen in the shadows.'

Before she could use them it had disappeared, but the sound of the engine grew in intensity and when next it appeared she saw that it was the powder-blue Buick. Kyriakou was its only occupant.

'Kyriakou,' she said, as if this were remarkable.

Black looked at her, wondering. 'I didn't know he was on visiting terms with van Biljon?'

'How d'you know he's going to see him?'

'It's a private road. Leads only to Altomonte.'

The car was lost to sight again where the road turned to the east, away from the ravine.

He said, 'Does Kyriakou know van Biljon well?'

'I don't know. He doesn't tell me everything.'

'I'm told you're close to him. I thought you might know.'

She flushed and he knew he was being a swine. 'Well, you thought wrong.'

'There's a buzz that you're his girl friend.'

'Yes,' she said defiantly, her dark eyes shining. 'I am. So you'd better be careful. He's jealous and he's a Greek.'

Black reined himself in. Why was he quarrelling with her? He needed her help. This wasn't the way to get it. When he'd caught up, he took her arm gently and pulled her round. 'I'm sorry, Manuela. I didn't mean it.'

She shook him off. 'Go to hell,' she said.

It hadn't been a good day. The man in the black beret, and Kyriakou's arrival on the scene were enough to worry about without this.

And Hassan? Black had almost forgotten about him. Compulsively he looked at his watch. Had Werner Zolde gone into action yet? And how? And for God's sake, was he going to be discreet? And, what was more, discreet and successful.

Later in the afternoon they reached a clearing above Altomonte and climbed on to a rock. From it they looked back over the valley and beyond to the Mediterranean. Black focused the binoculars on the sea.

'What are you looking at?' she said.

'The ferry. From Formentera.'

She's beginning to thaw, he thought, and passed her the binoculars.

She took them, and he saw that she was looking at

Altomonte.

'I can see his car,' she said. 'Parked just inside the gates.'

With forced obtuseness he said, 'Whose car?'

'Kirry's. I wonder what takes him to that house?'

'Expect they're buddies.'

She shook her head. 'How can they be? Van Biljon has no friends. Won't have visitors. Anyway, the last man he'd have anything in common with is Kyriakou.'

'Why do you say this?'

She held up her little finger, measuring off its tip. 'Kirry hasn't that much culture. Money, power, a good time. I guess these are the things that interest him.'

'And yet——'

She interrupted. 'Yes, I know—and yet I like him. I am often with him.'

'You said it.' He smiled thinly.

'He has some good things. He is kind. No one is all bad or all good.' She took a deep breath. 'Let us talk about something else.'

Black focused the binoculars on Altomonte; the plan in Haupt's office was in his mind.

In the centre of the patio the pool reflected the light of the dying sun, and the pergolas cast irregular shadows. On its western side the long gallery ran back into the slope of the hill, its extremity lost in shadow. He identified van Biljon's suite in the west wing, and the guest-suite in the east, and below and in front of them, the long hall off which led the reception rooms. He noted again the high barred windows along the length of the gallery, and the break in the stone wall surrounding the *finca* where the drive led in, the wrought-iron gates shut across it. Kyriakou's car was parked immediately inside them. As he watched, two dogs crossed the terrace in front of the house and disappeared into the shadows.

'It's a fine house,' he said. 'Van Biljon has good taste.'

'And lots of money,' she said. 'But I would not like to live there alone.'

'He has his pictures. I imagine that long building running back on this side of the patio is the gallery?'

'Maybe,' she said. 'It's big enough.'

He drew a deep breath, exhaling noisily.

'Why do you sigh?' she asked.

'I was thinking of those pictures. So close and yet I can't see them. I wonder what he really has? What they're worth? Can you imagine?'

'No,' she said firmly. 'I can't.'

'At Sotheby's the other day a Pissarro fetched three hundred and fifteen thousand pounds. In that gallery there are Pissarros, Cézannes, Renoirs, Monets, Degas, Manets, Sisleys, the lot. God knows how many. There they are, within five hundred yards of us. But nobody, not one solitary soul, is allowed to see them.' With a snort he added, '*Except* Mister bloody van Biljon.'

She felt his frustration and was worried because she liked him more than anybody she'd met for a long time. But she was afraid because she sensed the pattern of his thoughts and remembered the man in the black beret. Charles Black was being tailed, and he knew it. Yet he'd said nothing about the incident after he'd picked her up in the taxi outside Aviaco, other than to dismiss it as not worth worrying about. Somebody making a mistake somewhere, he'd said—you know what the Spanish police are like. Pretty good, she'd said, and he'd not looked pleased.

He was silent now, the binoculars still trained on Altomonte.

'You know, Charles, nobody could steal those pictures and get away with them. They're internationally catalogued. There's not a dealer worth the name who wouldn't know them.'

He put down the binoculars and turned towards her, and she couldn't make anything of his smile.

'I know,' he said. 'There's no future in that. And for your information, young woman, my interests are artistic and journalistic.' He patted her knee and she felt foolish. 'Let's go,' he said.

She stood on the rock. 'Good. The light will be gone soon.'

'Not to worry. It's a quick journey down. Once we've made the road it won't matter if it's dark.'

To the west the sun was a copper disc, its lower rim balanced on a strata of cloud stretched tenuously across the horizon. The temperature had fallen, and in the south-east dark banks of storm cloud were massing. She shivered. 'I need my jersey.'

He slid down from the rock, took the jersey from the basket and threw it to her. When she'd put it on, he reached up, pulled her into his arms and kissed her. 'Am I forgiven?'

She looked at him doubtfully, pushing him away, and said 'Yes.'

They had not gone far when there was the sound of a car starting. Altomonte was no longer in sight, but a few minutes later the Buick showed up on a turn of the road, making down the valley.

Black felt some of the tension go out of him. That was one complication less.

Chapter Ten

A large man in a skin-diving suit was on a ledge close to the water on the seaward side of the big rock which lay two hundred metres off shore. Less than a mile to seaward a white staysail schooner seemed scarcely to move as she reached to windward making up towards Botafoc lighthouse. The man on the rock, Werner Zolde, sat with his feet dangling in water which rose and fell, sucking and lapping at the base of the rock as the sea came in impelled by a light breeze from the north-east. On his lap were his goggles and schnorkel. He waited calmly, secure in the knowledge that he could not be seen from the shore, confident that at the appointed time he would do that which was required of him.

Now he looked at the diving watch on his wrist. It was 0602 and he thought of all the things that could go wrong: the man might not swim to-day, a stomach-ache perhaps, or a woman in his bedroom, or perhaps he would swim with a companion. Who could tell? But Werner Zolde was a phlegmatic man and he sat patiently, watching and waiting. And then, when a few more minutes had passed, he saw that from the truck of the schooner's mainmast, where a moment ago there had been nothing, there fluttered a small dark pennant.

He knew then that the man on the beach, on the landward side of the rock, must have entered the water, must now be swimming to seaward. Werner Zolde pressed the button on his diving watch and started the lapsed-time hand. The swim should take from ten to twelve minutes, but to play safe he would work on eight. While he waited, he looked down the coast towards Figuretes. Lejeune should be getting into position now. He waited stoically, too confident of Lejeune to worry as yet, but conscious that timing was vital if . . .

His thoughts were interrupted by a high whine, the monstrous amplification of a sound like tearing linen, and to the south-east he saw the bobbing blurr of a skimmer sweeping to seaward, turning in a wide arc to head up the coast towards him, the white plume at its stern unfolding into a long line of foam which lay like old lace on the indigo sea. Compulsively Werner Zolde looked again at the diving watch. 6.04. Another three minutes, and he would move. He checked over his equipment, wiggled his toes in the flippers to ensure that the circulation was all right and then, slowly, carefully, he eased himself off the rock and into the water until his feet found the submerged ledge and the sea lapped about his shoulders. Again he waited, alert, listening, his eyes constantly checking the position of the schooner and the fast moving skimmer.

When the lapsed-time hand showed seven minutes forty seconds, he slipped in the mouth-piece of the schnorkel, fixed the nose-clip, adjusted the goggles, and let himself down into a cavity between the flutes of jagged granite which screened him to right and left. By moving his head a few inches forward he could see either end of the long rectangular rock. What little wind and sea there was came from the north-east, so he judged the swimmer would come round the western side of the rock, taking advantage of its lee on the outward swim, knowing that he would have wind and sea behind him for the return. But Werner Zolde wasn't taking any chances, so he divided his attention between either end of the rock.

From where he waited, his goggled eyes almost at water level, the small seas lapping over his head, he could hear the note of the skimmer's engine rising and knew it was approaching. Once more he looked at the diving watch. Nine minutes and forty-seven seconds had lapsed. It must be soon now, he thought, feeling along his belt with his free hand to make sure of the knife and cosh. Then, above the slap and gurgle of the sea against the rock, he thought he heard a new sound and knowing that he would hear better under water, he submerged. A few seconds later he picked it up . . . the measured splash and beat of a swimmer—a long slow stroke, the sound coming from his right, from the western end of the rock.

Slowly he raised his eyes clear of the water and concentrated on that end. The unseen swimmer must be close now for the sound of his strokes was clearly audible. With eyes at water level, watching from behind the jagged flutes which concealed him, he saw first an arm and then a head round the corner. Even before he saw the man's face he knew it was Hassan—the copper bracelet on his left wrist, the white rubber skullcap, the muscular arms deeply bronzed.

The note of the skimmer's engine died suddenly. With a quick glance to seaward Werner Zolde saw the black rubber hull, not far off now, turning towards the rock. He submerged again until only the tip of the schnorkel remained above the surface. Behind the goggles his eyes searched the opaque water while his ears listened like delicate hydrophones to the sound of the swimmer which grew in intensity. Steadily they came on, until he estimated they were opposite him and comparatively close, although the man was not yet visible under water. The sound effects were moving now from the German's right to his left. He waited for a few seconds and then again raised his eyes just clear of the water, to see that the swimmer was about five or six metres away, moving towards the eastern end of the rock with deliberate, robust strokes.

Werner Zolde took a deep breath before he submerged. Then, bracing himself, he came away from the rock with the impetus of a racing turn and with flippers churning set off in silent pursuit, swimming beneath the surface. Soon he saw broken water ahead of him and then the undersides of beating feet. As he drew closer, he pulled the cosh from his belt and manœuvred so that he would come up behind Hassan and to his left. When he was in position he surfaced and sprinted alongside just as the other man completed a long slow stroke with his left arm and, looking back, saw him. Werner Zolde pulled off the schnorkel and shouted, 'Hallo, Hassan!'

The Lebanese stopped swimming and trod water. 'Hallo,' he said looking puzzled, wondering presumably whose face it was behind the goggles. 'How did you get here?'

'Cold, isn't it?' replied Werner Zolde, moving closer.

'Sure,' said Hassan, eyes still puzzled.

Suddenly, deafeningly, the sound of the skimmer's engine seemed to come from nowhere.

'Look out!' shouted Werner Zolde pointing with his schnorkel to the Lebanese's right. 'Look out!'

Hassan whipped round to see the skimmer coming for him, and in that moment Werner Zolde's cosh struck. The German grasped the limp figure beneath the armpits as the skimmer stopped alongside and Lejeune leant over the side, stretching out his hands,

'Quick!' he called. 'Get him down between the floats.'

When they had laid Hassan on the bottom boards, Werner Zolde stretched himself out alongside the recumbent Arab, and Lejeune, crouching, his backward stretched arm on the tiller, opened the throttle wide and the skimmer roared and bumped to seaward, making for the south-east at thirty knots —away from the white schooner which had gone about and was now standing out to sea. Werner Zolde looked at his diving watch. The act of snatching Ahmed ben Hassan from the Mediterranean, from cosh to full throttle, had occupied twenty-nine seconds.

The light breeze had fallen away but the schooner was moving faster now, and the wisps of blue smoke trailing astern told why. In the south-east storm clouds were massing, and to the west the sun was setting—soon it would be dusk and already the light on Dada Grande was flashing its warning message.

Chapter Eleven

They came out of the pines above Altomonte into a firebreak, crossed it and worked their way down the hill through bush and undergrowth. Black asked her to go ahead, saying he wouldn't be a moment. When she'd gone he went into a thicket, opened the fishing bag and took from it the Kodak carton. He removed the shoe and sock from his left foot, and making a bag of his handkerchief put the carton in it, feeling through the linen to take off the lid. He manipulated the handkerchief, holding the bees lightly against his ankle, and agitated it. He heard the bees buzz and felt the sharp pain of their stings. A few minutes later he ran his hand over the ankle, feeling for the stings. He pulled them out, using his nails as pincers, and replaced the sock and shoe. When he stood up the ankle was throbbing and he felt a slight nausea.

He rejoined Manuela and they came clear of the undergrowth and headed for the firebreak which flanked the woods opposite Altomonte. When they reached it they turned south, following it down, the trees on their right and the terraces of figs, olives and lemons on the left.

The light was going fast. 'We'll cross the terraces,' he said. 'The road's beyond them.'

They went down to a terrace of olives and made their way along it.

'Watch your step,' he called over his shoulder.

'I'm all right, but don't go too fast. Your legs are longer than mine.'

The ankle was hurting now, the swelling making the shoe tight. I can't delay it much longer, he thought, and jumped from the wall to the terrace beneath. In the dusk he could just see her standing above him.

'Here,' he said. 'I'll help you.'

She took his hands and landed beside him. 'Do we have to do this often?'

'A few times more, I expect.'

They walked along the terrace for some distance before he

86

said, 'Down here. I'll go first.' He jumped and fell and said 'Christ!'

She called out, 'What's wrong?'

'Twisted my ankle.' His voice was strangely, suddenly, hoarse. 'It'll be all right in a moment.'

She scrambled down and knelt beside him. 'Oh, Charles. What've you done?'

Her anxiety somehow pleased him. He clenched his teeth and emitted a well modulated groan. 'My bloody fault,' he said, propping himself against the wall and breathing heavily.

'Let me see it.' She reached towards the ankle. He moved his left foot gingerly and she began to undo the shoe laces.

'Christ!' He drew his breath sharply and pushed her hands away. 'It hurts like hell.'

'I'm sorry. I was clumsy.'

'No, you weren't,' he said. 'I'm a coward about pain. Let me take the shoe off.'

The bees had done a good job and taking off the shoe and sock hurt. There was not enough light to see the ankle. She said, 'Let me feel it. I promise to be gentle.'

She felt it, while he made appropriate noises.

'It's swollen,' she said. 'And hot.'

'Throbs like mad.' He was pleased not to have to lie about that.

'What are we going to do, Charles?'

'Not to worry. Just let me rest here for a bit. I'll be all right.'

'And if not?'

'We'll cross that bridge when we get to it.' He tried to change his position and released another small groan.

'Must be a bad sprain, Charles.'

For some time he sat huddled against the wall, Manuela beside him, the night growing darker and the stars gathering in the sky. Occasionally she would ask if the ankle felt better and he would grunt a noncommittal reply. She offered to go and get assistance.

'It's about three kilometres to the main road and another six or seven into San José.' He added, 'You can't go traipsing about the countryside in the dark.'

'I meant Altomonte. It's quite close.'

'Nonsense,' he said. 'I'll be all right if I can rest a bit longer. Anyway, you wouldn't get help there.'

'Of course I would. He's not inhuman.'

'Isn't he? How d'you know?'

'Because I've spoken to him and I can tell.'

'Like children and dogs?'

'Yes.'

He put out his hand in the darkness and touched her. 'You're sweet, Manuela. But I prefer to manage without his assistance.'

She put her head against his and he could feel the warmth of her breath. 'Oh, Charles,' she said. 'Why were you so goddam careless?'

The luminous dial of his watch showed it was well after seven. It was time to get things going. 'I'll put the sock on,' he said, 'and try walking without a shoe.'

When it was on he stood up and tested the foot. 'Come on,' he said. 'Let's give it a bash.'

'Can I help you?'

'No. If I can't do it on my own it's no good. We've got quite a way to go.'

He hobbled off, carrying the shoe in one hand, and she followed.

They walked for a few minutes, stopping occasionally, going slower all the time, until he leant against the terrace wall, breathless. 'It's no good. I can't make it.'

'Then I must go to Altomonte,' she said with decision. 'We cannot spend the night here. The ankle must be looked at.'

They argued for some time, but at last he acknowledged there was nothing for it but the *finca*. He told her to continue along the terrace until she came to the dirt road, then follow it up the hill to the gates of the house. 'Shouldn't take you more than half an hour,' he said.

When she'd gone a few steps, he called out, 'Better put a stone on the road when you reach it. So that you'll know which terrace I'm on when you come back.'

Her voice came out of the darkness. 'Okay. I won't be long.'

When he could no longer hear her footsteps he stood up and moved about to keep warm. It was dark, there was no moon, but the sky was bright with stars. He could smell the lemon and olive blossoms: and the chirp of crickets, the croaking of frogs and the rapping cry of a nightjar reminded him that he was not alone. It was cold and to keep up his spirits he whistled *Colonel Bogey.*

Long before she reached the gates the dogs were barking. She rounded a bend in the road and saw faint lights ahead. The iron gates showed up and not long afterwards she was dazzled by a strong light. A man challenged her in Spanish. Another voice silenced the dogs.

'I want help.' She was breathless because she had walked fast and the dogs frightened her. 'There has been an accident.' She spoke in Spanish.

'Wait,' said the man. She heard the gates being unlocked, then approaching footsteps, and presently he came into the circle of light.

'*Buenas noches, señorita.*' He was a thickset man, swarthy and gnarled and he wore a dark duffel coat. Somehow his face was familiar.

She said, '*Buenas noches, señor.*'

'What is it, señorita?'

'My friend has had a fall. His ankle is hurt. He cannot walk.'

The man looked at her uncertainly. 'Where is he?'

She pointed down the road. 'About one kilometre. Then along a terrace.'

'What were you doing on the terraces, señorita?'

'We had climbed the hill and were coming down.'

He gave her a strange look. 'It is late to be coming down.'

'No,' she shook her head. 'We started a long time ago. When he hurt his ankle we waited while he rested. He tried to walk but could not. I thought of going to San José for help. But this is much closer, so I came here.'

'What do you wish me to do?'

'Help me bring him in. He cannot walk. It is impossible that he should spend the night on the terrace.'

The Spaniard told her to wait, and went back through the gates. While she stood awkwardly in the glare of the light, waiting, she heard him talking to the other man. Then he came back. 'Follow me, señorita.'

She went in through the gates after him. As the spotlight went out arc lights on the terrace came on, and the big house stood out white and massive at the top of a flight of steps.

The other man joined them and with three Alsatians at their heels, growling and snuffling, they went up the steps.

The gnarled man rang the front door bell and almost immediately it was opened by a Spanish woman. She called him 'Juan' and his companion 'Pedro.' She watched Manuela with dark penetrating eyes, while Juan made his explanations. After some hesitation she said, 'Come in, señorita.'

Manuela went in with Juan, and the doors were closed leaving Pedro and the Alsatians outside.

They were in a large hall in which Persian and Aubusson carpets lay on white terrazzo floors, between walls panelled in dark mahogany. The furniture was Dutch and French, seventeenth- and eighteenth-century, while most of the pictures were by Dutch and Flemish painters of the same period. It reminded Manuela more of the interior of a French château than anything she'd seen in Spain. A log fire sparkled and spluttered in an open fireplace and the aromatic smell of burning pinewood hung in the air.

The woman pointed to a chair, 'Sit down, señorita.' Manuela took the chair but the woman remained standing. 'What is your name?'

'Manuela Valez.'

The woman looked puzzled. 'You are not Spanish.'

'No. I come from Puerto Rico.'

'And your friend?' She said *friend* with just enough inflection to colour the word.

'His name is Black. We live in Ibiza.'

'What are you doing there, señorita?'

'I am a painter.'

'And he?'

Manuela remembered van Biljon's aversion to art critics. 'He writes,' she said.

The Spanish woman looked at her for some time in silence before saying, 'I will see Señor van Biljon. Please wait.'

'I do not know if he will remember me,' Manuela said. 'We met once at the airport. He dropped his ticket and I picked it up. About two months ago.'

For a moment the Spanish woman's face softened, then her features set hard. 'I do not know whether we can help you. He will decide.'

Not long afterwards Manuela saw a tall thin figure come in through the archway on the west side of the hall and walk stiffly towards her. When she'd seen him before he'd been wearing a beret. Now she saw that he had a head of silken hair, more silver than white. Somehow it softened the ugly blemish of the scarred face and the sinister anonymity of the dark glasses.

She stood up, facing him, and he held out his hand. 'Good evening,' he said, 'I believe we have met before.'

'Yes. At the airport.' She felt the intense scrutiny of eyes she couldn't see, and looked away. It was difficult to focus on pieces of black glass which reflected the lights of the room.

'Techa, my housekeeper,' he waved in the woman's direction, 'tells me you have a friend who's damaged his foot on the terraces. That he needs help.'

She confirmed this, answering his questions, filling in the detail. He did not ask her to sit down but stood, arms folded, a hand shielding his mouth, eyes on the carpet between them.

'You say Black is a journalist.' His head came up and she knew that behind the dark glasses he was watching her closely. 'What is his first name?'

'Charles,' she said.

'Does he write for art journals?'

'Occasionally.'

'You know, I suppose, that he is determined to see my pictures. That he's been commissioned to do an article about them?' His voice hardened. 'And about me?'

'I know he is interested in the French Impressionists. You are said to have an exceptional collection.'

'That is an evasive answer.'

'I'm sorry. It was not meant to be. I'm tired.'

He shook his head emphatically, moving away from her. 'I don't have visitors here. Least of all his type. I know of him. I keep myself informed about what goes on in Ibiza.'

I'm making things worse, she thought. Charles has talked too much about those damned pictures, and this old man has heard that, and about his drinking. 'We are not visitors,' she said. 'He's had an accident. He's in pain. He cannot walk.' She had an idea. 'Can I telephone San José for a taxi?'

He was pacing the hall, hands clasped behind his back, forehead creased. 'There is no telephone.'

She sighed. 'He was right. He did not want me to come here.'

'Then why did you come?'

'When I saw that he could not walk, I insisted. It was already late.'

Van Biljon looked at the clock on the mantelpiece. It showed ten minutes after eight. He stopped pacing and turned to the housekeeper. 'When do you expect Tomaso?'

'He has gone to his brother at Portinax, señor. He is staying the night.'

Van Biljon clicked his teeth in annoyance. 'Her husband has the Land-Rover. Otherwise one of my servants would drive you into San José.' He began pacing again. 'Where on the terrace is he?'

She explained as best she could: about a kilometre down the road and something like three hundred metres along the terrace.

Van Biljon turned to the housekeeper. 'Tell Pedro to take the donkey cart and go with Señorita Valez to the terrace.' He addressed Manuela. 'You can bring Black here. Techa will give you what you need for his foot. When it has been attended to we can decide what must be done. Probably Pedro will take you in the cart to San José.'

Manuela wanted to laugh and cry. She had an absurd picture in her mind of riding into San José with Black in the donkey cart, while at the same time she sighed with relief at the prospect of help. 'Thank you,' she said. 'You are kind.'

'This has been forced upon me.' He spoke abruptly, turning his back on her. 'Do not expect me to play host. Techa will look after you.'

She mumbled a faint, 'Good night,' in the direction of the retreating figure, and the housekeeper said, 'Come. We will go.'

It was after nine o'clock when they got Black to Altomonte and helped him from the donkey cart. Techa led them along a passage past the store-rooms and kitchens to a butler's pantry in the east wing. There was a handbasin with hot and cold water, a stainless steel sink, a dish-warmer, cupboards, chairs and tables.

The housekeeper gave them a first-aid box, plastic basin and soap and towel. 'If you want anything else ring this.' She pointed to the bell push. 'I will get you something to eat.' Her manner was severe.

Black was taking off his sock and exposing his ankle in light for the first time. He let out a small groan. The housekeeper looked back from the doorway and saw the swollen discoloured ankle. 'It looks painful,' she said.

'It is,' he said as she left the room.

Manuela knelt and examined it. 'It looks horrible. I'll bathe it in hot water.'

'You fill the basin and I'll do it. Better that way. I know what I can take.'

She filled the basin with hot water. He felt it with his toes. 'It's too hot.'

'You're making a great fuss.'

'I told you I was a coward.'

She added the cold water and later made him bathe the ankle in cold water immediately after the hot. Then she took a tube of wintergreen from the first-aid outfit and told him to rub some into the swelling. He did, and the ankle felt better. But he insisted she bandage it although she said it was un-necessary.

'If it doesn't have support, the bloody thing'll go again,' he said.

She bandaged it, and he complained about the pain.

'You should have a baby,' she said. 'Then you could talk of pain.'

'I prefer not to. Anyway, how do you know?'

'All women know.'

It was while they were eating the plain meal the housekeeper brought them that they heard the first sounds of the storm. It began with the beating of rain against the windows which soon afterwards rattled in their frames to the gusting of the wind.

Later, after the meal, Black pulled the curtains aside and saw the rain outside whipped into streaks of spray by the force of the wind.

'Hell of a storm,' he said as the sky to the south-east was lit by forked lightning and a roll of thunder reverberated through the room.

Manuela shivered. 'I hate lightning.'

'Who doesn't?'

'It'll be nice in the donkey cart.'

'Marvellous. I can't wait.' He fiddled with his beard, shaking his head. 'Sorry I let you in for this.'

'Nobody *wants* to sprain an ankle.'

'Yes,' he said absentmindedly. 'I mean no. Of course they don't.'

He looked round the room. 'I wouldn't say we're regarded as distinguished visitors.'

'What did you expect, Charles? A five-course dinner. Cigars and liqueurs in front of the fire?'

'I didn't expect anything. I didn't want to come.'

'He has given us all we need. We're to be taken to San José. That is better than being out on the terraces in such a storm.'

'Yes,' he said wearily. 'I suppose you're right.'

A flash of lightning was followed almost immediately by thunder which drowned her reply.

The dining-room was lit by wall-lamps shaded with red silk. Van Biljon sat alone at the head of the long table, the light from the candles at its centre reflected in the silver and glass. He ate slowly and with long pauses, sometimes tasting the wine, at others savouring its bouquet. But he was too tense and rattled to enjoy the meal. He did not permit visitors at Altomonte, and two of them had been thrust upon him. What was more, the man was a journalist, an art critic.

But van Biljon knew he had no option. Above all things he avoided publicity. To have refused to help would have given the journalist a story which would have resulted in publicity of the worst kind. There could be no worthwhile story in the bare fact that he and the girl had sought and received help at Altomonte. But how different if it were refused. Van Biljon had no intention of seeing Black, or of allowing him anywhere near the gallery. Indeed, it had been in his mind that the accident had been contrived so that they could get into the house. But Techa had since told him she'd seen the ankle and that it was badly bruised and swollen. One does not, reflected van Biljon, damage an ankle to order with that severity. And it was not difficult to imagine what they had been doing up in the hills, notwithstanding the bird-watching story.

But it was the storm that really upset him. It was increasing in severity, the glass still falling, and before long it would be a full gale. It could be well into the next day before it had blown itself out. To send them down to San José in the donkey cart now would be impossible. Tomaso would not be back from Portinax until nine o'clock the following day. Because the little Seat was in Ibiza being overhauled, he had been reluctant to give Tomaso permission to keep the Land-

Rover overnight, but the gardener had to pick up plants in Santa Eulalia the next morning and it had all fitted in well enough, so he had agreed. Now he bitterly regretted his decision. There was nothing for it. The unwanted visitors would have to spend the night at Altomonte.

He pressed the bell and shortly afterwards Techa's voice came from behind him. 'Señor?'

'This storm,' he said.

'Yes, señor.'

He made a despairing gesture with his hands. 'These people will have to spend the night here.'

'Yes, señor. I will make up the beds.'

She turned to go but he called her back. 'When you have shown them to their rooms, lock the doors to that wing. The front and back doors. And bolt them on the outside.'

Her face showed surprise.

'He is a journalist. An art critic he calls himself,' said van Biljon. 'It is possible he may try to get into the gallery to see the pictures. I will not have that.'

'That is impossible, señor. The gallery doors are always locked.'

'I know, Techa. But I do not want to have strangers wandering about my house at night.'

'*Si, señor*. I shall do as you say.'

Van Biljon was tapping on the table with his fingers. She knew this was a sign that he was worried. He said, 'Tell Juan and Pedro of the circumstances. When Juan takes over from Pedro at midnight, he is to check that both doors of the east wing are locked. Do you understand?'

'It shall be done, señor.'

Later, in the gallery, he sat brooding over coffee and liqueur, the dark melancholy of Tchaikovsky's *Pathétique* matching his mood of presentiment.

He had chosen the music instinctively, almost as if he'd had no other choice. When in the first movement, the lyrical melody in D major took over, he got up and started his tour of the gallery. As he contemplated the pictures, each so familiar, so well understood, so well loved, he was sedated, tranquillity returned, he forgot his unwelcome visitors and pushed his fears into the background. '*Mein Liebchen*,' he called the pictures. They were his life's work. Everything that he had done, the long grim odyssey, had been dominated by them, by the determination to acquire them. Only when he was alone in the gallery did he feel wholly at peace.

He stopped before a Pissarro. It was a boat on the Loire. Consciousness of the picture faded and he saw instead Mrs. Heimann, large and helpless, overflowing her dress, sobbing quietly because her daughter had refused to come with them, preferring to stay with her grandparents. Karl Heimann had a cold and kept blowing his nose. In the van he was hesitant about signing. Apart from the Pissarro there'd been two van der Els, some jewellery and a snuff box set with rubies, reputed to have belonged to Tsar Nicholas II.

In the woods a dog had barked as the Heimanns set off down the path, and van Biljon had worried until he heard in the distance the border patrol's 'Wer Da?'

Then he had gone to the van and driven back into Zurich.

Chapter Twelve

The rooms into which Techa showed them were small but
adequately furnished. Not for important guests, Black decided;
perhaps for the children or servants of visitors. He had seen
something of the interior of the house, though not much: the
route they had taken past the kitchen and larder, along a
passage to the butler's pantry where they'd eaten. Afterwards
the housekeeper and Manuela, one on either side, had helped
him along a passage at the end of which steps led to doors
through which they passed into a long room with a high
ceiling. The housekeeper did not stop, so he had only a fleet-
ing impression of reed and grass mats on terra-cotta floors, of
rough-cast walls, lime washed, on them old maps and prints
of Africa and South America, carved headmasks in African
hardwoods, and others of copper and silver which he presumed were South American. There were ancient weapons,
spears, assegais and machetes; African drums serving as occasional tables; chairs and benches of exotic woods with hide-
thong seats; wild animals and figurines carved in wood and
modelled in clay; primitive tapestries with Picasso-like symbols
and figures, and reproductions of cave drawings; and karosses
from the skins of wild animals. It was a curious heterogeneous
mixture of African and South American cultures.

The south side of the room had windows across which
curtains were drawn. He presumed they looked out over the
terraces to the sea beyond. There was an archway on the left
through which he could see the long hall, and he knew from
Haupt's plans that the sitting- and drawing-rooms adjoined it
on the far side to form the first level of the west wing, but
there was not time to check this.

The housekeeper hurried across the room and drew curtains
at the back to reveal a flight of stairs up which they helped
him. At the top, gates of trellised iron guarded the landing to
the east wing. They crossed it and went down a passage. At
the third door on the left they stopped. The housekeeper said,
'This is your room, señor.'

They took him in and he sat on the bed. 'Can you manage?' asked Manuela.

'Of course.' He looked at the housekeeper. 'I'm sorry to have been such a nuisance. Thank you very much for your help.'

She looked at him and mumbled something in Spanish which he didn't understand.

Manuela said, 'Good night Charles. See you in the morning,' and she and the housekeeper left the room, shutting the door behind them.

He heard the Spanish woman showing Manuela to her room on the other side of the passage. They exchanged good nights and the woman's tone sounded more friendly than it had been to him. Soon afterwards he heard the iron gates at the end of the landing clang and the key turn. So that was that. Not that they need have worried. Not to-night, at any rate.

For the next few minutes he sat on the bed, head in hands, thinking how difficult it was to believe that this had really happened. Here he was in Altomonte. The event was as clouded and remote as a dream, and he felt no emotion other than exhaustion: not enough sleep after last night's pub crawl; a long strenuous day; faking a sprained ankle was in itself tiring, and there had been emotional strain . . . now there was nothing, only the bandaged ankle, scarcely throbbing, reminded him of reality. His thoughts went back to one of the early discussions, almost at the beginning. Kagan had said: 'I am not sure you are the man for this. You are too involved emotionally. It destroys objectivity. This is dangerous.'

The noise of the storm brought him back to the present. Tired as he was he must watch and listen. He forced himself off the bed and crossed the room. There was no need to limp now. He ran the cold water in the wash-basin and rinsed his face drying it vigorously, determined to wake himself up.

Somewhere a clock chimed ten. He turned off the light and moved to the window. It glistened with rain, but that side of the house was in the lee of the storm and he opened it enough to see out. Occasional flashes of lightning lit the patio and the pergolas at the side of the pool which reflected the lights of the house.

The patio was bordered to the south by the main house and to the east and west by wings which ran back into the hillside. He knew that the gallery was in the west wing, and through the driving rain he could see its high walls, ghostlike and unsubstantial. As he watched, the lights there came on and its long hidden flank assumed dimensions of warmth and reality.

It was seven minutes past ten. This was the fourth occasion on which he had seen the lights come on soon after ten. On three of them he had been alone on the hillside. To-night confirmed the pattern. Presumably van Biljon visited the gallery each night after dinner at a few minutes past ten. On the other occasions the lights had been switched off at about eleven-thirty. If that happened to-night the pattern would be complete.

He closed the window and, as a precaution, set the alarm on his wristwatch to eleven. He did not intend to sleep but lay on his bed, his mind numbed by problems. Because he was tired he was depressed, and the problems seemed enormously magnified.

He wondered if Manuela in the room across the passage was able to sleep. The more he thought about her the more confused he became, everything in him that was instinctive wanting her, everything that was rational rejecting her: *Kyriakou. Drugs. Tino Costa. Ahmed ben Hassan. George Madden.*

A discussion he'd had with her in the woods that day moved across his mind like a teleprinter tape. She'd been chiding him about his drinking.

'You drug, don't you?' He'd said it good naturedly, smiling, and she'd not been annoyed.

'Yes. If you mean hash and LSD.'

'Do you use them often?'

'Sometimes,' she said, and he wondered if the ambiguity were intentional.

'Why?'

'Same reason that you drink. For kicks.'

'What about your health?'

She shrugged her shoulders. 'They do less harm than alcohol.'

'That's a phoney argument.'

'It's not, you know.'

He shook his head. 'Every addict hooked on heroin or cocaine started on so-called soft drugs.'

'So what?'

'You'll become an addict.'

She looked past him with misty unseeing eyes. 'Maybe. Just like maybe you'll become an alcoholic.'

Outside the window there was a flash of lightning and his recollection of the conversation faltered, the thought sequences became irrelevant, and he fell asleep to the howling of wind and the rumble of thunder.

Uneasy sleep ended in the old nightmare: *pursuit in a dark forest, behind him the distant barking of dogs and gun shots. He fell into a hole almost covered with bracken, dank and wet, and waited, shivering with terror. Soon the sound of men running and the hunting howl of dogs, the pitch rising as they approached, then fading into the distance.*

He woke up wet with sweat, long remembered fear gripping him. He realised that the howl of the wind and the rattling of the windows had induced the dream. It was ten minutes to eleven. He switched off the wristwatch alarm and pulled aside the window curtain. The rain had stopped but the wind had become a gale and the house shook to its gusts. The gallery lights were still on, but van Biljon's bedroom suite and study were in darkness.

In a flash of lightning he saw for the first time that a steel ladder led from the patio to the roof of the west wing. As in all Ibizencan *fincas*, the flat-topped roofs were used for collecting rainwater. The ladder would be for access to the roof to clean the catchment area. He opened the window wider and leant out to examine the wall of the east wing, where his room was. There, ten feet to his right, was a replica of the ladder opposite.

Once on the roof of the east wing he would be able to see into the gallery; not only that, he would be able to see into van Biljon's bedroom.

For a few minutes he weighed the risks against the advantages. In other circumstances the risks would have been too great, but to-night there was a gale blowing, it was intensely dark, and there were intermittent squalls of rain.

He took off everything but his vest and underpants, unrolled the dark Pakamac from his fishing bag, put it on and sat barefooted, waiting. The rain came not long afterwards in fierce driving squalls, and he opened the window. Standing on the sill, he faced the wall and reached upwards until his fingers grasped the plaster rim of the roof, raised a few inches to contain the rain. His fingers searched for the roughness of cement between the terra-cotta tiles and finding it he tested his hold, increasing the load on his arms until he found he could support the weight of his body. He knew he would have some six feet to travel before he could put out his left hand and grip the steel ladder. But the short journey took several minutes and during it there were flashes of lightning which turned night into day and inflicted on him agonies of apprehension.

At last he reached the ladder, pulled himself on to it and clawed his way to the roof. Lying flat, he rolled inwards so that he could not been seen from the patio.

Slowly, on hands and knees, he worked his way along the roof until he was opposite the centre of the gallery. Then he lay on his stomach and inched towards the edge of the roof until he could look into the gallery. He found he could see through three different windows, but because of the height at which they were set in the wall his view began about five feet from the gallery floor. He saw the tops of two inner walls or screens, six feet or so high, and of the far wall, and tantalising views of the tops of pictures. Twice he saw van Biljon's head moving between the screens. He soon realised that the risks he was taking were not being justified, and he inched back towards the centre of the roof. The rain squall had passed, he was wet and cold and his teeth chattered. But he could not begin the return journey until the rain came again. From where he lay he could see the light reflected from the gallery windows. In a few minutes it would be eleven-thirty. If there was a fixed routine, the gallery lights would go off at that time. The minutes ticked away and then when the luminous dial of his watch showed eleven thirty-five, the glow of the lights went. Not bad, he thought.

Not long afterwards the rain came and he began the return journey. When he reached the head of the ladder, he lay watching van Biljon's bedroom windows. Presently the lights there went on and he saw van Biljon come into the room. But the old man drew dark curtains across the windows, and Black realised he'd seen all he was going to see. Not that he'd really expected any return, but it was always worth trying.

It was blowing and raining hard and he was soaked, water streaming down his face, his eyes and mouth full of it, his hair and beard holding it like flooded sponges. He lay facing the ladder, working his feet and body round to the left in a wide arc to bring them parallel with the rim. As his knees reached it he felt an obstruction and stopped. But it was too late. The loose tile crashed on to the patio below and immediately a dog began barking, the noise multiplying as others took up the alarm. With his nerves jangling, he rolled backwards, away from the edge of the roof, and waited. Almost at once arc lights came on around the house, evidently operated by one switch. He muttered, 'Christ! Bloody *son et lumière*,' and the observation steadied his nerves.

Above the noise of the storm he heard a man shout. There came an answering cry and the sound of running feet in the patio. The tension became traumatic as the beam of a torch reached into the sky opposite where he lay. There were more footsteps and men's voices, then, after numbing moments, the beam of light disappeared. The noise of the wind was too great to make out what was said, but he heard the Spanish words *teja*—tile—and *tormenta*—storm. The dogs stopped barking, the lights went out, and the footsteps receded. Shivering with cold and apprehension, Black waited for some time before continuing the return journey. When at last he reached his room he hung the wet Pakamac over the basin, wrang out his underclothes and put them on the steam radiator. He bathed aching fingers in water as hot as he could bear, then rubbed himself down with a towel and climbed into bed. He had learnt a number of things, but he doubted if Kagan would have approved. Just as he wouldn't have approved of what was being done about Hassan.

Sleep came to him while he was thinking about Kagan, envying the man his hard professionalism, and ruthless detachment, and wishing that he could be more like him and less like himself.

He was woken by a knock on the door. It was the housekeeper with rolls and coffee. 'My husband will be back at nine o'clock. He will drive you and Señorita Valez into San José. Please be ready.' Her manner was brisk and businesslike. Then came the sound of the iron gates being closed and locked on the landing. It was eight-fifteen.

Not taking any chances, are they, he thought. But at least her demeanour hadn't suggested that the fallen tile was his doing. He drew the curtains and looked at the weather. The rain had stopped, the wind had fallen and there were patches of blue sky.

Soon after nine, he heard the sound of a car. Not long afterwards there came a peremptory knock. It was the housekeeper. 'The car is waiting, señor. Please come at once.'

Manuela came from her room on the other side of the passage and Black remembered, belatedly, to limp as she and the housekeeper helped him along past the iron gates and down the stairs into what he'd mentally labelled the Tribal Room. Juan was waiting there. Black thought he looked tired. Chasing *la teja*, perhaps?

With the housekeeper leading, and Juan and Manuela now assisting him, they went down the passage past the pantries and kitchens to the waiting Land-Rover. Techa's husband, Tomaso, turned out to be a dark bulbous-nosed man. He looked gloomy, presumably at the prospect of driving into San José so soon after his return from Portinax. His reply to their '*Buenos dias, señor,*' was a gruff, '*Dias.*'

They thanked the housekeeper for all she had done, asked her to convey their thanks to Señor van Biljon, exchanged *adios* and sat back. Tomaso let out the clutch, the Land-Rover started down the drive which flanked the house, and Black felt like a runaway schoolboy being returned to his institution. As they approached the gates he made a mental note of their heavy iron-bound construction, estimated the height of the stone wall surrounding the house, and looked curiously at Pedro who was on duty with two Alsatians.

'Aren't they beautiful?' said Manuela as the Land-Rover drew away.

Black made a face. 'Absolute darlings. Those teeth!'

She gave him a sideways look. 'You don't like dogs?'

'Not that lot.'

Pedro closed the gates and Black looked back at the steps leading to the front door, but there was no sign of van Biljon. During the drive down the valley he checked as much detail of the road and terrain as he could, masking this activity with small talk with Manuela. Several times he attempted to draw Tomaso into some sort of conversation, but without success.

When the Land-Rover went over a bad pothole Black groaned. Manuela touched his arm. 'Is it very painful?'

He bit his lip as ostentatiously as he could, grimacing with what he hoped looked like pain. 'Pretty bloody,' he said.

She looked at him sadly. 'Poor Charles.'

At the bottom of the valley they reached the junction with the main road and turned right. A peasant working in the field at the turn-off leant on his fork and watched the Land-Rover travel down the tarmac towards San José. When it was out of sight he took a notebook from his pocket and wrote in it.

He was the man with the black beret and the mournful face.

Chapter Thirteen

Few were watching the white schooner as her crew made ready for sea: a handful of bystanders, people with nothing better to do, two small boys and, in the café across the road, the thin man who'd just put down the telephone and gone to a window seat where he could see the *Snowgoose* without fear of her crew seeing him.

In the engine-room Kamros was running the diesels dead slow, the propellers just turning, checking the thrust-block bearings, while the stern-line and after-spring strained and creaked as they held the schooner against the thrust of the screws. Dimitrio was in the bows oiling the windlass. Helmut and Francois were on deck checking the running gear.

'What time d'you make it?' asked Helmut.

Francois looked at his watch. 'Twelve minutes to. He's late. He'll delay us.'

'Maybe not. We said we were sailing at eleven.'

As he spoke a car came up the quay and stopped alongside the schooner. Helmut said, 'There he is,' and called softly to Dimitrio who looked up, nodded and went below. A man in uniform got out of the car, a file of papers under his arm, and stood on the quay thumbing through the file. Once on board, he introduced himself as Señor Manzala, representative of the Port Captain. Francois, who spoke good Spanish, took him down to the saloon where Helmut was waiting with a bottle of wine. After a preliminary exchange of courtesies they got down to business: the account for port dues was presented, inspected and paid. Francois explained that they were going to sea for a few days, to take photos and make notes of the coastline to the south and west of the port, and to visit Formentera and Abago.

They discussed the weather and the cruise of the *Snowgoose* thus far, and Señor Manzala asked if they might be so considerate as to show him examples of their work.

When this request had been satisfied, he expressed admiration for the schooner and inquired if they would be so kind as to show him round. Francois assured him that this would be a pleasure.

They started with the cockpit where he was shown the wheel, the compass, the repeater to the electronic log, the echo sounder, the engine controls, and the hooded chart-table. The watertight hatches to the engine-compartment were at his request lifted so that he might see the Gardner diesels. Then he climbed down into the compartment and examined the engines carefully, expressing surprise at their bulk and congratulating Kamros on their spotless appearance. Next followed a visit to the owner's suite, where he was shown, among other things, the two-way radio telephone and the radio direction finder.

They explained to Señor Manzala that they didn't use the owner's suite because the accommodation off the saloon was more practical for them since they were also crewing. While expressing admiration for the owner's suite, he assured them of the correctness of their decision. Next they visited the crew's quarters in the bows—a four-berth cabin—at present, they explained, occupied only by Kamros and Dimitrio. Finally, they returned to the saloon and looked into the cabins off it which were used by Helmut and Francois.

Francois pointed to the starboard door in the foremost bulkhead. 'Perhaps you would wish to see the galley, señor?' The señor thought he would, so they inspected it and he exclaimed upon its smallness.

Back in the saloon once more Francois beamed at him. 'And now you have seen it all, señor.'

But Manzala was looking over the Frenchman's shoulder to the port door in the foremost bulkhead—the door of the radio office. 'Ah, señor,' he said. 'What have you there?'

Francois smiled thinly.' A lavatory, señor.'

'Pardon, señor. May I? It is the wine.' Señor Manzala smiled as if in deprecation of his lack of fortitude.

Francois tried the door. From inside came Dimitrio's grunt.

The Frenchman shrugged his shoulders apologetically. 'Unfortunately Dimitrio is there. Poor fellow, he has an upset stomach. However, please use the lavatory in the owner's suite.' Without waiting for the Spaniard's reply he led the way aft through the cockpit, Señor Manzala following and Helmut bringing up the rear.

The Snowgoose had cleared the harbour and was past Botafoc

lighthouse when Señor Manzala reported to Capitan Calvi.

'I had a good look round,' he said. 'They took me everywhere. I went into the engine-compartment. The diesels are exceptionally large, but I saw nothing else of interest. All that I observed on board was consistent with the work these men say they are engaged upon. In the saloon there is much writing and photographic material, typewriters, cameras, paints. They showed me specimens of their work. It seemed professional. Of a high standard, I should say.'

The thin man looked at him doubtfully. 'I am more interested in what you did not see. The storerooms, forepeak, the bilges.'

The port official held out his hands, shrugging his shoulders. 'I could not ask to see these without arousing suspicion.'

'Of course, Señor Manzala. Do not worry. You have done your duty.'

There was a fresh easterly wind blowing and once they had cleared the harbour sail was set, the diesels were stopped and *Snowgoose* heeled over, clipping along to the south at eight knots.

'This is the life,' said Helmut leaning over the Perspex hooded chart-table.

At the wheel Francois nodded. 'Better than hanging round the harbour. There's nothing worse than waiting.'

To starboard, a mile or so away, the coast was slipping by: Figuretes, Playa den Bossa, the Malvin rocks, Sal Rosa, Punta Corpmari and Punta Portas. Astern, Ibiza, its buildings rising steeply on the hill above the harbour, was fading into the distance. There was a broken sea and at times the schooner dug her bows into it and sluiced spray over the deck, so that all was moist and fresh and the foot of the sails glistened in the sunlight.

Off Isla Ahorcados course was altered to the west and the schooner ran with the wind astern, making for the rocky pinnacle of Vedra, twelve miles ahead. At three o'clock in the afternoon they rounded Vedra and soon afterwards shortened sail and stood in towards the coast.

As they closed the land an engine was started, sails were lowered and the schooner anchored in the lee of the land off Cala d'Or.

For the next hour or so her crew were busy with cameras,

sketch-books and notebooks, and in the late afternoon they found time for a swim. Some time after six o'clock, anchor was weighed and *Snowgoose* stood out to sea on a southerly course. The wind had backed slightly but was still fresh. By nightfall she was well away from the land. At nine o'clock navigation lights were switched off, sails lowered, the engines started and course altered to the east, the schooner heading directly into wind and sea.

At midnight Helmut got a fix from the lights at Vedra and Ahorcados which put the schooner three miles south of Cabo Llentrisca. Course was altered to the north-east and they made for a *cala* to the east of Cabo Negret. Two miles from the shore the engines were stopped and the schooner proceeded under light canvas, moving silently through the water, showing no lights.

The land rose steeply round the base of the horseshoe bay, and once in it *Snowgoose* encountered sheltered water and lost the wind. Sails were lowered and her way carried her slowly inshore until the echo-sounder showed the water shoaling fast. The anchor was lowered, not dropped, and she came in to five fathoms.

There were no shore lights ahead of them. They had visited the *cala* by road a few days before and knew that there was nothing there but the road from San José winding down through land marked out for development but as yet not built upon. Nevertheless they had taken pains to conceal the schooner's arrival, and in this they had been assisted by the dark night and clouded sky.

A rubber dinghy was brought up on deck, inflated and put over the side. Francois, Helmut and Dimitrio, wearing dark clothing, climbed into it and paddled for the shore.

The best part of two hours later, Kamros heard a low whistle and the dinghy bumped alongside in the darkness. Helmut climbed on board, and Francois and Dimitrio manœuvred the rubber craft under the schooner's bow. A line was taken from the *Snowgoose* and made fast. Then Kamros and Helmut weighed the schooner's anchor and the men in the dinghy began to paddle. Slowly the *Snowgoose* responded to the tow and when the first breath of wind touched her a jib was hoisted, Francois and Dimitrio came back on board, and the dinghy was recovered, deflated and stowed below.

More sail was set, *Snowgoose*'s speed increased and she was put on a southerly course.

'How was it?' asked Kamros.

'Okay,' said Helmut who was at the wheel. 'We must anchor closer next time. There's plenty of water. The dinghy journey can be shortened quite a bit.' He looked at the deck watch on the chart-table. It was three hours and twenty-seven minutes past midnight.

'Did our guest give any trouble?'

'Not at all,' said Kamros. 'It seems seasickness makes him sleep.'

Francois shivered with cold. 'It would have been difficult without this reccy. Everything seems different in the dark.'

'Everything *is* different in the dark,' growled Dimitrio. 'Except women.'

Snowgoose was far out to sea by sunrise.

For the next two days Black kept to his room, going through the motions of nursing his ankle, deprecating the fuss Maria Massa made of him, and keeping her away from the injury. Several times he telephoned Manuela. When at last he found her in he asked her to come and see him. She expressed concern for his ankle, but said she was too busy. She simply had to get on with her painting. She'd persuaded a local gallery to take eight pictures for an exhibition in a month's time and she'd only done three. She promised to see him soon but could not name a day.

He found the story unconvincing and wondered how much of the time she'd be spending with Kyriakou. He shied away from admitting that he was jealous, ascribing his emotions to concern for her well-being. But another matter troubled him more seriously. He was desperately anxious to collect Werner Zolde's letter from the post office, for he still did not know if Hassan had been dealt with. For this and other reasons he found the enforced seclusion frustrating to a degree. But it was necessary, not only to maintain the ankle fiction, but because he needed time now, uninterrupted time, for planning. So he spent hours on his bed thinking, then at the table with pen and paper drawing up programmes and time-tables, making lists of possible courses of action and counter-action, for each of which he would work out responses.

Everything that he sketched or wrote he burnt, the salient facts he committed to memory. At the end of three days he consoled himself with the knowledge that in no other way could he have found the time to plan so thoroughly.

Maria Massa brought him a walking stick and on the third day he took his shopping basket and hobbled downstairs. The swelling had gone but the ankle was bandaged and he wore a slipper. By the time he reached the market he'd acquired a reasonably comfortable gait combined with what he believed to be a convincing limp.

His first call was the post office. There were two letters for him. One from Werner Zolde. Out in the *paseo* he sat on a bench, tore open the envelope and read the brief message: *All is well. Your friend is with us. Safe and sound. Do not worry.* No address, no signature—but, oh, what a relief. He took a deep breath and felt his whole body relax. For some minutes he sat in the warm sun, his mind emptied for the moment of its troubles. Then he opened the envelope with the Madrid postmark. In it he found an acceptance slip for the article on de Salla's *vernissage* and a cheque for twenty-five pounds. He took the cheque to the Banque Abel Matutes Torres and deposited it. The teller, who knew him, was friendly and asked why he limped. Black said he'd fallen climbing in the hills. The teller smiled politely, without conviction, and Black knew what he was thinking. After that he shopped in the market and at Spar. When he'd finished it was getting on for noon and he began to look for Manuela. She was not on the pavement outside the Alhambra or the Montesol, but several people he knew were and as he hobbled past he felt absurdly self-conscious. Ilse Berch, at a table by herself, was sympathetic. 'I know all about it,' she said. 'Manuela told me.'

'Seen her this morning?'

'Yes she was here half an hour ago. With friends.'

'Really. Who were they?'

'No idea, Charles. Two young men. They looked nice.' Ilse was enjoying herself.

'Any idea where they went?'

'Along Calle Rambau. Perhaps Malcolm's Boutique or Knack. I know she wanted to get some slacks.'

'I shouldn't have thought she needed two young men for that.'

Ilse Berch's eyes twinkled. 'You never know, Charles.'

'So long,' he said. 'If you see her, say I'm on the prowl.'

110

She wasn't at either of the boutiques, and although he didn't really think she'd be there he looked in at Mariano's, Bud's Bar and the George and Dragon, staying for a drink at each, and then, feeling better, he resumed the search, this time making for the waterfront.

It was a fine day, a few clouds tossed out like white candy floss straggled in the sky, and the sun was the warmest he'd yet experienced in Ibiza. It's good to be alive, he thought, even carrying this limp around. The plane trees were putting out new leaves and once again he was struck by the quality of light in Ibiza. It was of exceptional brilliance and opalescent. Ibiza was called the White Island, and he wondered whether it was because of this light or the limewashed houses. Perhaps it was both. He went past the church of San Telmo and came to the harbour. Manuela was not at the tables outside the Bar Formentera nor at the Pechet. He went on past the Plaza Marino Riquer, drew a blank at Juanito's, Delfin Verde, Les Caracoles and Can Garroves. He went along Calle de Carijo, the ships on his left and the old buildings of sa Peña on his right, the limewashed walls splashed with brightly painted doors and windows, and the small iron-railed balconies decorated with pots of geranium and fern. Up the side streets, lines of washing hung across from house to house like limp flag-hoists, children played in noisy groups, and neighbours resting from their chores chatted from balcony to balcony.

He had almost given up the search when he saw her at a table under the trees outside Clive's Bar. Though her back was to him, he knew at once that it was Manuela. There were two men with her, one big and burly with side burns and a full beard, the other slighter, with face fuzz, drooping whiskers, long unkempt hair and large gold ear-rings. Both men were dark-eyed and sun-tanned.

Black limped past the table, pretending not to see her, but she called his name and he turned and leant on his stick. 'Hallo. Thought you were painting.' He said it sullenly.

'I was.' She patted the seat next to her. 'Come and sit down.'

The young men shuffled in their chairs, not looking particularly pleased. Manuela inclined her head towards them. 'Do you know each other?'

They looked glum and shook their heads.

'Charles,' she said. 'Meet Helmut and Francois.'

The men grunted at each other, a waiter came up and Black ordered a beer.

Characteristically, she tilted her head on one side. 'How's the ankle?'

'Better, thanks.'

'I see you are using a stick.'

'It helps.'

She explained to the others how Black had injured his ankle. Helmut's eyebrows arched. 'What were you doing on the hills?'

'Bird watching.' Black yawned.

'*Bird watching.*' Francois' tone was a mixture of surprise and condescension.

Helmut turned to Manuela. 'Were you also there?'

'Yes. We had a marvellous day.' She laughed mischievously. 'And night.'

Helmut said. 'So. You sleep in the hills?'

'Kind of,' she said. 'As guests in a beautiful house.'

'So,' Helmut, nodding gravely, stroked his beard.

Manuela avoided Black's frosty stare. 'I met them last night. Kirry introduced us. They have a marvellous boat, Charles. Over there.' She pointed down the harbour.

'A schooner,' corrected Helmut stolidly.

'What's her name?'

'*Snowgoose.*'

'I've seen her. Not bad.' Black's lack of enthusiasm was a calculated snub.

Over the drinks he asked them what they were doing in Ibiza, his manner making it clear that he couldn't really care less. After they had told him, they expressed equally unenthusiastic interest in his activities. He was non-committal. Manuela stepped in and explained that he was a journalist, an art critic. Their shrugged shoulders and raised eyebrows seemed to indicate how little they thought of these occupations. A few minutes later they made their apologies and left.

Black watched them cross the street and make for the quay where the inter-island schooners lay. 'You've been elusive lately.'

'Have I?' she said.

'You couldn't see me, but you've had time for Kyriakou and those cretins.' He jerked a thumb over his shoulder.

112

'They're not cretins. They're nice. I met them by accident. And my date with Kirry was made ages ago.'

Gloomily he sat watching the beer bubbles effervescing, forming at the bottom of the glass, expanding, then rising hopefully through the amber liquid to explode into nothingness when they reached the surface. Like this thing if I fail, he thought.

Manuela sat watching him, her elbows on the table, cheeks resting on clenched fists. 'What did you think of Helmut and Francois?'

'I didn't think.'

'Not very co-operative to-day, are we?' She tried again. 'Fabulous jobs some people get. Fancy going round the islands in that lovely boat. Interesting creative work with fat royalties sticking out at the end.'

Black yawned again, more noisily this time. 'Possibly. I don't believe the story of a publisher's commission. Much more likely to be rich daddies at home footing the bill. A book at the end of it, *maybe, perhaps*. You know.'

'You were unpleasant to them, Charles.' Her eyes reproved him. 'Your trouble is that you're madly envious. You must have had an unhappy childhood. It's your nastiest characteristic. Otherwise you are a darling man.'

'I did,' said Black.

'Did what?'

'Have an unhappy childhood.'

'Tell me.'

'It isn't for discussion.'

Manuela worked hard on his mood and slowly he responded. They discussed the night at Altomonte and laughed about it. She said how much she'd enjoyed the climb in the hills, what a strange person van Biljon was, and what a lovely house he had. Once again Black complained about having been so close to the pictures without having seen them, but she got him off the subject.

Later they went over to La Solera and sat in the warm sun and ate *tapas*: *chipirones*, the baby squids, and *angulas*, and *sobrasadas* and black olives. Black drank half a bottle of the bar's speciality, a dry aromatic *fino*, and she had her inevitable orange juice. His mood improved steadily with the food and wine, and with her sympathy and affection which he so much needed.

He looked at her over his wine glass. 'Doing anything to-night?'

' 'Fraid so.'

'Who is it?'

'Kyriakou.'

His mouth set in a hard line. 'For Christ's sake! You live in his pocket.'

She shook her head. 'I knew him long before you, Charles. And I don't live in his pocket.'

'Why d'you go round with a bloody gangster?'

'He's not a gangster.' She leant forward, her manner suddenly changed. 'Look, Charles. Either you accept things as they are or you'd better not see me again. It's up to you.'

Every fibre of him wanted to tell her to go to hell and take the bloody Greek with her, but he was not going to give way to his emotions. She'd been invaluable once before. She might well be so again in the days that lay ahead. So he shrugged his shoulders and said, 'Sorry. It's just that I think you're wasted on that sort of man.'

'Let's not discuss it any more,' she said incisively.

The waiter came up and Black paid the bill. 'What about to-morrow?'

She shook her head. 'No good, Charles. But the next day's okay.'

'Right. At the Celler Balear at nine-thirty for dinner. Okay?'

'Lovely, Charles.'

'We'll dance afterwards.'

'Dance? What about the ankle?'

'I'd forgotten about that. Anyway we'll do something.' He *had* forgotten the ankle. He'd have to watch out. He was getting careless.

She smiled, collecting her things. 'Don't move,' she said. 'Rest your foot. I've got to rush.' She stood up, touched his cheek with the back of her hand and left him. He shifted to the other side of the table so that he could see her go. She was walking along the *muello* towards the town. Before she turned she looked back and waved, and he raised his hand limply. The futility of it all depressed him. He could no longer pretend she didn't mean something to him. And not only was that dangerous but it was hopeless. There was no future for them. Even the name she knew him by wasn't his own. He would be gone soon. And she? God knows what would happen to her.

When he got back to his room Maria Massa was mopping the stairs. She returned his greeting with a distant nod. He wondered what he'd done? The rent was paid. How had he offended?

Still worrying, he went into his room, put the stick and basket on the table and the things he'd bought on the shelves round the small stove at the end of the room. Then he went to the cupboard where he kept his files and stationery. Everything was in order, neat and tidy. But he was a man of careful habit and he soon saw that the order was not his. The drawers and the cupboard in which he kept his clothes told the same story. Someone had gone through them. He checked. Nothing was missing. There hadn't been anything incriminating anyway, so he had no fears on that account. But one thing was certain: his room had been searched. It would not be Maria Massa. But she knew who it was. And the reason she didn't tell him was obvious. It was the police.

Chapter Fourteen

The percolator gave a final hiss and bubble, the turbulence subsided, and van Biljon, cigar clenched between his teeth, leant forward, holding the coffee cup beneath the small copper tap, his hand shaking so that the cup trembled on its saucer.

The *Emperor Concerto* was approaching the end of the first movement, the music swelling, chord upon chord, its grandeur overwhelming thought. He went across to the cabinet and switched off. Silence was essential to the tangle in his mind.

Putting down the coffee cup he leant back in the armchair in a conscious effort to relax, a haze of cigar smoke gathering about his head as he tried to recall what Calvi had said.

Van Biljon had long been on cordial terms with the Gobernador Delegado and the Jefe de Comisario, as he was with other senior officials on the island, and he knew he enjoyed their respect. But Capitan Calvi, who had come ostensibly for a donation to the Widows and Orphans Fund of the Guardia Civil, had clearly had something else on his mind. In the course of a long and often inconsequential conversation he had brought up the names of Manuela Valez, Black and Kyriakou. Van Biljon had not met Calvi before: indeed, the thin Spaniard had told him that he had not been on the island long, having served formerly in Madrid. Nor had he arrived unannounced: the Comisario had sent him a note explaining that although Calvi's mission concerned a matter of small importance, it would be appreciated if van Biljon would see him personally.

When Calvi had asked if he knew Valez and Black—casually it is true and à propos of a remark he himself had made about Ibiza's attraction for artists and writers—van Biljon had said, 'I have met her. I do not know him.'

Calvi had looked out of the window and said quietly and without emphasis, 'I believe they were guests in this house a few nights ago.'

At once van Biljon had explained the circumstances, adding

with some warmth, 'They are complete strangers to me. I do not have visitors here. I prefer a solitary life.'

The Spaniard had assured van Biljon that he understood perfectly what had occurred, but after some further small talk he had brought up the name of Kyriakou.

'You do not know him, señor?'

'I have recently met him,' said van Biljon guardedly.

Calvi had gone to the window again and looked down over the terraces towards the sea. 'And he—has he visited Altomonte?'

'Yes,' said van Biljon. 'Once, a few days ago.'

'Oh. Did he, too, come uninvited?'

'He had expressed a wish to see me. A business matter. I wrote and asked him to call. He was not here long.'

Calvi came back from the window, the cheroot poking from the corner of his mouth at a jaunty angle, curiously out of keeping with the man's quiet civility. 'Señor Kyriakou is a rich man,' he said. 'He disposes much influence.'

'So I believe,' said van Biljon.

Calvi sighed. 'And you do business together, señor?'

'I would hardly call it that. I own a house in D'Alt Vila which he wishes to lease.'

Calvi changed the subject then to building activity in Ibiza, the rising demand for tourist accommodation, and the fortunes which land speculators were said to be making.

They discussed the tourist industry, its importance to the island, and the wide range of attractions Ibiza offered.

Calvi expressed the view that more and more yachts would visit the island and that harbour facilities should be expanded to cope with this. In these days of affluence, he said, the number of yachts in the Mediterranean ran into tens of thousands.

'What Ibiza needs is a marina. Something on a really large scale.'

'Probably you are right,' said van Biljon. 'But I for one do not welcome these developments. For me the attraction of Ibiza lies in what nature and history has provided. The climate, the terrain, the indigenous architecture. Above all the charm and integrity of the Ibizencans. The tourists and the developments they stimulate are to me excrescences. Tourists are parasitic. They leech on the island. I suppose I am selfish and old fashioned.'

Calvi smiled. 'Do not think we Spaniards like tourists any more than you do, señor. But they represent an industry of immense importance to Spain.'

Van Biljon sighed. 'I love this little harbour. I do not approve of the reclamations on the Talamanca side. It seems to me that they are making the harbour smaller. If this marina you speak of is built, there is going to be no room to move.'

'You have a boat I believe, señor?'

The old man nodded. 'The *Nordwind*. You have seen her?'

'Yes,' Calvi said. 'A fine craft.'

'You must come out in her one day.'

Calvi bowed. 'I shall be delighted, señor.' He paused before adding, 'There is another fine boat in the harbour.'

'Indeed?'

Calvi took the cheroot out of his mouth and examined it with a critical eye. 'The *Snowgoose*.'

Something in the way the Spaniard said it made van Biljon feel that Calvi believed he should have some knowledge of the schooner. This puzzled him.

'I have seen the *Snowgoose* in harbour,' he said.

'You know those on board, possibly?' Calvi tapped with his fingers on an African drum and its taut resonances vibrated through the room.

'No. I do not. My servants have told me they are cruising in the Mediterranean. Compiling a guide for yachtsmen. That is all I know.'

'Where,' said the Spaniard stroking the hide-bound sides of the drum, 'does this come from?'

'From the Congo. It is a Watusi drum.'

'Have you heard the African drumming?' Calvi's voice was wistful.

'Often,' said van Biljon. 'An unforgettable experience. It is as if the soul of Africa were throbbing.'

Soon after that Calvi had left, but his questions had nagged insistently throughout the day. It was not that they had been aggressively directed, nor had Calvi pressed him for answers. But the Spaniard had seemed to be searching for leads in a casual but persistent way.

At no time had he hinted at the reasons for his questions and in the end he'd switched the conversation to the weather and the small talk of the town.

And now, lying back in the armchair in the gallery, having recalled all that had been said, van Biljon was no wiser. He remained deeply disturbed: the coupling of Kyriakou's name with those of Manuela Valez and Charles Black, all three recent visitors to Altomonte—a house which did not receive visitors—and the questions about the *Snowgoose*. Van Biljon couldn't make sense of it, but he was left with the conviction that he'd been the subject of subtle cross-examination. What, he asked himself, lies behind this? What motive drives Calvi? And what is it these other people are up to which interests the police?

It was not in his nature to sit back and let situations develop. Too much was at stake. Resolving to find out more the next day, he left the armchair and began his tour of the gallery, moving slowly, savouring the pictures, knowing that it was for the van Gogh he was making. It would never have occurred to him to go straight to it, to vary the route he took, the order in which he viewed the pictures. When he reached it he stood before it, hands in the pockets of his velvet smoking jacket, rocking slowly on his feet, the cigar smoke spiralling above his head. The self-portrait had a macabre fascination. Was it, he often wondered, the self-inflicted mutilation, the bond of masochism? Or was it that van Gogh had been mad? There were times when van Biljon suspected that he himself was mad.

But always the van Gogh evoked another picture: white moonlight on a concrete path, a darkened villa in Bahia Blanca, slits of light edging the drawn blinds; the front door opening into a dark hall, a woman's voice saying, '*Pasa, señor*,' the door closing behind him and lights coming on to reveal a sharp-eyed, big boned woman—Torreta's nurse/housekeeper, his mistress, some said; the cool white walls of the surgery at the back, the single-bedded ward adjoining it; over all the prophylactic smell of iodoform.

He had spent seven weeks there before going on to Santa Fé. Even now he winced with recollected pain.

And Torreta himself: cold, impassive, compassionless. Above all, as befitted a man whose fees were exorbitant beyond belief, discreet.

Chapter Fifteen

It was a night of dark sky and bright stars, of light wind and the distant murmur of the sea, and closer at hand the clamour of traffic. Black had walked down from the old town, still carrying the stick, limping slightly when darkness did not cover him. He crossed the Paseo Vara de Rey and made for the Avenida Ignacio Wallis, the name evoking memories of a film he'd seen long ago and the abdication.

He got to the Celler Balear before she did and ordered a dry Martini. When it arrived, he leant against the bar dividing his attention between the Martini and diminutive mussels which he prised from their shells with a toothpick. Black liked the Celler. The food was good, the atmosphere authentic and the Spanish staff friendly and good humoured. The barman brought him a second Martini. As Black paid for it, Tino Costa and George Madden came up to the bar. He nodded briefly, the American said, 'Hi,' but the Cypriot ignored him. Black, irritated by their presence, turned his back and concentrated on the Martini, the mussels, and his problems.

The detail of the planning was settled, the timing balanced against the known factors. Only the imponderable remained, implacable and threatening, among them the dogs. If and when they'd been dealt with, a major problem would have been overcome. There was the possibility of an electronic alarm system, but he doubted it. It would have been superfluous. The outer windows were barred, there was the stone wall, the dogs patrolling inside it, and a night watchman on duty. There was no longer the problem of cutting the telephone cable because there wasn't one. That at least had been a pleasant surprise.

Before he saw her, he heard her voice. 'Hi, Charles. Sorry I'm late.'

She wore a red gardenia in her hair, and her eyes were misty and apologetic. He thought she'd never looked more lovely and wanted to take her in his arms, but all he did was lean on his stick and say, 'Not to worry. Have a drink.'

*

Over dinner she was quiet.

'What's on your mind?' he said.

'How d'you mean?'

'You're so quiet.'

She sighed and the lines round her mouth tightened as she looked over to the table where Tino Costa and Madden sat.

'I thought so,' said Black. 'Forget them. It's a free world.'

'Is it hell,' she said. 'Why do they have to come here to-night?'

He shook his head. 'For Christ's sake. Do they own you?'

'Of course they don't. Nobody does. But life's not as simple as you make out, Charles. No one is an island to oneself, independent, uninvolved. Every man and woman in this room is part of a complex structure of human relationships.'

'What does that long spiel mean?'

'You *know* what it means. I've known you for about ten days. Before that I wasn't sitting here in a vacuum.' She leant forward, tense, emphatic, trying to get through to him. 'Life goes on you know. I couldn't hang around just waiting for you to turn up. I was—I am like the rest of them.' She waved a hand round the room. 'Involved with other people.'

'Which means your night is spoilt because our friends are watching and will report back.' He jerked a contemptuous thumb in the direction of Tino Costa's table.

She nodded over the rim of her glass and he could see she was troubled. 'It's partly that,' she said. 'Don't you see, Charles, I can't just abandon Kirry. He's done a lot for me.'

For a time he was silent, then he said, 'I think I understand. I just wish your involvement was with another man, and . . .'

'*And* what, Charles?'

'And for another reason.'

She looked at him despairingly. 'I told you the other day. If you can't accept me as I am, forget me.'

'D'you want me to?'

'Of course I don't. Why d'you think I'm here?'

'Okay,' he said, suddenly cheerful. 'Let's get a taxi and go up the hill and give the Mar-Blau a thrash. Know it?'

'Yes. But . . .'

'But what?'

'I had thought of an early night.'

'Forget it,' he said.

She was silent for some time. Then she sighed again and

looking towards Tino Costa and George Madden she spoke in a low voice. 'Have you heard about Benny?'

'Benny?' he said with forced obtuseness. 'Who's he?'

'Ahmed ben Hassan. Our friend who was seasick in the steamer coming from Barcelona.'

'Oh, him,' said Black. 'No. Why?'

'He's been drowned.'

'Really. Where and when?'

'A few days ago. Bathing from the rocks below the military hospital. They found his clothes and towel there, but no trace of his body. They think the currents have taken it out to sea.'

'Poor chap,' said Black heavily. 'Was he a strong swimmer?'

'Very. He used to swim far out. He was an Olympic swimmer once. Maybe it was his heart or cramp or something. Who knows? Anything can happen in the sea.'

'I suppose so,' said Black, shaking his head. 'Poor chap.'

The taxi chugged up the hill towards Los Molinos, past the barracks where *Todo Por la Patria* showed up boldly in the headlights and made Black think how such exhortations meant different things to different people: and why not *Todo Por el Pueblo*?

Then an old shed of breeze-blocks and stone loomed up, the white patch on its wall crudely lettered Mar-Blau, Flamenco Night Club, beneath it an arrow. The taxi turned right, following the arrow, and they bumped along the road, climbing and turning. It stopped, they paid it off and went into the Mar-Blau.

A waiter showed them to a table well back from the floor and took their order. Black found Manuela's hand and squeezed it.

'Happy?' she said softly.

'Yes.' He sighed with content.

There was a breeze from the sea and the candles on the tables cast flickering shadows. A girl with a guitar and a flowing dress was singing an Andalusian song, stamping her feet, her eyes and teeth flashing defiance at the crimson spotlight. Pergolas surrounded the tables on two sides, a line of Chinese lanterns marked the bar, and to its left a terrace of tables rose to meet the slope of the hill; at its summit, the tiled roof of a *finca*, a windmill, clumps of cacti and aloes, were silhouetted against the rim of the night sky.

The girl from Andalusia finished her song, the spotlight switched to mauve and picked out the letters CHE COMBO on a drum in the background, and from the group behind it came the strains of *La-La-La* to remind the tourists that Spain had won the Eurovision song contest; underlying its cadences, the distant buzz of voices from the tables round the floor sounded like angry bee swarms.

'Like it here?' asked Black.

'Heaven,' she said. 'I adore sitting under the night sky.'

The music stopped and the waiter came up with a *coñac* and soda-siphon for Black and a Coke for Manuela. When he'd gone Black said, 'Know what? I've left the stick in the taxi.'

'Never mind,' she said. 'I'll prop you up.'

'Actually, the ankle's better. I think I can manage.'

'So I noticed.'

'You didn't say anything.'

She leant forward impulsively, laughing. 'Didn't want to spoil your act.'

Black felt the muscles in his stomach contract. *'My act!* What d'you mean?'

'You're a man, Charles. You made the most of that ankle. Got loads of sympathy.'

So that was it. His tension drained away. 'Well, it was bloody sore.'

'I'm sure it was.'

Ché Combo got going again and the lights went down. Black leant over and kissed her, feeling absurdly romantic yet knowing there could be nothing more than this moment. 'Come and dance. You'll have to support me.'

'I'll do that,' she said and pressed his arm.

When they got back to the table he called a waiter and ordered more drinks. Later, when he was paying for them, he felt her tug on his sleeve.

'Oh, God,' she said in a small voice. 'Look who's arrived.'

'Who?' said Black, counting the change.

'Kirry.'

The Greek was weaving his way through the tables towards them. His emphatically checked suit, the mauve shirt and orange tie, the magenta silk handkerchief lopping generously from the breast pocket, and the gilt band on the Havana cigar were colourful touches of vulgarity, as familiar to Black as the dark perspiring face; but he thought the Greek's smile lacked conviction.

' 'Allo, there!' Kyriakou called as he approached. Manuela smiled and murmured a subdued, 'Hi, Kirry.'

Black nodded unenthusiastically.

The Greek leant his hands on their table, his eyes on Manuela. 'Aha,' he said. 'So thees is why you cannot meet Kirry to-night. You tell me. *Kirry, I have just dinner with him. Then I make early night.*' He looked at his wrist watch, pushing back the cuff of his coat with an elaborate gesture. 'An' now is one o'clock.'

The Greek was trembling. Maybe drink, Black thought, maybe not. He's got this girl in his hair. If only he knew. He's got nothing to worry about.

Manuela shrank back in her chair, silent, fearful of the scene that was coming.

Black said, 'She wanted an early night. I talked her into this.'

'Aha,' said Kyriakou, hands on hips, cigar clenched firmly in strong white teeth. 'Is that so?' He glared at the Englishman.

A good deal of Black's caution had evaporated with the *coñac*, and he found the Greek's dramatics tedious. 'Yes, it is,' he said yawning. 'So what?'

Kyriakou's eyes reflected disbelief that this man could so have insulted him. And then, as the hard fact registered that he *had*, his eyes clouded and his hand moved towards the soda-siphon. But Black beat him to it and the Greek's fingers closed on air.

In the dim light of flickering candles, the combo swinging and throbbing its gay melody, Black, his right hand round the neck of the siphon, sat watching the Greek warily.

Kyriakou must have had second thoughts for he backed away from the table, puffing and blowing, to stop and stab with his cigar in Black's direction. 'You make beeg mistake, my friend, if you think you can take my girl.'

Trembling with emotion, he gave Black a final glare of hate and stumbled away. But the drama of his exit was spoilt by the bottle of wine he knocked off a nearby table. Its occupants were dancing, so with a characteristic flourish the Greek peeled a one-hundred peseta note from his wallet and fluttered it down on the table.

Because he knew he'd nearly been in a fight Black was tense, but the incident was not without humour and he was closer to laughter than anger. Beside him Manuela, pale and silent, shut her eyes, and he could hear her laboured breathing.

He said, '*Are* you his girl?'

'No.' She looked at him tearfully. 'I'm not anybody's.'

The taxi rattled down the road into Ibiza. To its right the high walls of the citadel hung like dark screens below the lighted windows of the houses in D'Alt Vila.

I'm tired and the *coñac* or the row with Kyriakou or something has given me indigestion, he decided. It would be good to be alone at this moment, to belch, to scratch, to fart, and to have no recollection of the night.

But Manuela is next to me. I can hear her sigh. She is worrying, so I hold her hand. She is thinking about to-morrow and the day after and all the other days because she's got herself hooked by this dope-peddling bastard who fixes her 'trips' or whatever they call them. And she is basically a nice girl. Much nicer than I am. But she is trying to escape from something and she never will because she's not tough enough. I think she's in love with me, if there is such a thing, and I suppose I am with her, if there is such a thing. But nothing can be done about it and I no longer really have any excuse for messing about with her. I'd like to be a Kagan; serious, unbending, so committed that there are no margins for lapses, so dedicated that even humour is eschewed, let alone thoughts about women and sex and one's future; so consecrated that the mind is not deflected from its houndlike pursuit of the objective by trivialities like beautiful sunsets, the flight of geese, or seas breaking on rocky headlands. And I am tight, and that's why these thoughts go tumbling inconsequentially through my mind. But to-morrow I will shed this frivolous mood, I will pick up my resolve where I dropped it, and I shall leave this island with what I've come for or bloody well die in the attempt. And *that* I mean, so held me God, and *that* I swear in the name of my forefathers. But all the same I hope I don't—die, I mean; or even find myself stuck in some foul smelling gaol.

And what is that you are saying, my little Manuela?

'Ah, here we are. Of course. How stupid of me.'

The taxi had stopped in Calle Mayor. He paid it off and saw from his watch that it was almost three o'clock. The *calle* was deserted and dark but for the dim glow of on occasional street lamp. The night air carried the stench of drains. He took her arm and they went up the steps and along a lane, turned right into another, then left, and came at last to the narrow alley high up on which crouched the tired old house where she lived.

The lane was steep and at the top he could see sky—and that was their first mistake—for he saw them coming out of a doorway, two of them, about fifty yards ahead, dark shapes blocking the stars, moving towards him.

The big man reached him first—and this disregard of Clausewitz's principle of concentration was their second mistake—for, as he lunged, Black stepped aside and kicked the Cypriot's genitals hard and accurately. Tino Costa doubled up and screamed, and Black slipped behind him and with the edge of a stiff palm chopped at the back of his neck.

These two movements occupied perhaps three seconds. It took about two and a half more to raise the Cypriot's right forearm and fracture it across his knee. That left Kyriakou, and to him the Englishman was kinder, administering only the kick in the crutch, an area to which he felt far from well disposed. Then, largely for aesthetic reasons, he lifted the fallen Greek's head in the crook of his arm and gave it two black eyes.

Manuela was pulling at him, crying, begging him to leave them alone, hissing that the police would be along at any moment for windows above them were opening, lights were coming on, and querulous voices were being raised.

Black said, 'Not to worry. I'm coming.'

Tino Costa was groaning. Black felt the Cypriot's heart beat and found it satisfactory. Kyriakou was sitting in the gutter, head in hands, sobbing quietly.

Black knelt down and said something. The Greek looked up, his face haggard in the dim light spilling down from a high window. 'Okay,' he said brokenly. 'Okay.'

Black said, 'Remember. It's that—or else.'

Kyriakou nodded emphatically. 'Okay. Leave me,' he sobbed. 'Just leave me.'

Black patted him on the head. 'Good boy,' he said. 'You put up a great fight.'

He took Manuela's arm and ran her up the lane clear of the window lights. They came out into the *calle* above and he hurried her along alleys and streets, twisting and turning, working their way down until they came to the fish market.

The lights there were on and women were busy cleaning and cutting fish from the early morning catch, so they steered off into Calle Antonio Palau and started back towards the church. There they stopped, leaning against the stone wall recovering their breath, their faces pallid in the light of a street lamp.

They had not spoken since the run from the alley.

'You all right?' he panted.

'God! It was horrible.' She was breathing deeply. She's not fit, he thought. It's that bloody muck.

'It was horrible, Charles.' Her eyes were frightened. 'I didn't know you were like that.'

'Nor did they.' He dusted his trouser legs where he had knelt.

She shook her head. 'There will be trouble. Kyriakou is a dangerous man.'

'Oh, bugger Kyriakou,' he said. 'What did you expect me to do? Let them sort me out?'

'No. But you needn't have been so violent.'

His sudden peal of laughter startled her. 'You mean I should have defended myself *gently*?'

'I am frightened, Charles. They will do something.'

'I'm bloody certain they won't.'

'How can you say that?'

In the distance he saw two patrolling policemen. 'Come on,' he said. 'Home now. To-morrow I'll tell you what I whispered in Kirry's ear. Then you'll know all is well.'

'Tell me now.'

'No. It's too late. But you've nothing to worry about.'

'For sure?'

'For sure,' he said, stopping and kissing her, and then taking her hand and hurrying her along so that she had difficulty in keeping up.

'Where did you learn to fight like that?' she said.

'Instinct.'

'Liar. Tell me.'

'Come on,' he said, thinking that maybe, one day, he'd tell her, but realising that he probably never would because there wasn't likely to be a *one day* for them.

He sat at a table outside the Montesol, waiting. It was a hot day, the sun just past the meridian, and he enjoyed its warm play on his arms and face. How considerate of God, he thought, to switch on that giant radiator, and how splendid that I no longer have to worry about Hassan. Jan and Vara Ludich waved from a table lower down the pavement and he raised his hand in answer, and ordered another *coñac*. He put on sunglasses and leant back in the chair, content for the moment because it was a fine day and he would be seeing her soon. Idly he examined the edge of his right palm, rubbing it where it had bruised on Tino Costa's neck. He wondered how the Cypriot was getting on. The arm would still be in a sling. A green-stick fracture, not a clean break. He had been that much considerate. He thought of Kyriakou sobbing in the gutter and felt contrite.

One should not humiliate such a man. His life was an act and if you jerked away the stage you destroyed him. Looking back on the night he was not proud of it. But how could it have been avoided? And what he'd done to them was probably a pale shadow of what they would have done to him. He wondered about himself. How such violence could be a part of him. It was so out of accord with the rest of his nature, with the things he set store by. Perhaps, its origins lay in the violence which had been done to him?

And yet without those things he would not be sitting there at that moment, he would not be involved in what had brought him to Ibiza, he would not . . .

He felt the light touch of fingers on his neck and Manuela said, 'Am I late?' There were shadows under her eyes.

'Get a decent sleep?'

'No. I was too worried.'

The waiter arrived, Black ordered an orange juice for her and another *coñac* for himself.

'I told you not to worry,' he said.

She looked round, leant towards him, lowering her voice. 'Tell me *now*. Tell me,' she said urgently. 'How do you know it will be all right?'

'Two days ago I wrote to the Jefe de Comisario. I gave the letter to a third person. If anything unpleasant happens to me— or to you—that letter will be delivered. It contains information about Kyriakou's activities on the island. Information the police would very much like to have.'

'And so?' she challenged, and he saw her expression hardening.

'Last night I told Kyriakou what I have just told you. He saw the point at once. I think his survival values are of a high order.'

For some moments she sat chin in hand, staring at the glass in front of her. Then she said, 'What do *you* know of his activities?'

He leant back in the chair, hands clasped behind his head, watching her through dark glasses. 'Perhaps as much as you do.'

She was not pleased, he could see that. His Pawn was threatening her Queen. Her move next. The lines at the corners of her mouth had tightened and the warmth had gone from her eyes. 'I suppose you realise that if your letter reaches the Jefe it will involve others,' she said.

'It will only reach him, my sweet, *if* something unpleasant happens to me—or to you. I thought it was rather a good idea, including you.'

'Brilliant,' she said in a brittle way, gathering up her things and frowning into the distance. But the frown changed to a smile as a shadow fell across the table and a man's voice, said *'Bonjour, mam'selle!'* and another's *'Guten Tag, Fräulein Valez.'*

It was the men from the *Snowgoose*.

'Sit down,' she said. 'It is lovely to see you.'

Black mumbled, 'Hallo,' in the flattest voice he could manage, looked at his watch and said, 'Be seeing you.'

Then, ignoring the new arrivals, he slung his shopping bag over his shoulder and slouched off.

The new arrivals sat down and Manuela watched Black's retreating figure. Francois laughed. Helmut smiled quizzically. 'Your friend is not pleased, *nein*?'

Manuela looked at herself in a mirror, patting her hair. 'Well if he is, let's say he shows it in the strangest way.'

'You know him long?' asked Francois.

She shook her head. 'Not very.'

'So,' said Helmut solemnly. 'Goot. Please what to drink?'

'That,' said Manuela, 'is a sensible question.'

She didn't tell him that Charles Black had just stood her up on a lunch date, and failed to pay for the last round of drinks.

Chapter Sixteen

From the line of lamps between the quay and the roadway, pools of light reached across dimly to the stacked timber, oil drums, orange cylinders of butane, pockets of cement, coils of wire, steel pipes, and straw-bound demijohns awaiting shipment to Formentera.

In the shadows beyond lay the island schooners, decklights throwing into relief sections of their upperworks and rigging, so that they were broken into unco-ordinated shapes like unfinished jig-saw puzzles.

The throb of diesel generators, the suck and squeak of bilge pumps, a cat miaowing, a faint thread of pop music from somewhere and the distant whine of a jet, were the only sounds of the night. At the end of the quay a solitary light burning amidships in a white schooner illuminated the gangplank and the white lifebuoy in the cockpit which had *Snowgoose* and *Piraeus* lettered around it in gold leaf.

In the town a clock chimed twice as a man came from the shadows and crossed the gangplank to the deck of the schooner. He went into the cockpit and down the forward companionway to the saloon. For a moment he stood in the doorway blinking in the strong light. The men round the table stood up and greeted him. It was evident that they were old friends.

The heavy bearded man pointed to the table. 'The charts and things are here. We can start when you're ready, Bernard.'

The newcomer swung round on him. '*Charles*. Charles Black,' he said with fierce insistence. 'Not *Bernard*. And for Christ's sake don't forget it.'

The big man said, '*Ach! Mein Gott:* I forgot.'

Black nodded. 'That's why I sheered off yesterday when you people pitched up at the Montesol. Scared me stiff. You should have kept away. What if Francois had called you Werner—or I'd called him André. Would've looked bloody good, wouldn't it?'

The German flushed but said nothing.

'*Elle est très jolie.*' Francois made a circle with his thumb and forefinger.

Black rebuffed the attempted humour. 'Security's paramount. Should have kept away when you saw me.' He stared them into silence.

Kamros said, 'Shall I fetch the coffee?'

The Englishman's frostiness disappeared. 'Yes. Good.' He lowered his voice. 'But first tell me about Hassan.' He looked round the saloon. 'Where is he?'

Helmut pointed forward. 'In the crew's quarters. Handcuffed. Locked up and battened down. You need not worry. He is co-operative. Anxious to keep clear of the police.'

'Is he well?'

'Very. But not happy at sea. He suffers from seasickness.'

'What did you tell him?'

'As you suggested. That we are from Cyprus. That we took him from the water on Kyriakou's orders because the police were about to arrest him, and it was necessary for him to disappear. Otherwise they could all be implicated.'

'What does he say about that?'

Helmut shrugged his shoulders. 'He thinks the coshing was unfriendly, that he might have been given the opportunity to co-operate.'

'Good point. What does he think will happen to him now?'

'We've told him that quite soon he will be put ashore—but not on Ibiza—and that he will then be a free man again.'

In a sudden gesture of affection, Black patted the German on the shoulder. 'Well done, Helmut.' He turned to the others. 'You too. You've saved the operation. I can't say more.' He looked at Kamros. 'Now for that coffee.'

They sat down round the table and exchanged notes about how they were and what they'd been doing. Helmut reported on the reconnaisance of the *cala* near Cabo Negret. Black told them of the night with Manuela at Altomonte, and of his observations there on other occasions. He mentioned the punch-up with Kyriakou and Tino Costa two nights back.

'I'm sorry it happened,' he said. 'But there was no way out. It was them or me. If they were going to the police, they'd have been by now. But they're too vulnerable. Apart from the letter threat, they know they started the fight. Manuela would testify to that.'

Helmut stroked his beard. 'To whom did you give the

131

letter?'

'No one. It doesn't exist. Except in their minds. And I don't know any more about Kyriakou than local gossip. But human nature being what it is, he'll assume I know the worst. And that must be pretty unattractive.'

The discussion switched to Manuela. Black told them of her involvement with the Greek.

'I don't understand their relationship,' he said. 'I think he's got her hooked. She's loyal to him, but she fears him. Some sort of love-hate complex, maybe. Whatever it is, I think drugs are at the bottom of it.'

'And *your* relationship with her?' Francois leant forward, the intensity of his dark stare, the gold earrings and mandarin moustache emphasising the aura of piracy.

'Entirely operational,' said Black irritably. 'But I'll be frank. Under other circumstances I'd have gone for her. She's got something.'

'They all have it,' Dimitrio grumbled, loading his pipe with calloused fingers. 'That's what half the trouble in the world's about.'

Black ignored him. Francois relaxed his stare. 'Does she know anything about *this* situation?' he said.

'Absolutely nothing.'

'And about you?'

'Only what is generally known on the island. What we have intended should be known all along: that I would very much like to see van Biljon's pictures, and the reasons why. That I'm a fairly dissolute character. Aimless. Not very successful.' He looked away, embarrassed. 'Some even say I'm a queer.'

Francois raised an eyebrow, cleared his throat and stroked his moustache. Black frowned at him before going on. 'At times I've been afraid that if I were to play this part too long I'd become Charles Black. To be dissolute and idle is not unattractive.'

'Especially in attractive company.' Francois lit a cheroot.

Black regarded him speculatively, his thoughts elsewhere. Then he said, 'That's pretty recent. But she's been invaluable. Without her I couldn't have got into the house. Anyway, let's get on with the job.' He looked at his watch. 'God, how the time flies.'

Kamros came back with coffee and rolls, and Black produced plans of Altomonte and its surroundings, a town plan of Ibiza, and a road map of the island. On it he indicated the route from Altomonte down into the valley, then westwards to San José, where it joined the road to Cubells, later forking off to the east towards Cabo Negret.

'That's the direct route,' he said. 'Eleven kilometres. But we won't use it. Here are the diversionary routes. Longer, but better tactically. If there's a pursuit we should be able to shake it off. Give the impression we're heading for San Antonio or Ibiza.'

He turned to Helmut. 'Fixed the car?'

'Yes. A Zephyr. From the Ford people on the Figueretes road. I said we wanted it for a few days to tour the island. Usual guidebook stuff. All okay.'

'Good,' said Black. 'An hour or so before you sail, park it here.' He made a cross on the town plan, close to El Corsario. 'Leave the key under the right front seat. Well back.'

He took the *Nautical Almanac* from the table. 'Now let's check the basic timetable. To-day's the tenth of May.' He turned the pages of the almanac. 'Here it is. Times of moonrise and moonset. Night of the eighteenth/nineteenth. Yes. It's slap in the middle of the period of no moon. So we didn't get that wrong.'

He closed the almanac and pushed it away. 'You must sail on the morning of the sixteenth. Keep to the south, well out of sight of land, and get the painting done. At daybreak on the eighteenth, make for Vedra. Go into Cala d'Or soon after midday and anchor. You two,' he turned to Helmut and Francois, 'go for a bathe in the afternoon. Swim ashore and wander about the beach. Get your bearings. Return on board at about five. Soon after dark Kamros will land you in the dinghy. Doesn't matter if you're seen. Perfectly normal. Yachtsmen having a run ashore. Wear dark slacks, wind cheaters and rubber-soled shoes. Carry the gear in a canvas beach bag. Start up the road towards San José about a quarter to eight. Don't go to the road immediately on landing. Wander about a bit first.

'I'll be along in the Zephyr to pick you up at eight-fifteen. It's an unlit winding road. Okay so far?'

There was a murmur of assent.

'Right. Now we'll stop the car here.' He pointed to the position on the map. 'About a kilometre below Altomonte. Helmut and I will get out on to the terraces. That'll be about nine o'clock. Then you turn the car, Francois, and drive back down the road. When you reach the junction, set off in the Ibiza direction.

'Give us until ten-thirty to get into position. In the woods here, alongside Altomonte.' He marked the spot on the plan. 'At ten to eleven, *exactly*, drive up to the front gate . . .' He paused, thinking of something. 'We'll synchronise watches by the noon time signal that day. Okay?'

They nodded.

'When you get to the gate,' he continued, 'hoot twice and turn the car so that it's facing down the road. Pocket the ignition key. They'll put the light on you, and the dogs'll raise hell. Pedro or Juan will be on duty there. Probably both, once the lights go on. They'll recognise you, which is a good thing. Neither of them has much English, so don't let on that you speak Spanish. It's better . . .'

Francois interrupted. 'We've already spoken to them at the harbour. Always in French or English. We do not forget our instructions. They're not much good at either.'

'Fine. Tell them you've an urgent message for van Biljon. Say you must see him. They'll stall on this and want to know what it's all about. Tell them you've come from the harbour where *Nordwind* is in trouble. They'll want to know what sort of trouble. Stall. Make the most of the language difficulty. When they press you, say that the boat is sinking slowly. Underwater damage or an outlet not properly shut, or something. That'll be difficult to put over in broken English. Say you couldn't raise anybody at the moorings at that time of night, but a man in one of the island schooners told you where van Biljon lived so you decided to come up.

'You know. A sailor's concern for another man's boat. According to Manuela, you'll probably be taken to the front door where the housekeeper will quiz you. She speaks good English. Keep up the chat with her, but at that stage ease up on the insistence to see van Biljon. It might look queer. Say that as long as she appreciates the urgency, etcetera, etcetera, and will give him the message it's all right by you. Okay? The important thing is to keep the chat going for as long as possible.

'When Helmut and I hear the dogs barking—we'll also have heard the Zephyr coming up and the two hoots—we'll go down to the wall on the west side and pop the meat over.

Then we'll double round to the back, go over the wall there and make for the gallery.' He looked round the table, 'Okay?

'From then on the drill will be as laid down by ZID. You've discussed and practised it often enough. The problem will be to adapt it to this house on a dark night in the circumstances which apply at the time. Now let's run through it using the plan of Altomonte. We'll make a number of different assumptions and vary our tactics to suit each. There'll always be the imponderable. We'll have to play them by ear as they come up.'

Almost an hour later Black said to Kamros. 'Now for your final part. Use an anchor light in Cala d'Or and when you leave keep the navigation lights burning until you're south of Vedra. Then switch off and start the run in to the *cola*. Be in position there from 2300 onwards. If all goes well, we'll make a torch signal from the shore between 2400 and 0200. Ideally at 0100. We may coast down the road to the beach. It's steep, so don't expect to hear the car, but you'll see the lights. Acknowledge our signal, then bring the dinghy in as fast as you can. Okay?'

'Okay,' said Kamros.

Black took a pad and pencil. 'I'll cable the standby to ZID from the post office this morning. They should have it a few hours later.'

He wrote on the pad: *Can let you have vernissage article on eighteenth nineteenth. Twenty-four pounds sterling.* He pushed it across to Helmut. 'Check it please.'

Helmut read it, nodded, and passed it to Francois. '*Bon,*' said the Frenchman.

'Confirm it with ZID direct by radio once you are south of Formentera. And confirm the rendezvous in the same signal.'

'Okay,' said Helmut.

Black leant over the chart of the Mediterranean. 'Now let's have a look at that rendezvous again.' Helmut marked the position with a pencilled cross.

Frowning with concentration as he set the dividers. Black measured the distance from the *cala* to the rendezvous. 'Okay,' he said. 'Any questions?'

'What about Hassan?' asked Francois.

'We'll stop in the lee of Abago Island on our way south,' said Black, 'and put him ashore that night. Provisions and water for three or four days. When we're well clear we'll make an anonymous signal to the harbour master here, reporting Hassan's presence on the island and asking them to pick him up.'

Helmut frowned. 'What story will he tell?'

'That's up to him. It'll be too late then to worry us.'

The town clock had not long chimed four, when Black went up on deck and made his way across the gangplank to the quay.

Soon afterwards a man came from behind a pile of timber near the *Snowgoose* and watched the Englishman disappear into the darkness.

In one hand the Comisario de Policia held the telephone, in the other a cigar the end of which he considered carefully, eyelids drooped over deep-set eyes.

Opposite him his deputy, Capitan Bonafasa, and the thin man, Capitan Calvi, looked out of the window, their faces expressing bored unconcern with the Comisario's end of a conversation to which they were listening intently.

The Comisario put down the telephone and sighed. He waved a hand at Calvi. 'Please proceed, Capitan.'

'We believe it will be stored overnight in a warehouse in the dock area and transferred soon afterwards to . . .' He hesitated. 'Another place.'

'And when will this consignment arrive?'

Calvi balanced his cheroot on the rim of the heavy glass ashtray. 'On May the thirteenth. The steamer from Barcelona that day will be the *Sevilla*. I think we . . .'

'Have you checked the manifests and passenger lists?' interrupted the Comisario.

A twitch of irritation showed on the thin man's face. 'I was about to mention them.'

'Find anything? Any features common to the occasion on which you *last* expected a consignment?' His superior officer's emphasis did not escape Calvi.

'A number, señor Comisario. Kyriakou and Costa are again passengers. The blue Buick will again be on board. Other items of cargo which interest us are again being carried. The same consigners, but different consignees.'

'And what are these items, Capitan?'

Calvi stiffened in his chair, lifting his shoulders and spreading his hands in a gesture of helplessness. The Comisario nodded, sensing what lay behind it. 'Ah, I see.' He stared at Calvi, speculating, trying to read the thin man's mind. 'You are sure these consignments come as cargo? That they are not in the hand-luggage of passengers. Or possibly brought ashore by crew members?'

'My information suggests that they come as cargo. That is our difficulty. No customs procedures operate in respect of cargoes shipped from one Spanish port to another. However, we shall on this occasion use certain checks. Here, and at the Barcelona end.'

'Can you develop this theme?'

Calvi sighed. It was not that he lacked confidence in the Comisario and his deputy, but his undertaking to the U.S. Narcotics Bureau was one on which he could not go back. The real information, the key to it all, he could not divulge. An agent in an exposed position had to be protected. If not, both the operation and the agent's life might be endangered.

'We believe,' said Calvi, 'that the drugs are placed in the ——.' He corrected himself. 'In cargo awaiting shipment in a dock warehouse at Barcelona—or on the voyage itself—probably by a workman or sailor who has access to it. Once unloaded here, it lies at the quay or in another warehouse. It is at this time, we think, that the drugs are removed. Again by someone who has official access. Then they are transferred to another place.'

'Have you confidence in this?'

'It is only a theory. We shall have to test it.'

'Other possibilities?' The Comisario leant back, drawing on his cigar, eyes half closed.

'We are watching the *Snowgoose* and *Nordwind*. Their movements shortly before and after the steamer arrives may be of importance.'

The Comisario leant forward, frowning with sudden concentration. 'You think, then, that van Biljon *may* be involved?'

'No,' said Calvi. 'I do not think so. But I am not so sure of his servants.'

The older man sighed with relief. 'Good,' he said. 'It would have been a shock to me.' He turned to his deputy. 'But not a surprise eh, Bonafasa? After thirty years of police work one is never surprised.' He turned back to the thin man. 'And so, Capitan, what are your plans?'

'At midnight on the thirteenth we'll pull in Kyriakou, Costa, Señorita Valez and Black, George Madden the American, and two or three others who we suspect are "pushers." Simultaneously we'll search the premises where they live and work, the cargo warehouse, and the *Snowgoose* and *Nordwind*.'

'Well, I wish you success. I want this finished.'

Calvi gave a wry smile. 'I, too, señor Comisario. I am anxious to get back to Madrid. I have a family there.'

The Comisario was silent, his eyes on the brass paper-weight balancing on the back of his left hand. 'Any trace of Hassan's body yet?' he asked.

'None,' said Calvi.

'I'm sorry he escaped our net,' said the Comisario. 'I think he was the big fish.'

Calvi nodded. 'I think so.'

Chapter Seventeen

The ferry steamer from Barcelona lay at the cross berth discharging cargo, her passengers long since landed and dispersed.

There was a hum of activity about the ship, the purr and rattle of winches, the noise of auxiliary engines, the shouts of men working cargo, and the cries of quarrelling seabirds. About the ship hung the smell of oil fuel, of wet decks, of food cooking in the galley, and the musty odours of cabins recently occupied.

In the yellow Land-Rover parked between the customs shed and the sea, sat a man in dark glasses, his silver hair showing beneath a beret, a tall upright figure, the scarred skin of his face drawn taut across the bone structure. But the immobile features gave no indication of the emotional forces at work, the reined-in excitement, the rising euphoria, as the thin packing case came clear of the ship's hold and the derrick swung out to lower it to the men waiting on the quay.

Among them were Juan and Pedro. Van Biljon knew they would ensure that the packing case was handled carefully. Even now he could hear Pedro shouting at the stevedores in Spanish to watch what they were doing, and their sharp rejoinders that he should mind his own business.

The cargo slings were removed from the wooden case and his servants lifted it, one at each end, and came towards him. As they approached van Biljon's elation grew, his hands and body trembled, and his mind was a jumble of recollection: the letter from his dealer in Paris suggesting the Utrillo might come on the market; his own urgent reply that he was interested; the delays after that, followed by Billiat's coded telegram confirming he would negotiate. Van Biljon had then made one of his rare visits to Paris, to see it and discuss price. He'd gone back to Ibiza two days later, and a long agonising wait had followed while Billiat haggled with the sellers in Zurich. Then had come Billiat's letter confirming that the picture was his, and van Biljon had arranged the finance.

Soon afterwards the papers and art journals had mentioned

the sale. As usual, Billiat had told them that he'd been acting for a U.S. collector whose name he was not permitted to disclose. And now here was the Utrillo in Ibiza, Juan and Pedro perspiring as they carried it, opening the rear doors of the Land-Rover, loading it carefully into the vehicle. When they'd finished they climbed back into the driving seat, the engine started and they moved off across the quay. On reaching the road they stopped to let traffic pass before turning to the right. When they'd made the turn, van Biljon, suddenly and with some agitation, told Pedro to stop outside the Bar Pechet.

Charles Black and Manuela were sitting at a table on the pavement outside the Bar Pechet when Black saw the yellow Land-Rover coming over from the cross berth. 'Hallo,' he said, 'here's our old friend.'

Manuela looked up. 'So it is.'

The Land-Rover stopped to let the traffic pass, then turned to the right and came down the road towards them. As it approached they saw van Biljon turn and say something to the driver who braked suddenly, the Land-Rover stopping almost opposite them.

Van Biljon, sitting stiff and upright, beckoned.

'He wants you, I think,' said Black.

Manuela got up and went across. Van Biljon greeted her and after they had spoken to each other she turned and waved to Black. 'Come here,' she called.

He went over, remembering the limp.

Van Biljon held out his hand. 'Good morning, Mr. Black,' he said. 'How is the ankle?' The scarred face and dark glasses gave no indication of his mood, but the tone was unmistakably friendly.

'Much better,' said Black, shaking hands. 'Practically back to normal. I don't even need a stick now.'

'I am glad,' said van Biljon.

'It was good of you to help me.'

'I could not have done less. I fear I was not a courteous host.' Van Biljon shrugged his shoulders. 'But I am old. I live alone and, well , , ,' he waved his hands expressively. 'You were strangers.'

'Of course,' said Manuela. 'You did more than enough.'

There was a disconcerting pause before she said, 'It's a fabulous day isn't it?'

Van Biljon looked at the sky. 'Yes.' He leant towards her. 'And for *me*, even more so.' He paused and the emphasis made them wonder what was coming next.

'This morning,' his voice dropped to a stage whisper. 'I have just picked up a *new* picture. For my collection. Something I very much wanted.'

'Oh, how lovely for you,' she said.

Black was about to ask him what it was, but the old man suddenly waved his hand. 'Good-bye. Good-bye,' he called and the Land-Rover moved off.

They stood watching it go down the road until it had turned the corner and gone up towards the Paseo Vara de Rey.

Black took her arm. 'Well, well. What was all that about?'

'Amazing.' She laughed in a puzzled way. 'Why, he couldn't have been sweeter. You know, I think he's terribly shy.'

Black was thinking, wondering what it was that had caused van Biljon to do something so out of character. 'Perhaps,' he said, 'it was excitement about the new picture. He just had to tell someone about it. You know.'

'Could be,' she said, 'He must be terribly lonely, poor old man.'

Juan and Pedro were working in the gallery. The packing case had been opened on the patio outside, and they had brought in the picture and carried it down to the far end of the second screen. Now they stood beside a folding steel ladder, holding the Utrillo.

Van Biljon spoke to them in Spanish. 'Good,' he said moving away from the screen. 'Raise it about the same height as the picture on the left.'

They lifted the picture and held it against the screen and he signalled with his hands the need to raise or lower it, to move it right or left.

'That's it. Hold it!' He stepped forward and with a pencil marked the screen at the lower corners of the frame. 'Right. Take it away.'

The men lowered the picture, turning its face to the screen. Pedro took brass hanging wire from a bobbin and attached an end to an eye in the back of the frame, adjusting the wire for length before cutting it. Then he and Juan lifted the picture again.

When it had been hung van Biljon stood back and viewed it

from various angles, his nervous enthusiasm communicating itself to his servants who, though they had no feeling for Utrillo, sensed its importance to him.

'*Bueno Juan, bueno Pedro,*' he said, and they knew it was the signal to go. They picked up the wire bobbin and the pliers, folded the steel ladder, and left the gallery.

When he heard the outer door close behind them, van Biljon relaxed. With a magnifying glass he examined the Utrillo, the brushwork, the state of the canvas, looking for flaws and cracks in the paint. But it was in good condition, confirming Billiat's report and his own impression in Paris. Then he stood back and spent some time viewing the picture, walking away, turning suddenly, seeking the best angle for light, analysing the composition, considering the subject, recalling the history. It was, he decided, Utrillo at his best, conveying exquisitely the fresh vision of the man, his finely planned design of the street scene, his warm affection for Paris. Van Biljon was well pleased with this addition to his collection and the pleasure he derived from it overlay, temporarily at any rate, his growing anxiety about other things.

When he left the Utrillo he walked slowly down the gallery, passing between the screens until he stopped before a Cézanne at the far end. Of all the French Impressionists none appealed to him more than this artist, and of the four Cézannes at Altomonte this picture of a water-mill at Argenton-sur-Creuse was the one he prized most.

Artistic merit apart, it had special significance because it had belonged to Johan Stiegel and it was in a sense Stiegel who had saved him. But for him he might have gone on until the end of the war and by then it could have been too late.

He thought of Stiegel and of the last and only time he had seen him. That had been a bad night. The launch delayed almost an hour because of the weather. Stiegel excited and argumentative, presuming to tell him how things should be done. As if he needed advice after so many had passed through his hands.

When the van broke down and he was doing his best to get the engine started, Stiegel had banged on the doors and shouted, and there were cars passing so that van Biljon had had to go back into the van to calm him down and explain why they were not heading directly for Zurich. Stiegel had waved a pocket compass in high excitement, said they were going in the wrong direction, that he could not understand the need for secrecy on Swiss soil. Van Biljon had said, 'Switzerland is full of German agents. How long do you think this would continue if it were known?' That had brought Stiegel to his senses, and he'd stopped gibbering like an idiot.

Mrs. Stiegel had given no trouble, smiling benignly; heavily sedated, van Biljon had judged. But the nephew, a boy of ten, had said nothing, watching him all the time with frightened suspicious eyes. This had hurt van Biljon, for children usually took to him at once.

In the woods he had given them a torch, shown them the path, and explained that when they heard the noise of traffic ahead they would know they were approaching the main road into Zurich. On reaching it they were to turn right. After walking a few hundred metres they would find a blue Peugeot van waiting by the roadside. He had given Stiegel the registration number. 'The van will take you into Zurich,' he had said. 'But hurry, you're late.' Stiegel had said, 'What if they are gone?'

Van Biljon had shaken his head. 'They will not have gone. But,' and he had held out his hand in a flurry of impatience. 'If they have, come back here. I will wait.'

He had not waited, it had been a violent storm-ridden night and it was not necessary, but the Stiegels had been the last. None came after them. Word came from Halsbach a few weeks later that the system had been penetrated, no more would come. Rosenthal had disappeared and van Biljon had left Zurich within twenty-four hours. That was late in 1943.

A cold wind blew in from the sea, sweeping across the harbour in gusts and eddies, buffeting the rows of houses piled upon each other in the old town, powdering them with fine dust from the reclamations at Talamanca.

The sun was setting behind the range of hills to the southwest and the temperature had fallen. Black pulled up the collar of his coat as he made his way up Calle Pedro Tur, then left into Calle Juan Roman and San Ciriaco, following their winding course to the higher reaches of D'Alt Vila.

At the top he paused to enjoy briefly the diorama spread beneath him; town, harbour and sea bathed in the glow of the dying sun.

He turned away and started up the old cobbled alley of

143

Obispo Torres, steep and twisting through the quarter where in earlier times the grandees and others of privilege had had their houses. It was for one of these, now the Galleria Rico Alma, that he was making.

The occasion was a *vernissage* for Klemens Prbnski, a young Polish artist whose work was beginning to attract attention. Black had met him and thought he showed more promise than most painters on the island. His imagination and sensitivity, his colour discipline, restraint and artistic integrity gave his work unusual distinction. Black knew the pictures, but he was going to the party because it was important he should be seen there. At a turn in the lane he went through an archway to a vaulted hall from which stone stairs led to the gallery.

As he went up he heard the buzz and clamour of many voices. Inside the door Prbnski and Paula Schönland, a hard-headed deep-voiced Swiss who owned the gallery, greeted him. He'd met her several times before and liked her.

She squeezed his hand, whispering hoarsely. 'Write nice things about Klemens or I'll slit your throat!'

He grinned, wished Prbnski well, went through the gallery to where people stood about in groups, found the drink table, took a glass of wine and moved off.

The gallery consisted of a long hall with two wings, and though Prbnski's pictures were hung in all three rooms most of the guests were in the hall within easy reach of the drinks. This in Black's experience was sound, and since there were few serious buyers at these functions it did not detract from the purpose of the occasion.

When he'd filled his glass for the second time, he stood back against a wall watching, sorting out the guests, the invited and the uninvited, listening to the brittle chatter, often about art, some of it informed, much of it phoney. Local gossip was having a good run, and with it the usual inanities from the usual assortment of people. A few serious painters and writers, others not so serious, those who were invited because they were interested in art, and those who were invited because they always were invited and they were many. Like a first night, thought Black: almost everybody who isn't really interested in the theatre.

There were young men with unkempt hair in high-necked jerseys and tight jeans whose beards and narrow thighs distinguished them from young women with unkempt hair, high-necked jerseys and tight jeans. There was Ilse Berch, the Norwegian, who looked to Black more handsome than ever in a black jersey with black jeans tucked into silver-studded riding boots, a Robin Hood hat with an insouciant feather, and a silver-bound pistol belt slung from her fine hips.

'You look terrific,' he said.

'Do I?'

'Yes. Can't think why we don't see more of each other.'

'Not my fault,' said Ilse. She held her head on one side, looking at him quizzically. 'Anyway your interests are strictly limited. There wouldn't be room for me.'

'What d'you mean?'

'French Impressionists and Manuela.'

'I'm glad you include her. At least you grant I'm heterosexual.'

She laughed, 'Who knows? Perhaps you're a Lytton Strachey.'

'On the contrary. A male Carrington.'

'I could have asked you something interesting, but here come the Ludichs.'

He turned and saw the Czechs making for them.

Ilse lowered her voice. 'Manuela's here. Have you seen her?'

He looked round. 'No. Where?'

'Can't see her at the moment. She's with an old friend.'

'Who's that?'

Ilse shook her head. 'You'll see.'

The Ludichs joined them and they discussed the pictures and Prbnski and Paula, before getting on to the small talk of the town. Black went to the drink table, switched to coñac, and moved slowly through the chattering groups, looking for Manuela. On the way George Madden, red-eyed and hollow-cheeked, gave him a furtive nod of recognition.

Haupt, the architect, came up. 'Any news of your friend?' he asked.

For an embarrassing moment Black, his mind on other things, wondered what Haupt was talking about. Then he remembered. 'I had a note from his secretary this morning. Intended to phone you to-morrow. She says he's very interested in the gen I sent him. He's in Japan just now, but he'll deal with it on his return.'

Haupt looked pleased. 'Well, let me know how things go.'

'I certainly will,' said Black.

Kyriakou and Manuela came in from one of the wings at the far end of the gallery. Preoccupied with whatever it was they were discussing, they had not noticed him. Kyriakou said something which made Manuela burst with laughter. Black knew her well enough to know it wasn't forced.

With some satisfaction he saw the puffy bruised circles round the Greek's eyes. That, he decided, has marred your fatal beauty, my friend. Manuela, looking up suddenly from her laughter, saw him and he watched with cynical detachment as the humour drained from her face. Kyriakou saw him too, and waved, shouting his inevitable, ' 'Allo there.'

So we're to be friends again are we, thought Black, returning the greeting coolly.

Manuela managed a forced smile. 'Hi, Charles. Didn't expect to see *you* here.'

'Why? It's my job.'

'Yes. But I mean I hadn't seen you here although I'd had a good look round.'

Kyriakou pointed to Black's glass. 'It's empty. Let's have a dreenk on the house. Leave it to me. I'll fetch them. What's it?'

'*Coñac.*'

White teeth flashed under the black moustache as he bowed to Manuela and made for the drink table.

'Orange for me, Kirry,' she called after him.

'Charming, gracious chap, isn't he?' said Black.

'Sarcasm will get you nowhere, Charles.'

He raised an eyebrow. 'I'm dead serious. He's witty, too.'

'Oh, stop it.' She opened her bag, took out a mirror and fiddled with her face.

'So glad to see his eyes are better,' said Black.

'Are you hell!'

'And since you're so close to our hero, perhaps you can tell me why's he's decided to be all palsy-walsy again?'

She wave him a frosty look. 'Because he's basically a decent man and he's behaving like an adult. And don't you, when he comes back with the drinks, carry on like an adolescent.'

Black didn't believe he deserved this outbreak, but he was too surprised by its intensity to do anything before Kyriakou was back, carrying three full glasses in the spread fingers of one hand.

I can't do that, thought Black, deciding that the Greek must have been a waiter: at a not very good hotel—the better ones used trays.

Kyriakou passed round the glasses, raised his and smiled blandly. '*Salud*!'

Since Black felt no compulsion to help the conversation along, and Manuela appeared to be deep in thought, there was a thoughtful pause while Kyriakou fidgeted with his tie. Then with a schoolboyish grin, he said, 'This is better than last time we meet, eh?'

Black, sensing that the Greek's friendliness was inspired by the mythical letter, smiled perfunctorily. 'Yes. Isn't it?'

Kyriakou became confidential, looking round to see who was near, leaning his head towards Black, lowering his voice. 'You know, Charles, trouble is dreenk. I have too much *coñac*. Make me leetle bit jealous.' He pinched Manuela's cheek playfully, but she pulled away and said, 'Don't.'

'Is lovely girl,' he went on. 'Make Kirry jealous. Then Tino comes and we dreenk more *coñac*.' His eyes grew large. 'Too much. And now we get leetle bit mad. So we make trouble for you.' He shrugged his shoulders, his hands appealing to them. 'How can man be like this? Because dreenk makes heem mad? You know.'

'How's your friend's arm?'

'Aha. Not too bad. Now get spleents and sleeng. Is all right.'

'I think he fell on it,' said Black.

The Greek looked at him doubtfully, the bruised eyes lugubrious. 'Yes. I suppose so. You know.' He looked at his watch. 'Aha. Late already. Well. I must hurry for appointment. You look after Manuela, pliz.' He beamed at them and was gone.

'Didn't I have behave nicely?' asked Black.

'Not bad,' she said.

'What are your plans for to-night?'

'They don't include you, Charles.'

'Why so scratchy?'

'Oh, I don't know.' She turned away, her eyes sad, and he was afraid she was going to cry.

'Let me get you a drink.'

She shook her head. 'No. I must go.' She looked at him uncertainly. 'I got a letter to-day. It concerns you, Charles.'

'Oh, did you?' He tried to appear casual. 'May I see it?'

'Yes. But not here.'

147

'Why not?'

'It's in my studio.'

'When can I see it?'

'Now, if you take me home.'

For a moment Black wondered if this were a trap. It had been out of character for Kyriakou to hand her over to him so easily, almost eagerly.

'Sounds very cloak and dagger,' he said.

'Not really. I should have brought it to-night.'

'So you're inviting me to your studio?' He looked at her thoughtfully.

'Yes,' she said. 'But *only* to see the letter.'

When they reached the old house in the lane about the *barrio* sa Peña, they climbed the stone stairs to the landing. Manuela unlocked the studio door and switched on the light. She went in first and Black followed, wary and alert, still beset by doubts about this girl who attracted him so much, yet whose behaviour posed questions he found difficult to answer.

It was his first visit to the studio, and he looked round curiously when she went to make coffee. It was a large, high-ceilinged room. On its north side, under a skylight, was the jumble of canvases, paints, easels and palettes he would have expected. Some pictures were stacked against a wall. For the exhibition, he presumed. There was a partly painted canvas on one easel, a finished one on another. He looked at her spidery abstracts, so evidently influenced by Miro, so amateurishly executed, and felt sad for her. She hadn't any real talent and yet she went on trying. Why, he wondered, was she leading this escapist life, trying to be something she must know she never could be.

The rest of the studio was comfortably furnished, mostly in Spanish wicker-work. There was a studio couch with Carnaby Street cushions, a writing desk, a coffee table piled with glossy magazines, several easy chairs, a hi-fi which looked good, and a complex of shelves and cupboards.

Looking at the couch, he wondered if Kyriakou was entertained there and his thoughts clouded and he grew angry. He decided he was being childish, and pulled himself together. On the bookshelves there were rows of paperbacks. He read the titles and approved most of her taste. The desk was untidy, a litter of papers and letters, old ballpoint pens, and pencils with broken points. There was a torn-up letter in the wastepaper basket, and an envelope bearing a Spanish stamp and a Barcelona postmark. He leant down to read the envelope. It was typewritten, addressed to *Señor G. Madden.*

Black would have given much for the opportunity to piece together its contents, but he heard the door of the kitchenette open and he moved away, wondering how the letter had come to be in her studio.

She came in with a tray of coffee and biscuits.

'Looks good,' he said.

She poured the coffee and offered him a biscuit.

'D'you sleep in here?'

'No. I have a bedroom.' She inclined her head towards the door at the end of the room. '*And* a bathroom.'

'Big deal,' he said.

'It's okay for me.' She looked at him evenly. Then she went to her desk and rummaged about until she'd found what she wanted.

'This is it.' She passed a sheet of note paper to him. Before reading it he saw that it was typed, headed Altomonte, and signed *Hendrik van Biljon.* It was dated 10th May. Two days back—Thursday. The day that van Biljon had stopped the Land-Rover outside the Bar Pechet to speak to them. He wrote in English:

Dear Miss Valez,

After I saw you this morning it occurred to me that you and Mr. Black might care to dine with me at Altomonte on May 14th—to celebrate the hanging of my new picture and see round the gallery. In this way, perhaps, I can make amends for my lack of courtesy on the occasion of your last visit. I have arranged for a car to pick you up outside Anselmo's in the Mercado Nuevo at 8 p.m. Please show this letter to the driver to identify yourselves. I do not normally have visitors here so I would, to avoid offence to others, be grateful if you would treat the invitation as confidential.

I shall understand if you cannot come since I have given such short notice, but please let me know.

With regards,
Hendrik van Biljon

Chapter Eighteen

When he got back to his room that night, Black made no attempt at sleep. There was too much to think about, too many new problems to tussle with. He lay on his bed, eyes closed, recalling the detail of what had been said in the studio. After some discussion, and a good deal of persuasion on his part, they had agreed to accept the invitation. Manuela had been curiously reluctant: said she realised how important it was to him that he should see the pictures, but they meant little to her; and the date was awkward—she didn't say why —so couldn't they reply thanking the old man and suggesting another? Black had pointed out that van Biljon's letter, while acknowledging the short notice he'd given, made no suggestion of alternative dates. In fact the last thing Black wanted was another date. If the invitation were what it purported to be it was, for him, providential. To see over Altomonte and its gallery from the inside, as a guest, at that juncture, was almost too good to be true. And in the end Manuela had agreed, and they would be going. But it probably *was* too good to be true—that was the trouble, and that was why so many questions posed themselves which Black could not answer. Why had van Biljon issued the invitation? Was it for the reason given in the letter? To make amends for a past discourtesy? Was it that he wanted to share the joy of a new acquisition?

In each case Black found the explanation unconvincing. That left him with the unpalatable fact that there must be another, and if it were the one he thought it might be, then somewhere along the line there'd been a failure of security. Had he been careless? Or Helmut or Francois, or others in the *Snowgoose*? Or someone at ZID?

Early on—that day in the hills near Altomonte—Manuela had said, *You know Charles, nobody could ever steal those pictures and get away with them.* And he had agreed, and whatever her suspicions then might have been he felt he had long since put them to rest.

It was on the morning of that day, hours before her

remark, that Manuela had seen the man in the beret trailing them. It was not long afterwards that Black's room had been searched. He had ascribed these events to police activity in connection with the drug traffic. There'd been a buzz that Madrid had become restless and was determined to put an end to it. Over a short period of time Black had been seen on a number of occasions with Manuela and Kyriakou, and hangers-on like George Madden. What more natural then, than that the police should check on him. But now, in the light of van Biljon's invitation, he wondered what connection if any there was between these events. Was there some quite other construction which could be put on them?

And, finally, three items in van Biljon's letter stood out for Black like lighthouses. He and Manuela were to treat the invitation as confidential, transport would be provided, and they were to bring van Biljon's letter with them. Manuela had not commented on any of these, and it had suited Black to say nothing. But whatever the answers might be to his doubts, there was one certainty: he'd have to go down to the harbour within the next few hours to see Helmut and Francois.

The original plan would have to stand, but an emergency one would have to be prepared, and an urgent signal made to ZID. In the morning *Snowgoose* would have to go to sea on some pretext or other to transmit it. It could not be sent through the post office, and the schooner was not permitted to transmit radio signals in harbour. He got off his bed and switched on the light to look at the faded wall calendar: a girl in a yellow bikini sitting astride a sixteenth-century cannon, a phoney siren with a cheese-cake smile enjoying the phallic ride. It was the twelfth of May. It would be the thirteenth at midnight. Dinner with van Biljon on the fourteenth. D-day on the eighteenth. He thought of the Sinai Desert. The long wait in the warm June night, the interminable hours before sunrise, before the tanks and trucks started rolling. He had felt then as he felt now: tense, apprehensive, irrevocably committed, longing for action that would mean the beginning of the end.

He set the wrist-watch alarm for one-thirty in the morning, switched off the light, and turned on his side and tried to sleep.

In the dusty undistinguished building on the Avenida Ignacio

Wallis the thin man leant back from his desk and closed his eyes, pushed his feet forward and stretched. Yawning loudly, he took a cheroot from the box next to the telephone. When he'd lit it and drawn on it several times, he balanced it on the rim of the ashtray and began to work through the pile of papers on the desk.

They were the drafts of the orders for the raids and arrests which were to take place the next day, the fourteenth of May, and he had typed them himself. Calvi was satisfied that he had precluded any tip-off since only he, the Comisario and his deputy, Bonafasa, knew what was in the wind. And even they knew little of the detail. Calvi intended to delay the briefing of his staff until the last moment. Not until they had assembled and were ready to move off, would they know *what* and *where* and *when*.

The day before he had been telephoned by the harbour-master who had reported that the *Snowgoose* wished to leave harbour for a short visit to Abago, a deserted islet to the south of Formentera. 'They say they will be back in a day or so,' he had added.

'Let her proceed,' Calvi had said, for he was pleased with this development. The pieces were falling into place.

The steamer from Barcelona, the *Sevilla*, had arrived that morning, the cargo in which Calvi was interested had been landed, and Kyriakou and Tino Costa had been among the passengers. The cargo concerned was in a warehouse under surveillance, as was the house in D'Alt Vila which the Greek had just leased from van Biljon. The principal suspects were being watched and would continue to be until the arrests took place during the night of the fourteenth.

Capitan Calvi picked up his cheroot. There was nothing more he could do now but wait. He thought about the *Snowgoose* and those in her. Where did *she* fit into the picture? What was her role? What part if any did Abago Island play? Van Biljon's boat, *Nordwind*, went there occasionally with parties of children. *Snowgoose* was on a visit to Abago now. *Nordwind* was in harbour. Would she put to sea to-day or to-morrow? Were these events in any way related?

That the *Snowgoose* had gone to sea the day before might have been no more than a coincidence. But if she returned to harbour that afternoon, it would complete the pattern of the last occasion. Then the steamer had arrived in the morning and the *Snowgoose* in the afternoon.

Calvi drew on his cheroot, pursing his lips to expel the smoke as he replaced the papers in the file and locked them away in the steel safe. Then he went to the window and looked out over the sea, his thoughts with his wife and child in Madrid.

When Black arrived at Anselmo's the tables in the little courtyard where he was to meet Manuela were empty, so he went to the bar and ordered a dry Martini. It was early and there were no familiar faces about. Anselmo's was a gathering place for the expatriate English, and he supposed that was why van Biljon had suggested it as a rendezvous. Taking the Martini from the bar, he chose a table where he could see the front door. While he waited he ate pecan nuts, drank the Martini and re-read van Biljon's letter of invitation.

Deliberately, he pushed away the temptation to speculate about the night ahead and the extent to which their plans would meet the new situation. For two nights now he had had little sleep, though he had managed a few hours' rest that afternoon.

It is better, he decided, that I empty my mind and relax. Stretch feet forward, he admonished, consciously relax thigh and leg muscles. Next toes. Uncrimp them and let them go slack. Now the arms. Lay them out along the chair and then go slack. Straighten the fingers, relax the muscles. Now, head back and let the neck and facial muscles go. After that, shoulders and chest. Last of all the stomach. Let go! More —*more*. Get rid of that knot of muscular contraction: the anxiety syndrome. There it goes.

How's that?

Better isn't it? Feel the tensions drain away? Stay relaxed. Absolutely slack. Now for the mind. Empty it. Think of RAJ. R—A—J JAR. ARJ. rja. ajr . . . concentrate on RAJ. Must look at my watch. Seven minutes to. Hope she's not late. Maybe she'll rat on me. Think of RAJ. Jar. JRA. Is it him? raj. RAJ. Jra. Why can't I remember his voice? How far back can one remember a voice? My mother's? Yes. My father's? Yes. Think of other people you knew long ago and try to . . . no. No. No . . . Think of raj. JAR. arj. jra. Check on the light switches as you go in. Mark them right away. I cannot empty my mind. And for God's sake, my muscles have contracted and I am all tense again, toes and fingers screwed up, neck straining, jaw muscles taut, and my stomach feeling as if someone has reached into it and tied my entrails in knots.

And what about Manuela? Poor Manuela. It is bad luck. You were born under an unlucky star, my sweet. You have lost your way and got mixed up in dangerous things.

The resolution of opposing forces and all that crap. It's too late now. And I don't really trust you though I think I love you. Which doesn't really make sense. Kagan would vomit. I can hear him. *The wrong time, the wrong place, the wrong girl*. But he needn't worry. I shall have to leave you to Kirry and Tino and your other queer friends. I wonder what will happen to you? And there you are now . . . coming through the door . . . pale and dark—such dark eyes—such dark shadows—*trips*? *happenings*? *psychedelic extravaganzas*?—so beautiful you are—high cheek bones—arching eyebrows—but so frail—not enough food.

And now you've seen me, but you don't smile. You are worried, my poor Manuela.

'Hi, Charles.' She looked at him inquiringly and her hand went up in brief greeting as she glanced at her watch. 'It's *exactly* eight o'clock.'

He stood up. 'Not to worry. See anything that looked like a car waiting for us outside?'

She shook her head. 'I didn't even look. I was hurrying. There are cars.'

'Come on,' he said. 'Let's go.' He led her out into the street. It was dark and the lamps in the square cast dim light at long intervals. The parked cars were empty, but there were people about, walking, sitting on benches, talking in low voices. A group of children played hop-scotch on the red and white chequers of the *paseo*, and the night air smelt of drains.

They walked a short distance down the pavement, then turned and came back to the corner outside Anselmo's.

'We'll have to wait here,' he said.

She made no answer. One of her preoccupied moods, he supposed. I would like to know what goes on in that little head. He looked down at the silent figure next to him and patted her shoulder. 'Cheer up,' he said. 'We're going to a party.'

She turned towards him and in the lamplight he saw her

sad smile. He was wondering what to say next, when a car pulled up alongside them. It was the yellow Land-Rover. Tomaso, the housekeeper's husband, the man with the bulbous nose, was driving.

He peered at them in the dim light. 'Señor Black? Señorita Valez?'

'Si. Buenas noches.'

The Spaniard nodded, leant over and opened the door. There was room for them all on the broad seat and Manuela sat between Black and the driver. They drew away from the kerb and went through the town to the San José road. Black was silent, thinking of van Biljon's note . . . *Please show this letter to the driver to identify yourselves* . . . Why was it necessary to identify themselves to Tomaso who already knew them? Black had not shown him the letter nor had the Spaniard asked for it. He was trying to make sense of this when Manuela said, 'I wonder what time we'll get back?'

He said, 'Haven't a clue. About midnight I suppose.'

She replied with a sigh that became a yawn.

After that there was only the roar of the engines and the hiss of the wind. Not until they had passed Figueretes and the turn-off to the airport, and the Land-Rover was well into the country, eating up the distance, its headlights revealing a fantasy of rushing stone walls and olive trees and verges of green grass, and golden wheat and marigolds and poppies and violets, and owls and night-jars—not until then did they speak. And all through the long silence he knew she must be busy with her thoughts, just as he was with his. And his were private, not for sharing, as must be hers. And anyway it was inhibiting to have Tomaso next to them in the darkness, sullen, silent, communicating nothing but the sour odour of his body.

At last, pressing her hand where it rested on her lap, Black said, 'You all right?' And she whispered, 'Yes,' and returned the pressure.

The Land-Rover left the tarmac and set off up the valley, following the dirt road through the foothills and coming presently to the terraces where the night air was sweet with the scent of almond and lemon.

Although he had walked along the road at different times in recent weeks, mostly in darkness, Black found the snatched glimpses in the headlights strange and unfamiliar, shadows and movement camouflaging features he would otherwise have recognised.

They slowed down for the final S-bend and the headlights illuminated alternating sweeps of terrace as the car swung first right and then left. Tomaso changed down and they started up the last slope, ahead of them the wrought-iron gates shut across the drive.

As the Land-Rover approached, its occupants were dazzled by a beam of light. Tomaso slowed down and switched off the headlights. There was the staccato barking of dogs, and a man came forward from the gate.

It was Pedro. He and Tomaso exchanged greetings and he went back, opened the gates, and they drove into the grounds of Altomonte, drawing up at the flight of steps which led to the front door.

There the housekeeper greeted them, unsmiling and formal, but at least she inquired after Black's ankle before taking them into the hall where a fire was burning.

'Please sit down,' she said. 'I will inform Señor van Biljon that you have arrived.'

After she'd gone Black said, 'I should have thought the dogs had done that.'

'I guess so,' said Manuela.

He looked at his watch. It was ten to nine. Moments later van Biljon came into the hall, tall and straight in a black velvet smoking jacket, scarred features immobile, eyes shielded by dark glasses. Black stood up. The old man went over to Manuela, bent to take her hand and kissed it. Afterwards he turned to Black, bowing faintly and clicking his heels.

'It is kind of you to come. I am delighted,' he said. 'Did Tomaso pick you up in good time?'

Black said, 'Yes,' and added, 'We were pleased to see him. Didn't have to identify ourselves.'

For a moment van Biljon seemed puzzled, then he said, 'Ah you mean my letter?'

'Yes.'

'I had intended to order a car to pick you up. Then Techa, my housekeeper, informed me her husband would be shopping in Ibiza this afternoon. So I told him to do so. He will drive you back to town after dinner.'

'That is very kind of you,' said Manuela.

'Not at all.'

A servant with a tray came from the archway on the far side of the hall. It was Juan.

'Now,' said van Biljon. 'You will join me, I hope, in an apèritif.'

Chapter Nineteen

It pleased Manuela that van Biljon proved over dinner to be a charming host, for it confirmed the judgment she had made when they'd met at the airport. He was a good though restrained conversationalist, always producing openings for his guests, ever solicitous of their needs. He listened with interest to Manuela's description of life in Puerto Rico, and to Black on the subject of contemporary art, to whom he explained courteously why he preferred the older school of painters. To Manuela his wide knowledge of the subject was impressive, yet he never sought to imply that it was in any way superior to theirs.

The French dishes, elegantly served and delicious, had been cooked by Techa, van Biljon told them. Manuela barely tasted the wines but she gathered Black was impressed. It was after he had remarked upon the excellence of the white *Montrachet* that van Biljon said, 'The things that have given me most pleasure have come from France. Her wines, her cooking, above all her art.' That led him on to the general statement that he had devoted much of his life to collecting the French Impressionists and post-Impressionists.

But Manuela noticed that he made no further reference to his pictures other than to say that they would see them after dinner when they could judge for themselves.

'Are you pleased with your latest acquisition?' she asked.

He hesitated for a moment. 'Ah. You mean the picture I collected on Thursday. When we met in the harbour. Yes, I am delighted with it.'

'What is it, Mr. van Biljon?' said Black.

The old man held up a hand. 'Wait,' he said. 'You shall see.' He turned to Manuela, changing the subject. 'Have you seen my motor-cruiser, the *Nordwind*?'

'Oh, yes. A fabulous boat.' She leant forward, clasping her hands together. 'Once I watched her go to sea on a rough day. It was beautiful. She cut through the waves. Such clouds of spray.'

'She is a fine boat,' said van Biljon. 'Built in England.'

'But you give her a Dutch name.'

'Yes. I *am* Dutch.'

She smiled apologetically. 'Of course.'

'There is another fine boat in the harbour. A recent arrival.' Van Biljon looked down at his side plate as he broke a roll with his fingers. 'The *Snowgoose*. A staysail schooner from the Piraeus. She has magnificent lines. I am too old for sail, but I must concede that it has something, a *je ne sais quoi*, that power-driven craft lack.'

They agreed with him and he went on: 'The *Snowgoose* has a most interesting mission, I am told. Two young men have chartered her for six months. They are cruising round the Mediterranean gathering material for a yachtsman's guide to the islands.'

'Yes,' said Manuela. 'I have met them. Helmut and Francois.'

'Really,' said van Biljon. He turned to Black. 'You know them?' he asked casually.

'Not really. I've bumped into them once or twice in bars. Haven't really sorted them out. I gather Manuela likes them.'

'Perhaps they are more attractive to young ladies.'

To Manuela it seemed that the Dutchman's voice reflected an amusement which contradicted the impassivity of the scarred face.

'And the *Snowgoose*?' Again van Biljon addressed Black. 'What do you think of her?'

'Looks all right. I'm no judge really.'

The old man worked the pepper-grinder vigorously over the cheese soufflé. 'I hear she has unusually powerful auxiliary engines.'

'I wouldn't know,' said Black. 'Never been on board.'

Van Biljon turned to Manuela. 'Do you approve of the soufflé, señorita?'

'It's fabulous,' she said. 'Delicious. Your housekeeper's a super cook.'

'She's a remarkable woman,' said van Biljon.

It seemed to Manuela that Black was unusually hesitant in replying to remarks addressed to him, and she had the feeling that his mind was not on what he was saying so much as on what he was thinking.

For the rest of the meal their host had to do most of the

159

talking, telling them of life in South America and of the manner in which his family had left the Transvaal and settled in the Argentine as refugees after the Boer War.

'To my parents it must have seemed a disaster of the first magnitude. To me it really meant nothing. I was born and brought up in South America.' He looked up at them quickly. 'You know it is my belief that all that happens in our lives is in the end for the best. It was in the Argentine that I made my fortune, and it was that which enabled me to collect my pictures and they . . .' he paused, to finish the sentence in a low voice . . . 'are my life.'

After dinner he took them to the drawing-room where Juan stood by a table with coffee and liqueurs.

While these were being handed round, van Biljon said, 'Normally I have coffee and liqueurs in the gallery. But to-night Techa insisted they be served here.' He chuckled. 'She is a great believer in the conventions. It is very much to her sorrow that I do not entertain. When I told her I was going to have a dinner party to-night, she looked at me as if I had gone out of my mind. But she was happy. Ah, yes, I could see that.'

When Juan had gone, van Biljon brought up the subject of Ibiza and its growing flood of tourists. While he spoke his eyes travelled round the room as if he were searching for something. Presently, he said, 'Please excuse me. I must have left the cigars in my study. I shall not be a moment.'

When the old man had gone, Black went over to Manuela. She looked up inquiringly and he caressed her cheek with the back of his hand. 'You're worried about something, aren't you?'

'And you?' she challenged. 'Why are you so silent? You should be excited. You are to see the pictures.'

'I know I am. Feel all dithery. But what's on *your* mind?'

She shook her head.

'Come on,' he urged. 'Tell me.'

'It's nothing,' she said and then, as they heard the sound of footsteps on the landing, she whispered, 'I'm afraid.'

Black went back to the other side of the room as their host came down the stairs.

'Please follow me,' said van Biljon, gesturing with the hand that held a cigar. He was standing before them, tall and elegant, the black velvet smoking-jacket emphasising the white hair which lent a curious distinction to the scarred face.

They followed him into the hall, through french windows and up stone steps to the patio where the long pool reflected the lights of the house and the bright scatter of stars. The tall figure moved ahead, skirting the pool, leading them along the white walls of the west wing on which the patio lights, shining through vine-covered pergolas, cast intricate shadows. The heady perfume of wistaria reminded Manuela of her childhood in Puerto Rico.

The line of windows on their left rose suddenly from eye level to high in the wall above them, and van Biljon stopped before a doorway. He unlocked the wrought-iron gate and swung it open. Beyond was a wooden door, massive and iron bound, and this, too, he unlocked. Touching a light switch, he went into the gallery, beckoning them to follow.

He shut the inner door, and led them across to the furnished recess at that end of the gallery which adjoined the house. Manuela saw many pictures on the walls and screens but since the lights which were on served only the entrance and recess, the greater part of the gallery was dimly lit.

She had a quick impression of leather armchairs and settees, of Persian carpets, walnut bookcases and cabinets, of glossy art journals, a mahogany desk, and a long, low hi-fi with a matching cabinet next to it. 'How lovely,' she said. 'You *have* done this attractively.'

Van Biljon stood facing them, his eyes invisible behind the dark glasses, but when with quiet modesty he said, 'I am glad you like it. I spend the happiest hours of my life here,' she knew he was pleased with her remark.

He lifted the lid of the cabinet. 'In a moment I shall show you my pictures, but first,' he paused, the cigar clenched between his teeth as he ran his fingers down the index sheet, 'but first music. Good music and good pictures. They go together. And now,' he went on. 'I look for something which is both Spain and France. Ah! Here it is,'

He straightened up and drew the record from its sleeve, slowly, almost reverently, while they wondered what he had chosen. He put it on the turntable and set the pick-up arm. With his back to them, he said, 'Ravel. You will know it.'

As the opening chords of *Rhapsodie Espagnole* broke the

silence in the great room, van Biljon went over to the screens, reached for a switch and the pictures in the gallery came to life with dramatic suddenness. He beckoned to them. 'Now,' he said. 'Come and see.'

Wall by wall, screen by screen, he showed them the pictures, keeping to the order in which he always viewed them. At each picture he would explain the period in which it had been painted, the history and character of the artist, his changing techniques and the influences to which he had been subject at the time. Van Biljon's excitement, his emotional involvement, communicated themselves to Manuela, and she felt a curious disquiet, a disturbing surfeit of emotion. It seemed to her that Black, too, might be experiencing the same thing, for she was aware of symptoms of stress: his constant throat clearing, the hands behind his back clenching and unclenching, the skin on his knuckles white where pressure forced the blood away. But he said little and she presumed he was dazzled by the scale and importance of what he was seeing.

Not once, she noticed, did the old man boast in any way about the collection; never did he say what he had paid for a picture, or what it might be worth, and Manuela found this modesty attractive, for she realised the collection was beyond any price she could imagine.

At the recess end of the third screen, van Biljon stopped before the picture of a water-mill at Argenton-sur-Creuse. 'That Cézanne is the picture I most prize,' he said. 'And of the French Impressionists, he is the painter I most admire.'

Manuela was puzzling at his subdued hesitant tone, when things happened of which afterwards she had only a confused recollection: at one moment Black was standing in front of her, chin in hand, silent, considering the picture—the next, she heard the door of the gallery open, then shut, as she turned to see Pedro and Juan come in: at first she thought they were holding out their hands in some sort of greeting, but then she realised that the hands held automatic pistols, aimed at her, and she let out a stifled scream. At much the same time she saw Black lunge towards the end of the screen, and the lights in the gallery went out as he fell to the floor. But the lights in the nearby recess remained on and she saw Pedro jump forward and stand over Black, and van Biljon was shouting, 'Hands up! Do not resist.'

Chapter Twenty

When he heard the gallery door open, Black swung round and saw the Spaniards. Instantly he lunged for the light switch, the position of which he'd so carefully marked. As he turned it he threw himself to the floor in anticipation of shots that never came, and at much the same time he heard van Biljon shout, 'Hands up! Do not resist.'

It was not possible to comply with this request lying on the floor, so he sat up, feeling that it was all rather theatrical and unnecessary, and lifted his hands above his head. He got to his feet as the main gallery lights went on again, to see that the Spaniards had ranged themselves on either side of him. Bad drill, he thought—if you have to shoot there's a chance you'll hit each other. Two or three feet ahead of him Manuela had her hands above her head, and in the sudden silence he could hear her breath coming in gasps.

Van Biljon moved towards him, stopping a few feet away, tall, sinister, the dark glasses concealing any emotion the eyes might have revealed. But he was breathing heavily and trembling, and Black, tense though he was, realised that he had the psychological advantage: he was calm, alert, and his mind was clear.

The tense silence was broken when van Biljon pointed an accusing finger at him. 'You told me at dinner that you scarcely knew the men in the *Snowgoose*. That you had never been on board.' The voice was hoarse, strangely subdued, and the pointing finger shook. 'In that case perhaps you can explain what you were doing in the schooner in the early hours of Thursday.'

Black said nothing, simply because there was nothing to say. And because it was difficult to outstare the anonymous black lenses, he concentrated on van Biljon's left ear, wondering how on earth the man knew that he'd been on board *Snowgoose* on Thursday. If that part of their security had blown, how much else?

The old man was off again.

'So you've no answer?' He took a step forward, thrusting

his face close to Black's. 'You and your friends are playing with fire. You must not be surprised if you get burnt.' The voice was rising, charged with emotion. Waiting for what might come next, Black thought of Manuela: what would she be making of all this? It was something he had half expected—if not quite in the form it had taken—but for her the shock must be immense.

As if she had read his thoughts, she swung round on him, frightened and confused. 'What are you trying to do? You . . .' Her indignation was too much for her. She turned to van Biljon in her distress, pointing at Black. 'He lied to me, too. About Helmut and Francois. Pretended they were strangers. He *never*,' her voice faltered, and she began again. 'He's *never* said a word about going on board *Snowgoose*.'

She switched to Black again. 'Why did you tell me those lies? Why have you got me into this?' Her face was ugly with frightened anger.

Black shrugged his shoulders. He knew what she was thinking: that he'd traded on her emotions, won her affection, used her. How right she is, he thought. And yet . . . but it was hardly the moment to explain that if he had used her, if he had landed her in this, at least it hadn't all been an act: his affection for her couldn't have been more genuine.

Van Biljon's voice broke into his thoughts. 'That story does not impress anyone,' he was saying to Manuela. 'Keep your hands up.'

With relief, Black saw that she was doing what she was told. He expected tears, but they didn't come. She was tougher than he'd thought.

Quietly, with resignation, he spoke to van Biljon. 'Manuela is telling the truth. She has had nothing to do with . . .' He hesitated, turning his head from side to side as if to indicate the gallery. 'I told her I didn't know them. I never let her know that I'd been on board *Snowgoose*. She's absolutely blameless.'

Van Biljon trembled with disbelief, his voice hoarse and menacing. 'You're lying, Black. You and the girl are always together.'

'I'm not lying,' said Black.

'Then if you're not lying to *me*, why did you lie to *her*?'

'Because I didn't want her to get mixed up in my business.'

'What *business*?'

'Drugs.' Black saw Manuela's head flick towards him,

'You're lying again, Black. Like you lied about bird watching when you came to the house last time. You weren't watching birds. You were watching Altomonte. It's what's in this gallery that interests you.'

Black shook his head. 'That's quite untrue in the sense you mean it. I *was* bird-watching. Manuela will confirm that. My interest in the gallery is professional. I am an art critic. It means good money and a scoop for me if I can do an article on your collection.'

'So you're an art critic *and* a drug smuggler.' Again van Biljon thrust his face forward, so close this time that Black smelt the cigar-laden breath, saw the white bristles on the bony chin, the spasmodic working of the sinews in the thin neck, and the uneven palpitations of the blood vessels at the temples. The Englishman took sardonic pleasure in these signs of agitation.

'I'll tell you what you are, Black. You're a liar. And a dangerous one.' For some moments he stared at the Englishman, then nodded briefly to Pedro and Juan. '*Un momento*,' he said and went to the recess.

Behind his back, Black heard the opening of a cupboard and the clink of metal. Soon the old man returned carrying handcuffs and a coil of nylon rope. Black felt the barrel of a pistol press into his neck as his arms were seized and pulled down behind him, then the cold touch of metal as handcuffs were snapped around his wrists.

Pedro kept them covered while Juan handcuffed Manuela's wrists behind her back to an accompaniment of noisy protestation and finally tears. Black was too concerned with other things to worry much about this, but it occurred to him that the more noise the better so he, too, raised his voice in protest until Pedro hit him across the face with a flat hand. '*Callarse!*—shut up,' the Spaniard growled.

Black was searched by Pedro, who returned everything to the Englishman's pockets except van Biljon's letter of invitation which he handed to the old man. Then they were made to lie on the floor and the rope was used to truss them. While this was being done the Spaniards' low mumbling was interrupted at times by interjections from van Biljon. With his scarred face, hoarse voice and agitated manner, their host looked so much the stage villain that Black had the curious feeling that it was all an act, that at any moment the curtain would drop to a round of applause, perhaps of booing. There had been other occasions in his life when he'd been in danger and then, too, he'd experienced this feeling of unreality, that what his eyes saw, his senses registered, could not in fact be happening.

When they were trussed—so tightly that Black feared for their circulation—and Manuela had stopped sobbing and instead was sniffing at intervals like a child after a long cry, gags of mutton cloth were produced and tied round their mouths. The moment this happened, Black knew with chilling certainty that van Biljon was not going to hand them over to the police. His worst fear was confirmed: van Biljon knew what it was that had brought him to Altomonte. That was why they'd been invited to dinner, why Tomaso had been sent to fetch them, why they'd been asked to treat the invitation as confidential, why van Biljon had asked them to use his letter to identify themselves . . . he had ensured that the essential evidence would be returned to him.

While Pedro and Juan picked up their automatics and returned them to their shoulder-holsters, the dominant thought in Black's mind was time. He could not see his watch, but he estimated that at least fifteen minutes had passed since he'd jumped for the light switch. He'd last looked at the time a few minutes before they'd reached the water-mill picture: it had then been ten twenty-seven . . . another fifteen minutes made it ten forty-two.

In the recess van Biljon was speaking to his servants in a low voice, almost a whisper. Black, concentrating, caught the words, *ahora—en seguida—Nordwind*.

What, he thought, is to happen *now, without delay*, which concerns the *Nordwind*. Before he could answer the rhetorical question, the Spaniards had seized him and Manuela by the ankles and were walking backwards, dragging them over the polished floor towards the gallery doors. Van Biljon, walking stiffly, went ahead.

As he was dragged along, Black raised his head and saw van Biljon go to the gallery door and swing it open, then turn back to them and step aside for Pedro and Juan to haul their loads.

What happened next appeared to him to take place in slow motion and, desperate and undignified though their situation was, Black felt it was not without humour: for into the doorway, directly in his line of vision—but unseen to van Biljon

166

and the Spaniards who had their backs to them—came two bearded, silent figures with Lugers in their left hands and coshes in their right. Black saw their surprise in the fraction of time they needed to take in the scene then, with traumatic effect, the silence was broken by Helmut's hoarse, 'Up with your hands—*pronto*!'

The new arrivals got quickly to work: van Biljon and the Spaniards were ordered to face the gallery wall and press their raised hands against it; then they were frisked, their firearms and handcuff keys removed, and their pockets emptied, the contents scattered over the floor.

Van Biljon began an agitated protest. Helmut at once interrupted, and in a voice and manner which left no room for doubt he told them that if there was any refusal to obey orders, any unauthorised movement, any talking or other noise, he would shoot or—and to make his point he went briskly along the line tapping the backs of their heads with his cosh.

Francois took off Black's gag, unlocked the handcuffs, and with his sheath-knife cut away the rope lashings. Black got to his feet, stiff and numb.

'You okay?' Francois' dark eyes were fiercely interrogative.

'For Chrissake. I thought you'd never come!'

'Are you okay?' repeated Francois urgently, 'We need you.'

'I'll be fine in a jiffy.' Black rubbed his arm and thigh muscles.

'Take this.' Francois kicked one of the Spaniards' automatics towards the Englishman, then set about freeing Manuela. Black looked at the wall where van Biljon's shoulders twitched curiously beneath raised arms, as if he were laughing. But Black knew that the emotion had nothing to do with humour. Then, with circulation returning and with it a good deal of pain and discomfort, he cleared his mind of irrelevances and concentrated on the task in hand.

Manuela, ashen and silent, was now free. Black helped her to her feet, but she had difficulty in standing. 'Sit down if you want to,' he said. 'Massage your leg and arm muscles.' He patted her shoulder. 'You're not in any danger now. Don't worry.' It wasn't quite true but it might help.

Helmut and Francois quickly handcuffed, gagged and bound van Biljon and the Spaniards while Black held them covered. Manuela, watching, wondered why they left the old man's left arm free. She was soon to know.

Francois produced a small box from a beach bag. Taking a syringe from it, he held it vertically and with the needle pointing to the ceiling depressed the plunger until he was satisfied that the free air had been expelled. While the Frenchman did this, Helmut grasped van Biljon's left arm and ripped the coat sleeve with a sheath-knife, pulling back the shirt sleeve and baring the arm to above the elbow.

With the quiet competence of a man who had done it many times before, Francois inserted the needle into the old man's forearm and injected the Pentothal. Ten seconds later he lifted van Biljon's eyelids.

'*Bon*,' he said, taking first the gag and then a set of dentures from the old man's mouth. 'He's out for about twenty minutes.'

Manuela watched, puzzled and frightened, as Helmut removed van Biljon's shoes and socks. When the right sock had been taken off Black said, 'yes,' in a taut way. After that Helmut took off the left sock and again Black said, '**yes**,' in what seemed to her a strange voice.

Black was putting on Pedro's shoulder-holster. 'Now,' he said as he adjusted the straps. 'Let's have the gen, and make it . . .' He was interrupted by Helmut's hissed, 'No you don't,' and turned to see the German dart forward, grab Manuela and clap a hand over her mouth.

'She was going to make a run for it,' said Helmut, holding the struggling girl in a lockforwards embrace.

Black went over to her, his eyes seeking desperately to convey the concern and affection he felt. 'Manuela. Don't try that sort of thing,' he pleaded. 'We don't want to get tough. You're safe as long as you keep quiet and do as you're told. If you don't you'll be soup before you know it. Take it easy. You've seen enough to-night to know that this isn't a vicar's tea party. There's a hell of a lot at stake and if you get in the way . . .' he paused, dropping his voice, 'you'll be put *out* of the way. I can't say it more plainly than that.'

'I don't know *who* you are,' she gasped, her eyes accusing them all. 'Art thieves, kidnappers, whatever. But you're a bunch of thugs, and I don't want anything to do with you. Just let me go.' She turned imploring eyes on Black. '*Please* let me go.'

He shook his head. 'We can't, yet. But we will before long. There isn't time to argue or explain. We're not art thieves and we're not thugs. Now calm down, or we'll have to use the hypodermic on you.'

She knew from the way he looked at her and his voice that he meant it. She stopped struggling and said a sullen, 'All right.'

'Now,' Black looked at his watch and turned to Helmut. 'Quick! What's the gen?'

'Kamros is waiting outside the wall with the stretcher. The Zephyr's parked according to plan. Can't see the Land-Rover. Must be in the garage at the back. We've not had time to look. On the way up we spotted a jeep of the Guardia Civil parked in a thicket at the foot of the Altomonte road. About five kilometres from here. You know, where the dirt road joins the main road? It was parked off the road behind some bushes about half a kilometre on the Ibiza side. Its windscreen reflected our headlights. We ran on a bit and stopped. Then I went back and did a reccy on foot. There were no police that I could see, but of course it's as dark as hell to-night.'

'Christ!' said Black. 'They've probably gone ahead on foot to watch the road junction.'

'Could be,' said Helmut. 'But they can't know about us.'

'I'm not so sure. Van Biljon knew a lot more about my movements than I'd bargained for.'

'Any way of rejoining the main road without using the junction?' Francois' face was strained.

Black thought, then snapped his fingers. 'Yes. There's a track near the bottom of the Altomonte road. Used by cattle. Goes through bush and joins up with the main road about half a kilometre west of the junction. Very rough, but I reckon the Zephyr could make it . . . With a little bit of luck,' he added.

'Thank God for bird watching,' said Helmut.

'You can say that again. But it'll be dicy. When they see our headlights they'll make for the jeep. It'll be touch and go.'

'There's a point I forgot to mention,' Helmut grinned complacently.

'What's that?'

'We took the precaution of removing the jeep's distributor-cap. Fixed the R/T set too.'

'At what time was that?'

'About nine o'clock—soon after you passed in the Land-Rover.'

Black frowned. 'Was that a good thing? If they've been back to the jeep they'll know it's been tampered with.'

'I don't think so. We replaced the distributor-cap after we'd taken a bit of wire out of the cable below the supply material. It'll take time to find that. When they do it'll look more like faulty cable than tampering.'

'And the R/T set?'

'Same thing. On the transmitting side. If those Spanish boys have got back to the jeep they've a lot of work to do.'

Black was thoughtful. 'Dogs okay? Any sign of Tomaso or the housekeeper?'

'About the dogs,' said Francois. 'You need not worry. They won't. That meat was lethal. I hated doing it. We saw Tomaso go to the gate when Juan and Pedro left it. Expect he's there now. Waiting for van Biljon and company to bring you and Manuela out. The housekeeper's probably in the kitchen or the servants' quarters. What d'you think he intended?'

'We were going for a short voyage in *Nordwind*,' said Black. 'On non-return basis, I imagine.'

'You always liked her lines.' Francois grimaced.

Black looked at his watch. 'Twelve minutes since you arrived. We must get cracking. I was hoping Tomaso might have come in by now to see how his chums were getting on.' He went across to where Manuela was slumped in an armchair, her eyes closed. He touched her shoulder. 'Manuela. Go with Helmut and Francois. Do *exactly* as they tell you. If you don't I can't be responsible for what happens. I'll be rejoining you outside.'

She didn't answer, and Black went over to the others. 'I'll go now and create the diversion in front. When you hear the shindy move off. Get him into the Zephyr *pronto*. Give him another shot when necessary. All being well I'll be over the wall about ten minutes after you. It's ten fifty-seven now. You should reach the car by eleven-fifteen. Give me five minutes' grace unless it's obvious I've come unstuck. In that case, don't wait. Look out for the track. On the left, about two to three hundred metres before you reach the main road. Unfortunately you'll have to use lights. If I have time, I'll try and fix the Land-Rover. But I doubt it.'

Helmut shook his head. 'You'll be with us. Don't worry.'

'I sincerely hope so.' Black patted him on the back, touched Francois' arm and then, taking a set of gallery keys and handcuffs, he slipped the thong of a cosh over his wrist and took the automatic from the shoulder-holster. When he reached the gallery door he opened it quietly and went out, shutting it behind him.

A few minutes later Helmut and Francois checked the lashings on Pedro and Juan and went over to where van Biljon was lying. Helmut called to Manuela, 'Come. Help us, please.'

She went across, frowning and sullen, her eyes on the cosh dangling from Helmut's wrist.

He stared at her. 'I'm going to carry van Biljon out. At the wall we may need assistance. Francois will keep next to you. Please behave. He also has a cosh.' With that he bent down, picked up the long thin body of the old man and with little effort slung it over his shoulder.

'Okay,' he said. 'Flick the lights.'

When Francois had flicked the lights on and off, he led the way out of the gallery with Manuela, hesitant and fearful, at his side. They stopped in the patio for a moment while Francois shut and locked the double doors.

Chapter Twenty-One

Once out of the gallery Black made for the nearest pergola, moving silently in the shadows, past the long pool, until he reached the french windows to the hall.

Before entering he looked in. From where he stood he could see not only into the hall but into parts of the rooms adjoining it. There was no one about. Taut, wary, he went in and made his way to the Tribal Room. He chose it because it was on the side of the house nearest the kitchen and farthest from the wall down which Helmut and the others would pass once they'd gone over at the back. It helped, too, that he was familiar with the layout in that wing.

The curtains were drawn and the lights on. The doors leading to the pantry and kitchen were shut, but the iron gates on the guest-suite landing were open and he marked that as an emergency exit. When he'd locked the other doors, he knew that the Tribal Room could only be entered from the hall or the guest-suite. On the south side of the big room, where the windows overlooked the main gates, he moved a curtain an inch aside and looked through. The gates were about fifty yards away, the lights along the terrace in front of the house still on, as they had been when Tomaso had driven them up in the Land-Rover. There was nothing to be seen of the Spaniard. Then he heard the sound of his voice, faint at first but growing louder. He was calling the dogs, alternately whistling and using their names.

The sound came from the east side of the house, and Black watched the corner there. Presently Tomaso appeared, still whistling and calling, making for the gates, using a hand torch to search the clumps of cacti and shrubs. When the Spaniard had almost reached the gates, Black picked up a wooden stool and flung it at the front windows of the Tribal Room. It struck the thick curtains, smashing the glass behind them with a shattering noise. The whistling stopped, and Black looked through the chink in the curtain. Tomaso was standing at the gate, watching the east wing of the house, his mouth wide open with surprise.

Black took a wooden giraffe by its neck and beat with it on an African drum, with excellent results. Next he seized a great earthenware bowl, Amerindian in origin. This he threw at another of the front windows and it, too, made a rewarding noise. Highest decibel register yet, he decided. Again he went to the window and looked out. Tomaso, bent low, was running up the steps to the front door. Simultaneously, Black heard knocking on the door from the kitchen passage and a woman's voice, fearful and querulous. 'What is happening?' she cried. 'What is the trouble?' It was the housekeeper.

Affecting a throaty hoarseness, he shouted in Spanish, Murder! Run for your life.' There came immediately the sound of footsteps scampering on terra-cotta tiles, fading rapidly into the distance.

'Now for the reception committee,' he muttered as he slipped into the hall and stood against the wall beside the front door. He could hear Tomaso inserting the key, and watched fascinated as the handle turned. The door was opening against him so he edged back, cosh in his right hand, Luger in his left. It was happening in slow motion, and again he was reminded of a Buster Keaton comedy. Why did dangerous moments seem so unreal, so funny that he wanted to giggle? It was a weakness. Kagan would not approve. Tomaso was doing his best to be careful, but he lacked training or he wouldn't be coming into the room like that. Didn't he know the standard drill?: *Kick door and jump aside. If door hits soft object fire through it, if in doubt challenge.* Tomaso did neither, relying on stealth in slow motion, apparently convinced that where the noise had been the people must be.

As the Spaniard came through the door, slowly, like a stalking cat, his eyes were fixed on the Tribal Room, and there they were when Black's cosh descended and Tomaso lost all further interest in the proceedings. Black looked unhappily at the prone figure twitching on the floor at his feet. He had no quarrel with Tomaso. 'Definitely not first eleven,' he sighed as he took the Spaniard's automatic from a limp hand and slid it under a settee. He looked at the clock in the hall and then at his watch. It was seven minutes since he'd left the gallery. The others should be over the wall by now and making for the car, Helmut and Kamros carrying the stretcher while Francois covered them and brought along the girl.

Black dragged Tomaso to the foot of the stairs and hand-cuffed him to the wrought-iron banisters. After a last look round, he ran through the hall, out on to the patio and on past the pool to the gallery. There he unlocked the doors and went in, locking them again behind him. He checked the Spaniards' lashings and found them secure, but Juan's gag had worked loose and this he tightened, warning the men that if they wanted to see the sun rise, they'd better play dead for the next few hours.

That done, he went to the far screen and took the Cézanne water-mill picture from its frame, and with a heavy pocket knife lifted the tacks which secured the canvas to the stretchers. He rolled the canvas and thrust it inside his trousers, wedging it between belt and body. When he left the gallery he locked the doors, and in the subdued light from the patio made for the outbuildings. Beyond them and the screening clumps of figs and cacti, he found the wall and moved westward along it, checking the rough surface with the beam of a pencil torch. Soon the bottom of the nylon ladder showed up.

Grasping it, he climbed to the top of the wall, pulled it up after him, dropping it over on the far side and climbed down.

Moving as fast as he could in the darkness, he went along the side of the *finca* keeping to the wall, the top of which was outlined against the sky by the lights from the house. At the corner the wall turned east across the front of the property, and he left it and went into the trees. A few minutes later he came to the road and started down it. The night was cold and clear, the sky bright with stars, the light southerly breeze charged with the scent of almonds and lemons from the terraces.

When he reached the S-bend, he followed it to the bottom of the ravine. There he went into the trees again and walked in a half-circle, sniffing the wind until he picked up the synthetic odour of petrol and oil and rubber. He followed it until he almost walked into the car.

'Everything okay?' Black's dry throat made him hoarse.

'Okay,' said Helmut. 'Bloody hard work carrying him, though. Even with the stretcher. And you?'

'Fine,' said Black. 'I had to clobber Tomaso. He's out for

a bit. Handcuffed to the banisters.'

'And the housekeeper?'

'She's lying low somewhere. Badly frightened, I'd say.'

'What about the girl? Drop her here?'

He had almost forgotten Manuela. 'Not yet,' he said, climbing into the driving seat. 'All in?' He turned but could see nothing in the darkness.

Francois said, 'Okay. He's between me and Kamros. Stretcher's in the boot. I've given him another shot.'

Black started the engine and switched on the headlights. In the glow of the facia board he saw that Manuela was next to him. He touched her hand reassuringly, but she snatched it away. The car came clear of the trees and they turned south on to the dirt road, climbing the long slope out of the ravine. At the top he switched to sidelights and then, as they began the descent, he used the headlights again.

'Time?' he called.

Helmut held his wrist against the dashlight. 'Eighteen minutes past eleven.'

'Christ,' said Black. 'It's taken twenty-one minutes.'

'Feels like twenty-one hours,' said the German.

Black said, 'I'll drive down at an easy pace. They'll see and hear us before we reach the turn-off, but they won't know whether it's the Zephyr or the Land-Rover. They'll reckon on stopping the car at the junction to check. We've got to reach the main road via the cattle track before they realise we're by-passing the junction. When we reach the track we'll give it stick.'

Helmut said, 'I wonder if that jeep's serviceable yet?'

A voice came from the back seat. 'You'll soon know.' It was Kamros at his gloomiest.

The lone olive tree showed up in the headlights and Black slowed down, his eyes straining for the cattle track. He knew that the police, a few hundred yards ahead at the road junction, would long since have seen the Zephyr's headlights although he'd kept them dipped. If they'd got the jeep going or requisitioned a passing vehicle, it would be a close thing.

He saw the track and swung right. 'Hold tight,' he called. 'It'll be bumpy.' To Helmut he said. 'Keep a look-out for snags. Shout if you see anything.'

With the car in second gear, he switched the headlights on

and accelerated. Then began a wild dash through trees and scrub, the Zephyr swerving and bumping along the dry track braking and skidding as unexpected hazards loomed up, then accelerating on to the next one, the car sometimes leaving the ground as it hit a furrow or grass hump. Twice it seemed to Black that they would go over as he fought skids with wheel and accelerator. Several times Helmut shouted warnings, once when the headlights dispersed a shadow cast by bushes and a yawning burrow showed up close ahead. Black wrenched the steering wheel and the car lurched dangerously, a rear wheel sliding and spinning as the rim of the hole collapsed.

But somehow they kept going until Helmut shouted, 'See that! Police maybe.' Ahead and to their left the headlight of a car came sweeping up out of the darkness and they knew that they had almost reached the main road.

'Christ!' said Black, and as the Zephyr dry skidded round a bend on the cattle track, he switched off the lights and slammed on the brakes. Those in the back seat were thrown forward and the car juddered to a stop behind a clump of pines. The air was thick with dust, and from the wheels came the acrid smell of burning rubber.

He switched off the engine. 'Sorry to have stopped so untidily, but there's good cover here. We'll hold on.'

The headlights of the other car disappeared. 'Must've gone into a dip,' he said. 'They'll slow up soon.'

Before he'd finished speaking they appeared again, the beams reaching towards San José. In their lights, through gaps in the pines, Black could see the road ahead of and below them, no more than a hundred yards away. In the Zephyr the only sound was that of breathing, and even it seemed to stop as the other car swept up the main road, came opposite the thicket of pines, and raced on in the darkness.

'Don't think it could have been the police,' he said. 'That car must have seen our headlights before we stopped. If it'd been the police, they'd have slowed down to check.'

'Unless they reckon we made the road ahead of them,' suggested Helmut. 'And went round the bend.'

'We'll probably do that anyway,' said Black dryly. 'Let's give them a minute or two to get clear. Watch their headlights as long as you can. They may be aiming to stop ahead of us and wait.'

Francois leant forward from the back seat. 'Are you going

to take the Ibiza direction?'

'It's tricky.' Black took a deep breath. 'Means going back on the main road past the junction—that's past the jeep if it's still there. I think we'd better take the San José route. Unless somebody has a better idea. Whatever we do is a gamble. But the San José route'll get us to Cabo Negret quicker.'

The minutes ticked away as they waited for the other car's headlights to disappear. When they had, Black said, 'They should be five or six kilometres away now.' He started the engine, switched on the headlights, and they moved off down the track. It became rocky and rutted, growing steeper as they approached the main road where the line of the ditch was marked by a long shadow. At its edge, Black stopped the car and was about to get out to examine it when Helmut leant across and grabbed his arm. 'Look! Something coming down from Altomonte.'

Black swung round to see distant fingers of light probing the darkness like antennae as a car made its way down the valley. 'Must be the Land-Rover,' he said.

It seemed to him unlikely that Tomaso could have recovered in time to have been of much use. Anyway, he was handcuffed to the banisters. Techa must have overcome her fear, got into the gallery somehow, and released Pedro and Juan. But speculating didn't help, it was the fact of the pursuit he had to deal with. 'I reckon we've got five minutes' start,' he said. 'And a lot more speed.'

'D'you think the police will stop them at the junction. Then join in the chase?' asked Helmut.

'Could be. Now for this bloody ditch.' He turned in the driving seat. 'Everybody out. Get ready to shove. Not you,' he said to Manuela gruffly as she began to move. Immediately contrite, he added, 'You're too light to make any difference.'

She said nothing and he climbed down and had a good look at the ditch before engaging low gear and taking the Zephyr into it. The car moved ahead, meeting the ditch at an oblique angle, lurching first one way and then the other, its body groaning as the metal twisted and strained. It started up the slope towards the verge, hesitated, stopped, and the engine roared as the wheels spun. Black slipped the gear lever into reverse and backed. 'Now! Shove as we try again,' he called. It was not until the fourth attempt that the Zephyr staggered out of the ditch and Black pulled it up on the side of the road.

They'd lost at least three minutes.

The others ran up and climbed in, and he let the clutch out and accelerated through the gears until they were making for San José. On the straight stretches the speedometer needle hovered between the 120 and 130 kilometre notches, the roar of the wind drowned all other sounds, and the bends and undulations in the road made it difficult to see if they were being followed. Nothing was said, but Black knew that his men—and for quite other reasons, Manuela—were thinking of the police, expecting a road block round every corner, over the brow of each hill, looking back for the headlights of a pursuing car.

The lights of San José showed up as the car breasted a hill, then disappeared as it descended into the valley. The next time they showed, Black said, 'San José must be four or five kilometres. Look out for a turn to the right. Any time now. It's a country road. Leads to Santa Gertrudis. Once on it, we'll come to cross-roads after about five minutes. There we'll turn east on to a really bad road. More of a track, actually. That'll take us round behind and to the north of San José and San Augustin.'

Shortly before they reached the turn-off to Santa Gertrudis, they saw headlights coming towards them. Tension in the car mounted, but Black kept the speedometer needle on the 140 kilometre mark. The lights flashed by and Francois and Helmut shouted 'Truck' simultaneously. Almost immediately afterwards the Zephyr topped the brow of a hill and Black slammed on the brakes. With tyres shrieking they swerved past a car which was backing out of a lay-by alongside a gravel pit. As they accelerated away, there were shouts from the roadside and the flash of torches. In the brief moment that the other car, standing half-way across the road, had been illuminated by their headlights, they'd seen the white letters GUARDIA CIVIL on the front door, and the big external roof lamp.

'Police!' shouted Black. 'That was going to be a road block.'

At the bottom of the hill the Santa Gertrudis road showed up. They slowed down and turned on to it. As the Zephyr gathered speed, Francois called out urgently, 'They're coming down the hill.' Soon afterwards he said, 'Now they're turning on to this road. About a kilometre and a half behind.'

Black was silent, concentrating on the driving as they raced down the road skirting the hills which seemed to shut out the sky to the west. Conscious of the tension in the car he said, 'The big hill on the left is Reco. Very good name I thought, first time I saw it. More than three hundred metres. Excellent for birds of prey. I've seen a Golden Eagle there.'

'Must have been sick,' said Francois. 'They like two, three thousand metres at least.'

'Are you doubting my word?'

'Of course,' said Francois. 'Bird watchers are famous liars. I think we are drawing ahead. About two kilometres now.'

Black smiled dourly in the darkness. He was enjoying the chase, every muscle and nerve stretched, the future balanced on a knife edge. That was life as it should be.

The stars in the western sky showed the break beyond the big hill and then they were at the crossroads and the car swung left on to a stony track. He dimmed the headlights, turned the car off the road and ran it into the trees. 'Now,' he said quietly switching off the lights and engine. 'It's a three to one chance. They can go straight on, left or right.'

They heard the noise of the engine first, then the trees and bushes by the crossroads reflected the lights of the approaching car, faintly at first, but with increasing intensity. It stopped at the crossroads and they heard, above the noise of its engine, the voices of men arguing. There followed the rising note of the engine, and they waited breathlessly as the car moved forward. Its lights traversed slowly right, and it bumped off down the road towards San Rafael—away from the direction they had taken.

Black breathed deeply. 'Thank God for that.'

'Thank him for diversionary routes,' said Helmut.

They waited for a few minutes before reversing out of the trees and starting down towards the coast, the rough track which they had taken ascending and descending, winding through the hills and valleys. Soon after midnight they crossed the tarred road that ran from San José to San Antonio, and drove on in darkness. The country road curving steadily southwards was more suited to farm carts than motor cars, and Black had to reduce speed and brake often. The shadows of trees and bushes contrived strange shapes on the road, and at times he found himself avoiding things which were not there. It was then that he realised how tired he was.

It was a night which seemed to have endured for an infinity, to stretch endlessly ahead, to hold no promise of finishing. Sleep before daylight was not on, and he doubted if any would be possible then. He fumbled in his coat pocket for the small bottle, found it, and passed it to Manuela.

'Open it,' he said. 'Give me one.'

She took the bottle and held it to the dashlight. 'Here,' her voice was hard. 'I thought you didn't approve of drugs?' It was the first time she'd spoken since the journey'd begun.

'Benzedrine,' he said. 'Doesn't count. Anybody else like one? We won't get any sleep for a long time.'

Kamros was the only taker. Age, thought Black. We haven't the stamina of these kids. Thirty-five. Christ, I'm old.

They struck a pothole and the car bounced, coming down heavily on its springs. He thought he heard the exhaust pipe hit the road, and there was a muffled thud in the back seat, followed by a moan.

'Who's that?' snapped Black.

'Van Biljon,' said Kamros.

Francois said, 'He's okay. Bump knocked him off the seat.'

There were sounds of exertion in the back, interrupted by the Zephyr hitting two more potholes, the second one so violently that they were thrown from the seats. Manuela let out a frightened, 'For God's sake!'

Black braked and the car dry skidded. 'Sorry,' he said taking a deep breath and shaking his head to clear his eyes. 'I'll be more careful.' After that he gave up trying to beat the road.

The track curved left and dipped down between the hills, the rutted surface alternating with outcrops of rock which made steps over which the car bounced. At the foot of the hill, stone walls bordering olive groves showed up in the headlights, and presently the walls of a *finca*, white and ghostly, slid by. After that the road improved and he increased speed until they ran into clouds of dust from which a red light winked intermittently. It turned out to be a truck, lurching and rattling down the hill, laden with vegetables beneath its green canopy. Black hooted several times before it pulled aside and let them pass. 'Making for market,' he said.

Later, descending a hill to the road fork where they would turn east below San José, he felt the steering gear go and slammed on the brakes. There was a jarring metallic noise, and the car sheered over to the wrong side of the road before juddering to a stop. 'My bloody oath,' he said desperately.

'What's the trouble?' several voices inquired at once.

'Steering's gone.'

They got out and he and Kamros examined the underside of the car. In the thin beam of the torch they saw the track rod hanging down asymmetrically between the toed-in front wheels.

'Well, that's it,' said Black.

Helmut swore in German. 'Must've been the smack that knocked the old bugger off the back seat.'

No longer able to order his thoughts, overwhelmed by despair, Black could only mumble, 'Christ.' It was an expression, not of fear, but of the shock of failure at the very moment when success had seemed, if not assured, at least probable. In an instant the situation had become hopeless. They were at least ten kilometres from Cabo Negret. Even if it were physically possible in the time available—and it wasn't—they couldn't carry the old man through those hills and valleys without encountering someone, if not the police. The entire island was only about fifty by twenty-five kilometres, and now that the alarm had been given, every unit of the Guardia Civil would be out looking for them. He felt an overpowering sense of personal guilt. Why had he driven so recklessly? Once the police car had been shaken off, another ten, fifteen minutes on the journey would have been neither here nor there, and it would in all probability have meant the difference between success and failure. He had let excitement get the better of his judgment and he was appalled at the results.

Thoughts of those he had let down ran through his mind: Kagan, the men on the operation with him, the people at ZID and, beyond all these, faceless and anonymous, the others—those vast uncountable numbers whose eternal muteness was in itself the ultimate reproach.

He was contemplating the enormity of his failure when Helmut's calm, 'Well, what now?' broke into his thoughts and he felt suddenly ashamed that he had given way so easily to despair.

He took a grip on himself, shook off the mood of defeat, and his mind cleared. He recalled Kagan's, *You're not beaten until you give up*. Well, he wasn't giving up. Standing there in the darkness, silent, his mind now seeking feverishly for a solution, an idea came to him—flickering at first, then

181

steadying and growing like the flame of a newly lit candle. He called the others. 'That farm truck isn't far behind. Let's push the Zephyr into the middle of the road.'

'What then?'

'The truck'll have to stop and we'll borrow it.'

Helmut laughed hoarsely from the depths of his belly. 'Anything you say, boss.'

With difficulty the four men pushed and lifted the Zephyr until it was parked in the middle of the road at an angle of about forty-five degrees to the centre line, and there they left it with the side and rear lights burning.

Black turned to Kamros: 'When we see the truck's lights, get under the car. Make as if you're working at something. We'll stop the truck about fifty metres back. Soon after we begin talking to the driver, come and join us. You, Francois, stay in the car with Manuela.'

He went back to where she was sitting huddled in the front seat. He could just make out her features in the reflection of the dashlight. 'Manuela,' he said, 'I don't want you to get hurt. But if you try anything when that truck pitches up ... You know what I mean?'

He was waiting for her reply, when Helmut shouted, 'The lights have just come over the hill. Not too far, I reckon.'

'Okay,' said Black. 'Let's get cracking.'

Chapter Twenty-Two

The truck rattled down the hill, the engine misfiring and the brakes squealing as the driver controlled its descent. Rounding a corner, its headlights revealed two men on the road waving their arms: behind them the tail lights of a car glowed brightly, spilling pools of vermillion on the road and illuminating feet which projected from it.

With a final groan of brakes the truck stopped and the men on the road went up to the driving cab.

In the darkness Black couldn't see the face of the driver, but he greeted him in Spanish, explaining that the Zephyr had broken down.

'We are tourists,' he said. 'It is a hired car. We are not sure what the trouble is. A part is loose underneath.'

While the driver spoke to someone in the cab, Black heard Kamros coming up the road from the Zephyr.

'How far is it to San José?' asked Black.

'About two or three kilometres, señor,' said the truck driver.

'Can you take a message for us?'

'At this time they will be in bed. There is an inn. You can spend the night there.'

'Can you look at the car? Tell us what the trouble is?'

There was a pause and then the voice from the darkened cab said, 'Señor, I would like to do this, but my son and I are not mechanics. Also we must get our load to the market in Ibiza and be back to the farm by daylight. We are late.'

Black said, 'I understand, señor. But we cannot move the car. Something is stuck. Can you and your son help us push it to the side of the road so that your truck may pass?'

They heard the man's low rumble as he spoke to his son. The cab doors opened and they stepped down on to the road. When they reached the front of the Zephyr, Black explained what had happened, and the farmer's son bent down and with Black's torch looked underneath. He called to his father, saying that the track rod had broken.

With exclamations of surprise, Helmut and Kamros discussed the implications of this with the farmer, while Black watched the Zephyr anxiously, checking what could be seen in the truck's headlights. But it all looked normal enough: the windows closed against the cold night air; the old man in the back leaning in a corner, evidently asleep; the woman and the man in the front seat close to each other, the man's head next to hers.

Francois got out of the front seat and the five men pushed the car slowly and with noisy exertion to the side of the road. Black opened the door, pulled on the handbrake and then, walking round the car, he took the automatic from his shoulder-holster. 'Stand-by,' he warned in a low voice. To the farmer he said, 'I am sorry, señor, but we must borrow your truck. We have urgent business in Ibiza.'

The Spaniard looked in astonishment at the muzzle of the automatic, and Helmut grabbed the boy who had jumped forward to help his father. The farmer called sharply, 'Do not resist, Manuel,' and Helmut released him.

'We will leave the truck in the Paseo Vara de Rey,' said Black. 'The vegetables will still be marketable. I am sorry. We have no option. Have you the key?'

'In the cab,' said the farmer sullenly.

Black turned to Helmut. 'Get in. Start the engine and park ahead of the Zephyr.'

When the truck had drawn ahead, he ordered the farmer and his son to walk up the hill away from the vehicles. 'Don't try any tricks,' he said, sounding as villainous as he could, 'or we'll use our guns.'

The farmer and his son walked away in the darkness, and Black posted Kamros as a rearguard at the back of the Zephyr. Then he called to Manuela and helped her into the driving cab. Van Biljon, still in a state of torpor, was lifted on to the top of the vegetables and lay at the back well under the canopy, Kamros and Francois on either side of him.

Black leant out of the cab and called to Helmut, 'Okay. Come along.'

The German jumped in beside Manuela, slamming the door as the engine revved up and the truck creaked forward.

'We'll have to take the road through San José,' said Black. 'It'll save time and distance, and the police won't be looking for a farm truck yet. What's the time?'

Helmut looked at his watch. 'Twenty-seven minutes past midnight.'

After that there was a long silence in the swaying, rattling cab. Later, Black felt Manuela's head resting against his shoulder and it reassured him, though he knew it was sleep and not affection. He'd not had much time to think of her since the chase had started and now, in the darkness, he wondered what to do about her. She knew a great deal. Too much to let her loose yet. But soon he would have to make the decision. Already he had a vague sense of guilt: a feeling that he'd already made the decision, that now he was looking for excuses to justify it. And though he was able to mask this with considerations of security and other things that were not related to his emotions, he knew that even the desire to get her away from Ibiza, from the tangle she'd got herself into with Kyriakou, was not paramount in his mind. He began an involved argument with his conscience: if I cannot be honest with them, at least I can be honest with myself. *It is because I want her.* Now that the time of decision has come, I don't want to lose her. And what does she want? This is a question I cannot answer. For she does not and cannot yet know the truth. But how can I, at this time, in these circumstances, with so much at stake, so much dependent upon my judgment, sit here and worry about a Puerto Rican drop-out I've known for a few weeks, who at this moment detests and fears me? What sort of future can there be for us . . .?

Helmut's voice brought him back to reality. 'What time d'you reckon we'll make Cabo Negret?'

'We can't do much in this outfit. But we'll be in San José any minute now, and it's about eight kilometres from there. Let's say, at the beach shortly before one o'clock.'

'Goot,' said the German, and there was once more silence in the cab.

The truck struggled up the winding road, past the cultivated terraces and outlying houses into the village of San José. As the gradient levelled, Black changed gear and the truck rolled down the tarred road between the houses, their walls sliding silently by, shadowy and spectral, encapsulating their sleeping inmates, the darkness broken only by the headlights. Towards the end of the village they were slowing down for the turn on to the Cubells road, when Helmut hissed '*Achtung!*' as the headlights picked up the white crash helmet and dark uniform of a policeman astride a motorcycle. It was parked in the shadows where the road forked right to Cubells. He was smoking a cigarette.

Black hissed, 'Watch Manuela, and look straight ahead.' There was a scuffle beside him and he realised that Helmut was pushing her on to the floor boards: with a hand over her mouth, judging by the muffled protests.

Slowly the truck's speed picked up, the policeman was passed, and the houses fell behind. Black relaxed. 'My God! That was a near thing,' he said hoarsely.

Helmut lifted Manuela back on to the seat, where she burst with indignation. 'You swine—you bloody swine of a man,' she gasped. 'You nearly choked me.' She turned on Black. 'You said that if I . . .'

'Shut up,' he interrupted. 'He had no option. No way of knowing you'd co-operate.'

'Co-operate,' she spluttered indignantly. 'With *you*?'

After that she was silent, but Black felt her body shaking and knew she was crying.

'We have missed the Cubells road,' announced Helmut lugubriously. 'So what now?'

'There'll be another on our right shortly. Just before Cova Santa. We couldn't have turned in San José. Loaded vegetable lorries don't go down to Cubells. That policeman would have been on to us. It's a million to one he's watching for the Zephyr.'

Helmut said, 'I reckon so.'

Not long afterwards they reached the turnout before Santa Cova and set off down the country road through stone-walled terraces of olives and caribs. A few kilometres later they joined the Cubells road, and were soon turning and twisting through heavily terraced undulating tree-strewn countryside, dark and anonymous save for an occasional *finca*. The final descent to the beach was by way of steep bends which necessitated low gear and heavy braking, the engine coughing and spluttering in protest. Coming out of the last bend the road straightened abruptly and in the headlights they could see, beyond the stone parapet which marked the end of the road, the dark ripple of the sea.

Black stopped the truck and switched off the lights. At the back he found Francois and Kamros already busy man-handling van Biljon from the top of the vegetables.

'How is he?' he asked.

'Okay,' said Francois. 'I gave him one more shot. He'll be all right for at least another fifteen minutes. Heart and pluse okay.'

Black said, 'Good. Get him down those steps and on to the beach. I'll look after the signalling. Helmut will see to the girl. We had a close shave in San José. Policeman on a motorbike at the road fork. See him? Just as we were about to make the turn.'

'Didn't see a thing,' said Francois laconically. 'Is she . . .'

'Just as well,' said Black. 'Bad for the heart.' Ignoring Francois' interrupted question, he went round to the driving cab. What the hell. He'd made the decision long ago, even if he hadn't admitted it to himself. He called to Helmut. 'Down here. Quickly!'

'And the girl?'

'Forget her for a moment.'

Helmut joined him and they moved away. Black lowered his voice. 'We'll have to take her. She's too heavily involved now. If we leave her she'll talk. They'll know how we left, and from where. We need all the start we can get. When we're on the other side she can do what she likes. By then the story will be out. ZID will see she's okay.'

'This is logical,' said Helmut censoriously, 'if highly un-usual. Anyway, we have not the time to argue.'

'Who with?' said Black dryly. 'Take the girl and join the others on the beach.'

Black went down the stone steps to the beach, feeling his way in the darkness. Close ahead he could hear Francois and Kamros talking in low voices. As he passed them carrying their human load, he said, 'Keep close. I'm going to signal.'

He stopped at the water's edge and looked at the wall of darkness over the sea. Behind him, and to left and right, the land rose steeply, the rims of the cliffs outlined against the starlit sky. Ahead the bay opened out, narrow at first but widening like a bell-mouth, and across the water to the south-east the lights at Ahorcados and Formentera flashed their warning to seamen. A cold breeze smelling of kelp and salt water came in from the sea. Except for the lapping of wavelets on the beach, the night was without sound.

Black aimed the pencil torch, flashing groups of shorts and longs. He had begun the third group when the answering flashes came, from a good deal closer in than he'd expected. Good man, he thought. Must have seen the truck's lights coming down the road.

On the screen of Black's mind there were two persistent images: the farmer and his son walking along the road, encountered by a searching police car; and, later, the policeman on the motor-cycle at the road fork in San José confirming that the truck had gone towards Ibiza. He looked at his watch. Twenty-seven minutes to one. Daylight at six-thirty-one. Six hours at most.

In the darkness he found the others. 'Dimitrio's answered,' he said. 'Not long now. Dinghy'll take four. Five with him. As soon as it shows up we'll put van Biljon in. Helmut and Francois must shove the dinghy off. Then hang on to the lifelines and swim.' He chuckled. 'You'll have a wet ride.'

He became serious again. 'Keep your automatics with you while you're on the beach. As we leave, chuck them into the dinghy. There's no sign of anyone yet, but if there's a last minute show up, you may need them. Fire to frighten, not to kill. We've no quarrel with the Spanish.'

'Tell that to the farmer and his son,' said Kamros.

Helmut made a rude noise. 'And to Pedro, Juan and company.'

'What about the girl?' asked Francois. 'Leaving her here?'

'No,' said Black. 'She's coming with us.'

Next to him he heard Manuela say, 'I'm *not*.' It was a pathetic gesture of defiance. Black, nerves stretched taut, felt smothered in guilt. 'You *are*,' he said wearily. 'Conscious, if you play ball. Unconscious if you don't. It's up to you.'

Her voice became suddenly small. 'Where to?'

'Can't tell you *yet*. But we won't hurt you. In a short time you'll be free. Then you can do what you like.'

She said in a broken voice, 'I never thought *you* would do this to me.'

The reproach stung him. 'Nor did I,' he said. 'But van Biljon decided the time-table. There were no options.'

'I don't know what you're talking about, and I . . .'

'Shush! Listen!' he interrupted.

In the silence which followed, only the lapping of the sea,

the deep breathing of van Biljon, and the lesser respirations of the others, could be heard. Then, faintly, a new sound obtruded, a minuscule splash and swish of water. It grew stronger and Black said, 'That's him. Get ready.'

Soon afterwards they heard a soft scraping on the beach, followed by Dimitrio's low call.

Chapter Twenty-Three

The hull of the schooner loomed suddenly above them in the darkness and the next moment they were alongside and climbing on board. Helmut and Francois clambered from the water into the dinghy and helped lift van Biljon out. The dinghy was brought inboard and deflated, a jib hoisted, the anchor weighed, foresail and mainsail set, and slowly, silently, without lights, *Snowgoose* moved to the south-west. Twenty minutes later, when they had cleared Cabo Llentrisca and the light on Vedra was broad on the starboard bow, the diesel engines coughed and boomed into life, the sails were lowered and the schooner shook purposefully as she drove through the water at fifteen knots.

Van Biljon, his lashings removed, had been locked in the single cabin adjoining the owner's suite. The lights there were on and he could be seen through a portlight from the cockpit, lying on the bunk, his manacled hands resting on the rug which covered him. Francois had reported that he was in good shape and recovering from the effects of the Pentothal.

Manuela had been given a cabin off the saloon. When he'd shown her to it, she'd complained to Francois of a headache. He told her she was suffering from nervous exhaustion and gave her two Codis tablets. 'Take them in water,' he said. 'You will sleep well. To-morrow when you wake up everything will be okay. *Bon soir, mam'selle.*'

She had given him a look which he described to Black later as, 'A stiletto from the eyes. You know,' and slammed the cabin door.

It was dark in the cockpit but for the dim shaded lights over the binnacle and hooded chart-table where Black was busy with dividers and parallel rulers.

He switched off the light and went over to Dimitrio who was at the wheel. 'How are we heading?'

'Two zero-five,' said Dimitrio.

Black looked at the automatic log repeater. It was reading 15.3 knots.

'Won't be a moment,' he said, taking the chart and going

190

down the companionway to the saloon. Helmut and Francois were there.

'Signal sent?' he asked abruptly.

Helmut nodded. 'Yes. ZID has acknowledged.'

'Dinghy stowed away?'

Helmut made a circle with his thumb and forefinger. 'Also, yes.'

With a start Black remembered something which the torrent of the night's events had pushed to the back of his mind. 'Hassan,' he said. 'What happened?'

Helmut smiled slowly. 'Dimitrio and Kamros landed him on Abago this afternoon. Blindfolded until he reached the shore. He still does not know the name of this schooner, or where it is from.'

Black felt again something of the pity and kinship of the night at Rafah. He would have liked to have seen Ahmed ben Hassan, if only to have apologised for the uncavalier treatment he'd been accorded. 'How is he?' he asked quietly.

'Very well,' said Helmut. 'He laughed and joked with us on the skimmer going into Abago. When we took the blindfold off and handed over the provisions and water he bowed and salaamed in Arabic style. After we had shown him the fisherman's shelter, he insisted on shaking hands.'

'He gave us a message,' said Francois.

'What was it?' asked Black.

'To tell Kyriakou, when we next saw him, that he was the son of an infidel dog.'

Black was puzzled. 'Why the hate for Kyriakou?'

'Hassan reckons the police story and the snatch from the island was a frame-up.'

'With what object?'

'So that the Greek wouldn't have to pay him for his last consignment.'

'Their next meeting should be interesting.' Black yawned. 'I see you've changed.'

'Too cold for midnight swimming.' Francois' teeth chattered.

Black looked at the shut door to Manuela's cabin. 'She all right?'

The Frenchman shrugged his shoulders. 'She sleeps, I expect.'

For a moment Black seemed undecided, then he laid the chart on the table. 'Here. Have a look at this.' He pointed with a pencil. 'That's Rendezvous Gamma. Thirty miles north of Cape Matifu. See Matifu there? On the eastern side of Algiers Bay. The wind has dropped and we're making a good fifteen point three. We're here now. The Vedra light is coming up on the beam. At this rate we should make the rendezvous by eight-thirty in the morning. Daylight's at six thirty-one. Things that worry me are the two hours in daylight, and that all this is happening four days ahead of schedule. ZID's had less than forty-eight hours' warning of the possible change of plans. And now it's happened. Here we are, asking to be met on the fifteenth instead of the nineteenth.'

Helmut looked at the chart and measured with dividers, making notes on a pad. 'Weissner was off Benghazi on the tenth. If ZID moved him westwards on the thirteenth, when they got our stand-by signal, he'll make it.'

'It's a big *if*, Helmut. We don't know his movements between the tenth and thirteenth. Anyway we've no option, so let's get on with it. Check that we can make the rendezvous by eight-thirty.'

Helmut got busy with the dividers again and when he'd finished he confirmed Black's estimates.

'Right.' Black took a signal pad and, calling out the message word by word, he wrote: *Prospect embarked. ETA Rendezvous Gamma 0830 to-day fifteenth. Request early confirmation.* How's that?'

'Goot,' said Helmut.

'*Bon.*' Francois waved his cheroot in a gesture of approval.

Black yawned, stretched his arms, and then dropped them suddenly. 'What are you waiting for?' he barked at Helmut. 'Get it off to ZID. *Geschwind Dummkopf!*'

Helmut gave an exaggerated Nazi salute. '*Jawohl, Herr Oberleutnant.*'

Francois made a rude sign and hissed.

An hour later when the light at Vedra had dropped out of sight astern and Punta Rotja, the southernmost light on Formentera, was abeam ten miles to the east, course was altered to 130 degrees. Now Rendezvous Gamma was dead ahead, distant

73 miles, and Black breathed more freely for they were clear of territorial waters. Anything that happened from now on would be on the high seas.

Not that he had any serious qualms. Even if Weissner failed to make the rendezvous in time, Black felt they were comparatively safe. At daybreak *Snowgoose* would be some eighty-five miles to the south of Ibiza. He accepted the possibility that *Nordwind* would be used for seaborne pursuit *if* the Spaniards knew in which direction the schooner had sailed. But how could they know? By daylight, when the farm truck was found abandoned at Cabo Negret, all they would know was the point of departure. From it, *Snowgoose* might have sailed anywhere. They would assume, of course, that she'd keep clear of Spanish territory. But that still left a host of options around three-quarters of the compass. The imponderable which worried him was the extent to which the Spanish authorities might decide to become involved.

The Guardia Civil had known early on of van Biljon's abduction—the road chase had followed—and there was the hold-up of the farm truck. But somehow he did not feel that these offences, serious though they were, would be regarded by the Spanish as sufficient to warrant activity other than that normally undertaken by the police. There were no naval or airforce units in Ibiza at the moment, though there might well be some not far off. But he discounted the likelihood of their being used for a special search, particularly at such short notice.

The breeze from the south-east had dropped and the sea was calm, the schooner rolling gently to the remains of a westerly swell. The dark blanket of the night was pierced occasionally by the steaming lights of ships, distant and anonymous, and sometimes the whine of high-flying jets could be heard above the thump of the schooner's diesel, and the splash and tumble of water along the hull.

Black stayed in the cockpit with Dimitrio, silent most of the time, on the edge of physical exhaustion, yet his mind restless, busy interminably with what had happened and what lay ahead. Deliberately, as from the first days in Ibiza, he fought against thinking about van Biljon, conscious always of Kagan's injunction: *emotional involvement is dangerous: maintain always your objectivity*. But what of Manuela? Kagan knew nothing of her, of *that* emotional involvement.

He went back in his mind over all that had happened since they'd met on the Barcelona ferry steamer. How had he allowed himself to become emotionally involved? What were the insidious steps by which these things happened? He decided it couldn't be explained. Why was one woman suddenly more important to you than all the others you'd ever known. The elements were always the same: eyes, nose and mouth; breasts and broad thighs; flesh and skin and bone; ninety per cent water, it was said, the body regenerating itself entirely in a seven year cycle. What then made Manuela important to him? Her eyes? The bones in her face? The way she could look sad? Her smile of recognition? Her voice, the strangely inflected English, North American with a Puerto Rican accent? Her helplessness? How could one say?

He thought of her sleeping in the cabin, not ten feet away. Miserable, exhausted, frightened, not knowing in what she had become involved, believing that he had somehow betrayed her. When they got to the other side, would she stay with him? He didn't know much about drugs. What if she were an addict? There were clinics, he supposed, where she could be treated, even cured. If he could arrange that, would she co-operate?

The door to the forward companionway opened and shut, and a man came into the cockpit. It was Helmut.

'Signal from ZID,' he said.

Black put out his hand in the darkness and took it. Switching on the chart-table light he read: '*Your 0107. Meeting Rendezvous Gamma 0830 to-day fifteenth confirmed. ZID.*'

'Thank God,' he said wearily. 'I'll be glad to hand over.'

'You know,' said Helmut, 'I won't. This has been terrific. Now it's just about over, I feel kind of flat. You know. I mean, what's there to look forward to?'

Black started as he felt someone touch him. It was Francois. 'I must have dozed,' said Black. He was sitting on a flap seat, huddled in the corner of the cockpit.

'You should have rested in the saloon. You weren't needed here.'

'Thanks for the compliment,' said Black. 'What's the trouble?'

'He insists on seeing you.'

'Who?' Black rubbed his smarting eyes.

194

'Van Biljon. He's over the worst of the Pentothal. Quite lucid. See for yourself.'

Black went to the portlight and looked in. Van Biljon, back to him, was sitting at the desk beside the bunk, his head in his hands.

The deck-watch showed nine minutes past three. 'Get Helmut to bring him to the saloon,' said Black. 'You take over here.'

When Francois had gone, Black went across to the wheel, spoke to Dimitrio and checked the compass course and log repeater. He looked down the half-open hatch to the engine compartment where Kamros was making an adjustment. 'Okay, there, Kamros?' he shouted.

Kamros looked up, his face stained with grease and sweat. 'Fine. We can manage a few more revs if you need them.'

'Not at the moment. We're logging fifteen point two. What've you got in hand?'

'About a knot, if I open everything. Prefer not to, though.'

'Nice to know, but I don't think it'll be necessary.'

Black went down the companionway and forward to the saloon. While he sat there waiting, arms folded, eyes half closed, fighting off sleep, he wondered what line van Biljon would take. I must keep calm, he thought. Think of what I'm saying. Mustn't bully. Remain detached. Outside it all. Leave to him, at least, the dignity he denied to others.

The saloon door opened and a tall angular shape came in. The dark glasses had gone, lost in the mêlée in the gallery, and for the first time Black saw that van Biljon's eyes were narrow slits with puffy white surrounds, so little of the eyeballs visible that at first no colour could be ascribed to them then, later, they took on a faded blue against the scarred face. Because of the low deckhead the old man stooped, his manacled hands and his head held forward, the overall effect so predatory that Black was reminded of a mantis.

Standing in the corner of the saloon, silent and motionless, he gestured van Biljon to the settee. Awkwardly, because he could not use his hands, the old man edged in between the table and the settee and sat down, his breathing laboured. Francois remained standing at the door until Black nodded to him; then he, too, sat down.

'You wish to see me?' said Black.

Van Biljon's head came up, his body stiffened, and the old air of authority returned. He thumped the table with his manacled hands. 'I demand an explanation of this outrage. I am a Spanish citizen, well known to influential members of the Spanish Government. You may think you will get away with this . . .' He paused, wheezing with the effort he was putting into what he was saying. 'This *violence*. But you won't. The Governor is a friend of mine. The full resources of the State will be used to track you down. *You and your gang.* Then you will receive the punishment you deserve.' The tightly compressed lips, the pink tongue tip spitting the words through them, reminded Black of a snake.

He stared into the narrow eyes, set in the scarred face like coin slots in a vending machine, raking his memory, searching for a spark of recognition, but none came.

'I doubt if the Governor will do anything,' he said. 'By nine o'clock this morning he'll know that you are Kurt Heinrich Gottwald, formerly of Zurich, wanted by the Israeli Government for war crimes against the Jewish people.'

Again the old man raised his hands in protest and banged the table, the handcuffs rattling like chains. 'Lies,' he hissed. 'Damned lies, and you know it. I am not Gottwald—whoever he may be. And as for war crimes—that is childish nonsense. I am not and never have been a German. I can prove that. And I can prove that I was not in Germany for one day of the war.'

Black sighed wearily, not so much that he was tired, but that he was sick with emotion, sick with remembered horror; too sick to shout accusations at this carrion-like old man, to pour on him the hatred and loathing of a lifetime. Instead he said, 'Something of what you say is correct. You are *not* a German. You were in Switzerland from the beginning of the war until November, 1943, when you moved to South America. Whether these facts will help you, will be seen when you are on trial. In the meantime, save your energies for that occasion.'

Van Biljon stared at him, leaning forward across the table, baring uneven yellow teeth. 'You concede that I am Swiss. That I was not in Germany during the war. So this nonsense you talk of war crimes is not going to help you. What is this? A cloak for crime? For abduction?' He stopped, closing his eyes and pressing the tips of his fingers against his eyelids. 'I will not play that game: ask what the ransom is. How it is to be paid? Where it is to be collected? I am too old for that.' He sighed. 'I will leave it to the Spanish Government to deal with you. Do what you wish with me. I have had my life. But you will end your days, you and the others, rotting in a Spanish gaol.' The words came spitting from the twisted mouth, as if their emission hurt.

Black watched him, unmoved. 'There is no ransom, Gottwald. No easy way out. No escape. Eichmann discovered that, and many thousands of others. *There is no escape.*'

Van Biljon shook his manacled hands in a final gesture of despair. 'Stop this absurd act. At once! It is preposterous that you should subject an inoffensive old man to such indignities. In the name of God, stop it.'

Black shook his head. 'We met many years ago, Gottwald. Of course you look different now.'

The old man's neck muscles worked as he glared at his captor. 'I *never* forget a man's face. We haven't met before.'

'It's not a man's face you have to remember. It was longer ago than that.'

'I don't know what you're talking about.'

'I think you do,' said Black. 'That Cézanne picture. The water-mill at Argenton-sur-Creuse.'

'What of it?'

'It was my uncle's.'

Gottwald's face crumbled and his head sagged forward as if its means of support had been suddenly withdrawn. 'You mean, you mean . . . ?' he whispered.

'Yes. I am Bernard Falk. Johan Stiegel's nephew. You sent us up that path in the forest.'

Gottwald closed his eyes. '*Mein Gott!*' he said. '*Mein Gott!*'

Chapter Twenty-Four

After Helmut had taken van Biljon back to the owner's suite, Black sat hunched on the settee in a corner. Drained of emotion, exhausted yet unwilling to sleep, his mind blurred with thought, he tried to concentrate on the rendezvous: Helmut would have to get a star fix at dawn, plot *Snowgoose*'s position, make the necessary alterations of course to reach Rendezvous Gamma by eight-thirty. With luck they would have a little time on hand. If not, use would have to be made of those extra revolutions.

The legal niceties must be observed. Fifteen minutes before they were due at the rendezvous they'd transmit a MAYDAY signal. *Mistral of Monaco in distress 50 miles N.W. Algiers. Hull leak. Sinking rapidly.* Providentially, Weissner would show up. A schooner sinking on the high seas. He would take them off. Return to his base. Hand those he had rescued to the appropriate authorities. Everything had been thought of. ZID was an organisation manned by people of intelligence, determination and infinite patience. Its director, Kagan, was the embodiment of those virtues. Black's thoughts trailed away, interrupted by the sound of a door opening. He looked up.

Manuela stood in the doorway, pale and uncertain, steadying herself against the schooner's corkscrew motion.

Her hair was untidy, she had no make-up, the soft lips glistened and there were dark smudges under eyes which regarded him as if he were a stranger. 'I couldn't help it,' she said. 'I heard what was said.'

Black had not moved. Now he looked away, running his hand over his forehead. 'With Gottwald, you mean?'

She came over and stood above him, her hand on his shoulder. 'I am sorry,' she said. 'I will not repeat it. But the ventilator over the door was open. It was terribly stuffy.'

'So you know,' said Black, feeling that it wasn't a very bright remark.

'Yes,' she said, 'and I am—well—sad *and* happy. You know.

Mixed up.'

'Happy that you're safe. But why sad? For him?'

She shook her head emphatically. 'Happy that you are—what you are. Sad that I have thought such unkind things about you.'

He felt an enormous relief and pulled her down beside him.

'I had to *do* pretty unkind things to you.'

She said, 'Yes,' and he put his arms round her, burying his face in her hair, holding her tight, restraining thoughts and fears he preferred not to face.

Gently she pushed him away. 'You know I can't call you *Bernard*. It is not *you*. For me you can only be Charles. I don't mind the Falk. I never thought much of Black.'

'I thought it was rather good. Sort of strong-silent-man name. *Killer* Black. You know. But Charles is my second name. Bernard Charles Falk.'

She put up a hand to stifle a yawn.

'You must sleep,' he said.

'Impossible. My brain is too active. There's too much I don't understand.'

'What, for example?' He held one of her hands, marvelling at its softness, the wrist almost transparent, the veins and arteries showing through the skin like threads in marble.

'What you were talking about to van Biljon. How could he commit war crimes against the Jews *outside* Germany? How could you, an Englishman, be involved? How did you escape? Can't you tell me?'

'It'll all come out at the trial, Manuela.' He looked at her with tired, inquiring eyes; then, seeing her disappointment, he said, 'All right. I'll tell you. But don't repeat it. You could ruin me if you did.'

'Look at me,' she said impulsively, leaning towards him. 'Do you think I would ever do that?'

'No. I don't.'

'Oh, Charles,' she said, 'I wish I'd known before.'

'Sit over there, not too close.' He said it sternly, moving away from her. 'I can't think clearly with you next to me.'

He put his legs on the settee, wedging himself in the corner. 'It's a long story. Gottwald was a Swiss. At the beginning of the Second World War he was a small, not very successful art dealer in Zurich. He was in his early thirties then. For several years before that he'd had connections with an art dealer, Rosenthal, on the German side of Lake Constance. In 1940, Rosenthal persuaded him to operate the Swiss end of an escape route across the lake for Jewish refugees. These were wealthy people. They brought easily transported valuables. You know. Diamonds, gold, jewellery, pictures.

'Gottwald's reward for his services was the sole right to dispose of these for their owners. He got a twenty per cent commission. It was a lucrative business. After he'd worked in this way for some time his reliability and discretion were well established, and a steady trickle of Jews was getting through.

'By then he'd got a taste for money, and an obsession about the French Impressionists. He'd handled a number of their pictures which refugees had brought over.

'But to acquire these required a lot more money than he had. Anyway, it seems that some time in 1942 he saw the possibility of getting rich quick, and without risk, by introducing a simple but important variation into the escape routine.

'Gottwald's work from the Zurich end was to meet an incoming motor-launch at varying but pre-determined points on the Swiss side of the lake, and transfer the refugees to his panel van. There they would sign documents appointing him sole agent for the disposal of their valuables, which they then handed over. This done, he would lock the doors and drive into Zurich by roundabout routes, dropping the refugees in outlying parts of the city. He had to vary the routes and points of disembarkation on each occasion so that no pattern was built up which might be detected by German agents. Then . . .'

Manuela broke in. 'What was this variation you spoke of? In the escape route, I mean?'

The schooner trembled as the bow smacked into a sea and they heard the spray sluice over the deck above them.

'Wind and sea increasing.' Black's red-rimmed eyes emphasised his weariness. 'Now where was I? Oh, yes. The variation. After he'd met the launch, he'd put them in his van. There they'd sign the documents and hand over their valuables. Then he'd lock the van, but instead of driving into Zurich, he'd go to a point on the Swiss-German, or Swiss-Austrian border. He varied them. The distances were never great. He would tell the refugees that they were just outside Zurich, that they must follow a forest footpath he showed them which would lead them to a main road in a kilometre or so. He

200

explained that these precautions were necessary for the safety of other refugees who would be using the escape route in future.

'The refugees would set off up the path and soon run into the arms of a German border patrol which was expecting them.'

Manuela shivered. 'What a fiendish thing to do. But he was making money anyway. Why did he do it?'

'Greed. Also, perhaps, some complex hate motive. He was a German Swiss.'

'Why did he help in the beginning?'

'Money, I suppose. He got a lot of money from the commissions. But the only way he could get the lot was to get rid of their owners. Once he'd done that it was easy.'

Manuela brushed the hair away from her eyes. 'How did the German border guards know the refugees were coming?'

'Gottwald had a cousin in Bavaria. A man called Halsbach. Well placed in the middle echelons of the Nazi Party. Through him, Gottwald evolved this system for returning refugees. He even claimed out-of-pocket expenses for his services. This was probably done to keep from the Germans the real purpose of his activities.'

'He must be like an animal,' said Manuela.

'You're a bit hard on animals.'

For a moment she watched him in silence. 'I heard you say that he went back to South America in 1943.'

Black ran his hands over his face as if to refresh himself. 'God, I'm tired.'

She was at once contrite. 'Oh, Charles. How selfish of me. I will go. You must sleep.'

'No. Don't go. It does me good to get this out of my system. Anyway I would never sleep. This'll help to pass the time.'

'You mean until Rendezvous Gamma?'

He looked up quickly. 'You know that, too?'

'Of course. Everything you discussed I could hear in the cabin.'

'Lucky we didn't get on to Helmut's favourite subject.'

'It might have been interesting.' She tilted her head on one side, regarding him curiously. 'Why don't you people speak to each other in Hebrew?'

'Two of us don't speak it well. In any case when this

operation began we had orders not to speak Hebrew at any time, in case we gave away our cover. English is the one language we all speak reasonably well. And it suits me. I am English.'

She repeated an earlier question. 'Why did Gottwald go to South America in 1943?'

'Because that year the escape route dried up. Rosenthal disappeared, and Gottwald's cousin in Bavaria sent word that the Jewish underground in Germany had got wind of the double-sell.

'Gottwald left Switzerland for South America almost immediately. I expect he was terrified of reprisals. He took with him the pictures. You've seen many of them at Altomonte. A good part of that collection was built up during the war years. Either with the wealth he stole from refugees, or simply by keeping their pictures. Like my uncle's Cézanne.

'In the Argentine, he took the name "van Biljon" and had extensive plastic surgery. The idea was to simulate facial injuries and burns in an air crash.'

Manuela said, 'He certainly succeeded.'

'Afterwards he moved from the Argentine to Peru, shifting to Brazil when the war ended. In 1949 he moved again, this time to the Paranà area of Brazil. Bormann, Mengele, Gluck and others were in those parts, and Gottwald evidently wanted to be near them. I expect it gave him a sense of security. But there is no evidence that he had any connection with them. From the start he chose the life of a recluse.

'As it happened, his first serious mistake was to take the name of van Biljon, although he had good reason for doing this. But it provided the first, the essential, clue to his identity. He had been married before the 1939-45 war to a woman who came from a Transvaal family which had settled in the Argentine after the Boer War. In this way he had an intimate knowledge of the background he'd adopted.'

'What happened to her?'

'She died of leukemia in Zurich less than a year after their marriage. There were no children.'

'I believe he adored children,' she said. 'Is it not strange?'

'No. I understand this. He had to live with his conscience. We all do. He had sent many people to their death, some of them children. I imagine he thought in a twisted way that he could come to terms with himself if he gave happiness to children.' Black pulled at his beard. 'It is impossible to know what goes on in such a mind. Perhaps it also was that they gave him company, and were too young to menace him with awkward questions about the past.'

'Tell me about yourself.' She looked at him curiously. 'What happened to you?'

'I must get a drink,' he said. 'I'm getting hoarse. Something for you?'

'A Coke or milk. Anything.'

As Black stood up, Dimitrio flung into the saloon. 'Quick! Aircraft flares astern,' he shouted and ran back.

After a moment's hesitation, Manuela followed. As she emerged from the companionway into the wet windy darkness, she heard Black's urgent shouted order, 'Reverse course. Stop engines. Hoist sails,' and she saw by the reflection of the compass light that he was at the wheel.

There was a flurry of activity and the schooner's bows came round until she was heading for Ibiza. The big diesels coughed to a stop and the hull vibrations ceased. Kamros came from the engine-compartment and lent a hand with the running gear.

Halyards were run to the winches, sails hoisted, sheets slackened and the booms swung broad-off to catch the wind. Within minutes *Snowgoose* was under sail, moving slowly through the water, making the most of the wind from astern, her navigation lights burning.

Fine on the starboard bow, Manuela saw a flare flicker faintly then go out, leaving behind a night which seemed blacker than ever. She heard Black say: 'How many flares were there?'

'Two,' said Francois. 'One about thirty seconds after the other.'

'Could you hear the aircraft?'

'No. At first I thought they might be distress signals. But they came down so slowly that I realised they were aircraft flares.'

'Did they illuminate anything?'

'Nothing that I could see. I reckon they were about eight to ten miles off, or we'd have heard the aircraft.'

'Could be closer,' said Black. 'The wind's carrying the sound away from us.'

Helmut said, 'Aircraft don't drop flares over the sea unless they look for something.'

'That,' said Kamros, 'is a fabulous deduction.'

'*Magnifique.*' Francois cleared his throat. '*Deutschland über Alles.*'

'Shut up,' said Black urgently. 'And listen.'

After that the only sounds were the slap and gurgle of water along the schooner's side, and the creaking of running blocks and rigging.

It was Dimitrio who heard it first. 'On the port bow,' he called.

'What?' snapped Black irritably.

'Aircraft engines.'

A moment later Black said, 'Yes.' What had at first seemed no more than a pulsing in the atmosphere, had grown in intensity to become a rhythmic pattern of sound somewhere out on the port bow.

'Twin piston engines.' Black's voice was laconic. 'I'll stay at the wheel. The rest of you get under cover. If they drop a flare it'll look odd if the cockpit's stiff with bodies at three o'clock in the morning.'

'Three-twenty-seven,' corrected Helmut, calling back over his shoulder as he shepherded the others down the companionway, shutting the door after him and switching off the lights.

There was a porthole in the door and through it Manuela watched Black's bearded face and intense eyes lit by the dim lights of the compass binnacle. Like a bird of prey, she thought. He was watching the compass card, looking up occasionally at the sails and turning the wheel a few spokes at a time to correct the yaw. His calmness reassured her.

In the darkness at the foot of the companionway, Manuela's thoughts were of him and not of the unknown aircraft. He seemed to her now such a strong determined character, so different to the good natured, feckless yet attractive man she'd thought him to be. The puzzle that he'd represented, the apparent aimlessness of his life, the unpleasant feeling she'd had that he lived by his wits, perhaps as an art thief—fears which seemed to have been so amply confirmed by the earlier happenings of the night—all were now explained. It was as if she'd been granted a reprieve from a sentence the nature of which she'd not dared contemplate. She sensed that he was in love with her, and she felt a deep contentment. There were difficulties still. The business with Kyriakou must finished. If Black wanted her then, she would begin a new life.

She started, her thoughts interrupted by Helmut's voice. 'It close now,' he said. Through the skylight she heard the noise of engines growing louder, the pitch rising, passing overhead, then fading into the distance.

Soon afterwards the cockpit lit up as if night had been turned into day. They couldn't see the flares, but they knew they must be somewhere above the schooner, the parachutes descending slowly, the *Snowgoose* naked for all to see. They heard the aircraft pass overhead again, the noise of its engines this time so deafening that they knew it was flying low. Manuela, watching the cockpit, frightened and uncertain, sensed that something about the schooner was different. The external paintwork was no longer white but a bright blue, and the lifebuoy had *Mistral* and *Monaco* on it, not *Snowgoose* and *Piræus*.

She whispered to Helmut, 'Aren't we in the *Snowgoose*?'

For a moment he was silent, then he saw the point. 'Sure we are.'

'But she was a white schooner. And the name?'

'Paint,' said Helmut gruffly. 'Just paint.'

The brilliance of the flares was fading, the cockpit looking like a stage with the lights going down. Darkness returned suddenly as if a switch had been thrown, and they heard the drone of the aircraft's engines receding into the distance.

Helmut opened the doghouse door and they went back to the cockpit.

Black said, 'They had a bloody good look. Came really low on that last run.'

'What did you make of it?' asked Francois.

'Nothing. Couldn't see a thing except the navigation lights. Might have been civil or military. Probably military. Must have had radar and flare-droppers. I don't like the look of things. One—they've flown off in the direction of Ibiza. Two —they're probably in radio touch with something seaborne, possibly *Nordwind*. If it's her, she can do twenty-five knots to our sixteen. Depending upon where she is at this moment, it could be tricky.'

Helmut was gruffly optimistic. 'Is it not for them confusing? The blue hull and change of name? And that we are steering for Ibiza?'

'That's what we've got to hope,' said Black. 'But the changes are more effective in daylight than at night. Anywa an aircraft flying that fast couldn't read our name, flare or flare. What they're looking for is a staysail schooner, Bermu rigged, about thirty-five tons displacement. And that's wh they've just found.'

'There must be others much the same,' said Kamr stolidly.

Black ignored him. 'We'll stay on this course for anoth five minutes. Then, if there's no sound of the aircraft retur ing, we'll lower sails, start the diesels and get back on cour for Rendezvous Gamma. We've lost valuable time a distance.'

Manuela, looking out over the sea, thinking of the *Nor wind*, recalled the unsympathetic faces of Juan and Pedro, gu in hand, as they came into the gallery. She shivered.

Chapter Twenty-Five

Once again *Snowgoose* was heading for Africa, steering 138 degrees now to correct for the northerly drift she'd experienced while under sail. Helmut estimated that six miles had been lost in distance and about twenty-five minutes in time. Even with the extra revolutions from the diesels, the schooner was only logging fourteen knots in the freshening southerly wind. In the cockpit, the lamp under the chart-table screen reflected on the faces of Helmut and Black as they bent over the chart. Francois was at the wheel.

Black tapped the chart with his pencil. 'Check our distance from Rendezvous Gamma at daylight.'

Helmut took the parallel rulers and dividers and checked the course and distance. 'Thirty-six miles,' he said.

'Two and a half hours' steaming.' Black whistled. 'No good. Daylight's at six thirty-one. That means Gamma at about nine o'clock instead of eight-thirty. If there's anything after us—and we must now assume there is—we'll be steaming in daylight for two and a half hours. That's not acceptable.'

'Have we any option?'

'We can try. Let's plot a new rendezvous which we can reach half an hour after daylight. At 0700. Then we'll ask ZID if Weissner can manage it.'

Helmut went to work on the chart again. 'Here it is,' he said. 'Twenty-eight miles west of Gamma. Fifty-eight miles due north of Pointe Shersel. That's still in Algeria.'

Black looked at the new position. 'We're adding to Weissner's problems. I wonder if he can make it?'

'You're worrying about that aircraft.'

'Too bloody right I am. They weren't doing night flips for tourists.'

Helmut regarded him thoughtfully. 'The Spanish authorities wouldn't assist if they knew who van Biljon was, would they?'

'Probably not. But the protocol's very dodgy. Until Weissner has *rescued* us on the high seas, Israel has no official knowledge of Gottwald. Officially he remains a wanted man, thought to be in South America, exact whereabouts unknown.

The Israeli Government will have no part in abductions on other people's territory. You know that. That's why ours a private venture. Why ZID's a private organisation.'

Francois called to them from the wheel. 'After Weissno has picked us up, will the Spanish Government be informe immediately of the identity of van Biljon? Or will ZID wa for our arrival at Haifa?'

'Haven't a clue,' said Black. 'I can't say. ZID must decide Now. Quick! What's the course and distance to the ne rendezvous?'

Helmut looked at the deck-watch and log repeater befor plotting *Snowgoose*'s position. Then he drew the course lin to Rendezvous Delta, rolled the parallel ruler on to th compass rose, and with the dividers measured the distanc against the latitude scale. 'One-six-five degrees, fifty-nine miles.

Black went across to the compass. 'Steer one-six-five.'

Francois turned the wheel to starboard and steadied th schooner's bows on the new course.

When they had agreed the signal to ZID, reporting th searching aircraft and requesting the new rendezvous, Helmu went off to the radio cabin to transmit it. Black straightene up from the chart-table and yawned loudly. 'I'm going alon to the galley to see how Dimitrio's getting on with that coffee.

'Have a rest,' called Francois. 'You're not as young as yo were.'

'Go to hell,' said Black, as he went down the companionway

Dimitrio came into the saloon unsteadily, balancing himsel against the schooner's pitching, and put the coffee and sand wiches inside the fiddles on the saloon table.

Manuela poured two cups and put aside some sandwiches and Dimitrio went off with the rest to the cockpit.

'Why don't you try to sleep?' said Black. 'It's just after four. You can get a few hours still.'

She shook her head. 'Oh, no. It's too stuffy and everything keeps jumping about. I would never sleep. I'm too excited. Have some coffee. It will chase away the tiredness.' She passed him a cup. 'Now tell me about Gottwald. And about what happened to you. Tell me,' she said insistently.

'Oh, it's a hell of a long story. I could never tell it all.'

She drew her legs on to the settee next to him, wedging herself against the edge of the table. 'Tell me a little,' she coaxed.

He waved a sandwich at her, his mouth full, and pointed to his coffee cup. 'First these.'

Later he said, 'In Brazil, Gottwald led the life of a recluse. Concentrated on looking after his investments and collecting pictures. He had a lot of money in South Africa and South America. On three occasions he visited South Africa. Partly to support his claim to Boer descent, partly to make investments. One of our most valuable clues came from a Johannesburg stockbroker.'

'What was it?'

He shook his head. 'Sorry. Those are things that will never be told.'

'Doesn't matter. Just my feminine curiosity.'

'Well, after fourteen years of that sort of life he began to get bolder. He must have believed the world had forgotten Kurt Heinrich Gottwald. Probably he began to feel that he really was Hendrick Wilhelm van Biljon. I've been Charles Black for nearly eight months now. You know, you begin to believe that the part you're playing is real. That you *are* the other man.' He chuckled. 'That's how I fell for you.'

She made a face. 'You say the nicest things.'

'Gottwald's undoing was his longing for Europe. He must have become obsessed with the idea of getting back. But he appreciated the risks, and I imagine that's why he chose Ibiza. It's an attractive place. Europe, yet not *in* Europe, you know. And island life is easier for a recluse. He settled there eleven years ago. Always had the same staff. They were highly paid by local standards. Very loyal. We believe they have no knowledge of his identity.'

'Did he ever leave the island?'

'Occasionally. At very long intervals. He would go to Paris, or London, or Madrid—never to Zurich, incidentally —to look at a picture a dealer had put him on to.'

'Now tell me about *you*. And that Cézanne picture.'

Black smiled. The way she said *you*, as if he were something special, touched him. 'My family was English,' he said. 'My mother Jewish. Her sister married a German, Johan Stiegel. When the war started I was on holiday in Germany staying with the Stiegels. I'd been sent over because Mother was having a baby—my sister. The Stiegels hadn't been touched by anti-Semitism then because Stiegel wasn't a Jew. He was

209

wealthy and had influential friends. About two weeks before the war started I got scarlet fever and was sent to an isolation hospital in Munich where the Stiegels lived. When I got back to my uncle's house it was too late to return to England, the war was already on, so I stayed with my aunt. Everybody thought it was going to be a short war.

'As anti-Semitism grew, the Stiegel family went underground—me with them. Eventually, in 1943, we escaped across Lake Constance. Gottwald met us that night on the Swiss side. I was only ten but—I can't think why—I knew somehow that things were wrong. I didn't trust Gottwald. I suppose I was terrified. Also my uncle seemed suspicious. He had a little compass with him and after we'd got into the van and started on the journey he made a great fuss because we were going in the wrong direction. But Gottwald explained why it was necessary. Said also that the compass was affected by the steel body of the van. Anyway, he pacified him. I should have explained that among the valuables my uncle brought over that night was the Cézanne picture of the water-mill.'

'So it's really your picture? I mean a family picture.'

Black stared into the corner, at nothing. 'Yes. And it's come back to the family. Temporarily. It's in my cabin.'

'I am glad,' she said.

'So will ZID be. It will pay for many things.'

'Go on about that night.'

'Oh, yes. Where was I? In the van. Well, after quite a journey it stopped. We were in a clearing inside a forest. It was dark. Gottwald took us a hundred metres or so along a footpath, well into the forest. He said we must walk about a kilometre down the path, when we would come to the main road into Zurich. There would be traffic on the road, he said. When we reached it, we were to turn right and start walking towards Zurich. After a few hundred metres we would find a blue Peugeot van waiting at the roadside. He gave my uncle the registration number and said it would take us into Zurich. He particularly stressed that if we were questioned at any stage we were under no circumstances to say how we had got out of Germany. Gottwald said it was vital not to compromise the escape route. It meant the difference between life and death for those who still had to come. There were, he warned, many German agents in Switzerland. Then he left us.

'As we went up that path without him, I had a feeling of impending disaster. Something I couldn't explain. The night was dark and violent. Lashing rain and wind, and although it was summer it was very cold. Gottwald had given my uncle a torch and he kept using it to keep us on the path. It seemed a long walk, and then, at last, the wind brought to us from somewhere ahead the distant noise of traffic. I remember my uncle saying to my aunt, "Stella. Do you hear that? It must be the Zurich road. We are safe."

'But I didn't feel safe, though I was too ashamed to admit it. I hung back and they would call me to hurry. I remember there was a flash of lightning and then, with appalling suddenness, two black shapes stepped out from the trees ahead of me. They shone torches on my aunt and uncle and shouted to them in German. My uncle called out and my aunt screamed. They were about twenty metres ahead of me. When I saw the Germans come on to the path, silhouetted against the beam of my uncle's torch, I slipped behind a tree. Then, when they shouted, I ran. I don't know how far I ran, but I stopped only when I fell into a hole in a clump of bracken. It must have been an animal burrow. I was cut and bruised and half dead with fright. It was raining hard and that saved me. I could hear the hunt going on. Men running, shouting in German, dogs barking and howling, and once there were shots. But the rain had destroyed the scent and washed away my footprints. I knew they'd be back at daylight, so I moved while it was still dark. I had no idea of direction. Didn't know whether we'd crossed the frontier or not. But I assumed we were in Germany or Austria, and I decided to keep to the forests. Luckily it was summer and I had warm clothing and a raincoat. I used to lie up in the forests by day and move only at night. Because of the mountains I followed the river valleys and always I tried to keep going east—to reach Italy. I didn't trust Switzerland any more. I lived on wild berries and fruit I took from the orchards at night. On the tenth or eleventh day—maybe the twelfth, I'd lost count—a woodcutter found me asleep in the forest where he worked. I was in pretty poor condition by then. Must have covered about eighty miles, mostly in Switzerland as it happened. Afterwards we worked out that I'd followed the valley of the River Inn to near its confluence with the Adige. Then I must have crossed over into Italy.

'Anyway, to shorten a long story, the woodcutter was the son of an Italian family—farmers in the mountains above Siladron—and they kept me until the end of the war. Even then they didn't want to part with me. They were the most wonderful people. I've been back several times.'

'How marvellous, Charles.'

He smiled. '*They* called me Bernardino.'

'And then you went back to your family in England?'

'Yes. It was quite a homecoming. They'd long since given me up. But we weren't together long. In 1947 they were killed in a car accident, with my sister. That was the end of the Falks, but for me.

'A spinster aunt tried to cope with me after that but it was a losing battle. I was pretty impossible and the war experience had done things to me. I was only half a Jew but I'd lost faith in the Christian world, and I felt my Jewishness intensely. When I was seventeen I went to Israel and worked on a kibbutz. Near Beth Saida, by the Sea of Galilee. Later I became interested in fine art. Studied it in my spare time. Worked as an art critic in Israel, England and Canada at different times. My only other real interests in life were ornithology and sailing. I served in the Israeli army. Fought in 1956 and the June war. I was a paratrooper. Commando unit.'

Manuela pointed an accusing finger. 'So that's where you learned to fight. I mean like the night you attacked Kirry and Tino.'

His eyes narrowed, but soon the frown changed to a smile. 'I thought they attacked me. Never mind.'

'You know what I mean,' she said.

He stifled a yawn. 'Well, that's about all. Except that some years ago I learnt that the ZID people wanted to hear from anyone who'd used Gottwald's escape route. So I got in touch. A lot happened after that. It took three years' work to get me to the moment in time when I had to rescue a damsel in distress on the steamer from Barcelona.'

She moved up the settee and leant against him, her head on his shoulder. 'Oh, Charles,' she said. 'What a sad life you've had.'

'Not especially sad,' he said. 'Just a life. Some of it grim. A lot of it dull. Some exciting. Some enjoyable.'

He put his arm round her and kissed her.

'Tell me one thing,' she said. 'Why did you take off the old man's shoes and socks in the gallery? Then put them on again?'

'That was quite a moment for us,' said Black. 'Over the years ZID built up a dossier on him. Slowly and with enormous patience. Bits and pieces of evidence came in from various places. Contact was made with people he'd had dealings with in South America and South Africa. People he'd known in Zurich, some he'd been at school with. That sort of thing. The circumstantial evidence was strong. But the only way to identify him beyond doubt was to see his feet. He had no small toes.'

She looked at him strangely, half fearing to ask what was in her mind. 'Now that you've got him, has the hatred gone? I ask that because they say the end of revenge is pity.'

He shook his head. 'It was not a question of revenge. When I was young, yes. I was obsessed with the idea. But that was a long time ago. The motives now are quite different. We pursue these people for two reasons. One, because the world is full of reactionaries. What Hitler did to the Jews, can be done to them again. And it can be done to non-Jews.

'By hunting down those who committed these crimes, by pulling them out from where they believe they are safe, we teach a lesson which all can understand. *There is no escape.* Only the certainty of punishment can deter people with the same inclinations as Eichmann and Bormann and Mengele.'

He took a deep breath. 'It is not just that they must know that they will hang. That's not enough. They must live with the knowledge that they *will* be pursued—if necessary for a quarter of a century—that they will be found, that they will be hanged, that each day they wake up may be *the* day. In this way a man dies many times.

'That is one of our motives. The other is that the public trials of these people inform new generations of something they should know. Something that would otherwise be forgotten because many would like it to be. But we intend that it shall not be.'

'What will happen to Gottwald?'

Black shrugged his shoulders. 'You can imagine. In some ways he was worse than the others. He can't plead that he did it in the course of duty, or on orders from his superiors. He isn't a German. He wasn't even in Germany. He did it for

greed. To enrich himself. And he did it in the most callou
revolting way, betraying at the moment of rescue the ver
people he was employed to save, sending them to the
death so that he could steal their possessions. There is n
punishment severe enough for that.'

He stood up to stretch and yawn, then looked at his watc
and saw that it was nearly four-thirty. 'Hell's delight! I
must go and see what's happening. We should have had
reply from ZID by now.'

He saw her tired eyes, the smudges under them and the hig
cheek bones giving her face an almost skeletal appearanc
'Manuela, *please* try to sleep.'

She shook her head, patting her mouth as she yawned. 'N
Impossible. I don't want to be alone. I'll wait here for you.'

She curled up on the settee in a corner and waved to hir
jauntily. 'Bye. Don't be long.'

There was some delay before ZID's reply came. It was a
terse as it was welcome: '*Your 0348. Weissner will do Rendez
vous Delta 0700. Regret aircraft.*'

'So do we,' said Black. 'But thank God for Weissner.'

The fresh wind had built up the sea and increasingly th
schooner's bows threw up sheets of spray which blew bacl
over her, stinging the faces of the man in the cockpit despit
the spray-dodgers which had been rigged.

'Lot of cloud,' said Black. 'Nearly nine-tenth. Don't thin!
you'll manage star-sights?'

'*Verdammte Wolke,*' Helmut grumbled. 'It will be difficult.'

Black looked astern into the darkness. 'Wish I knew wha
was there. If only we had radar.'

'*Nordwind* has,' said Francois. 'We should have borrowe
hers.'

'Very funny,' said Black. 'But I imagine she's using it.'

His fingernails bit into the palms of his hands and he trie
consciously to relax, but the tension remained. It is the dark
ness, he decided, and exhaustion, nature's morale busters. Wit
daylight everything will seem different. Half an hour of i
will bring us to the rendezvous with Weissner. Then I'll han
over. Get rid of my responsibilities. All of them, but Manuela

It was ten minutes to six. Soon it would be daylight. Throug
the portlight in the cockpit, van Biljon could be seen lying o

214

e bunk, manacled hands on his stomach, eyes open. Fran-
ɔis, noting his restlessness, had gone in and offered him
eeping-pills or an injection. But van Biljon had declined.

Black had just come up from the engine compartment where
e'd relieved Kamros for a short spell.

'Starsights will be impossible,' said Helmut. 'Unless I get
ɪck. A cloud break in the right place at the right time. You
now.'

'If you can't, our D.R. position shouldn't be too bad,' said
lack. 'We haven't been all that long at sea. Even if it does
em a bloody lifetime.'

'Pity the rendezvous is so far from the African coast. Other-
ise we could get a radio fix.'

'We'll manage somehow,' said Black.

He left them in the cockpit and went back to the saloon.
Ianuela was still curled up in the corner but she'd wrapped
erself in a blanket. She opened her eyes. 'I was dozing,' she
ıid.

'It'll be daylight soon.'

'Is everything all right?'

'It's okay. Weissner will be at the rendezvous.'

She looked round the saloon. 'The boat seems to be moving
bout much more. Such vibrations.' She shivered. 'I'm cold.'

'Wait till you see the sun. You'll feel better.'

'Yes,' she said, looking at him gravely. 'I suppose so. But it
 terribly stuffy. Such a smell of food and—' she hesitated.

'Men?' he said.

She laughed. 'Yes. Men.'

He stood watching her, ready to go back to the cockpit, but
ɪere was something nagging at him. 'Manuela,' he said.

She'd sat up and was arranging her hair, gathering the long
lack strands behind her neck, smoothing them back. Now
ɪe stopped, looking at him, head on one side. 'Yes.'

'What are you going to do when we get to Haifa?'

'Go back to Ibiza, of course.'

His apprehension and disappointment changed to anger.
Vhy?' he asked coldly.

She looked away and went on with her hair. 'Because I live
ɪere, and . . .'

'And what?'

'The exhibition. My pictures. Other things.'

'Like Kyriakou?'

'Him, too, I suppose.'

'So you must go back? Nothing you want to do more tha[n] that?'

'I'm confused,' she said in a subdued voice. 'I don't know Maybe.'

Frustrated, hurt, he watched her with hopelessly mixed fee[l]ings, hating her because he loved her, because she was makin[g] it clear that he wasn't as important to her as she was to him Determined to hurt her, to bump her into reality, he sai[d] 'Typical little junkie, aren't you?'

She looked at him sadly, her eyes moist with tears. 'Wha[t]ever I say *you think I am*, so I suppose I must be.'

He was exhausted and his jumbled emotions spilled ove[r] 'Well you bloody well are. So why not have the guts to adm[it] it?'

She winced and he knew he'd hurt her. But standing ther[e] feeling brutal and helpless, he had no idea what to do or sa[y] next. As he turned to go, Helmut almost fell in the saloon. H[e] was breathless. 'There's something coming up astern.'

'What?' said Black.

'Can't say. Not enough light yet.'

Chapter Twenty-Six

The wind from the south-east brought the dust across from Talamanca, swirling it along the Avenida Ignacio Wallis, clutching at left-over newspapers in the racks outside the news agency, picking up discarded wrappings and dead leaves, rustling them along the side walk, whirling itself into a vortex which rattled the windows of the tired looking building, scattering red dust in the big office where Capitan Calvi was making his early morning report.

The Comisario interrupted him. 'Close that window, please, Capitan.'

Calvi shut the window, picked up the papers which had blown on to the floor, and sat down again.

'You were saying,' said the Comisario, 'that the arrests were made at midnight. You mentioned Rosetta. Who is he?'

'A cleaner in the funeral parlour. The procession met the Barcelona steamer yesterday morning. Padre Dominco officiated. Family and friends were there of course. The funeral is to take place this afternoon. Last night the coffin was left in the funeral parlour. We kept it under observation. At nine o'clock Rosetta was seen to go in through a back entrance. From a little-used lane. Capitan Sura's men went in ten minutes later. Rosetta had already opened the coffin. They caught him lifting out the drugs. Heroin, cocaine, opium, LSD, cannabis.'

The Comisario leant forward. '*Madre de Dios*! Was there a body in the coffin?'

'Yes. The drugs were packed round it.'

'Incredible. Are the family—any members of the church—involved?'

'No, no,' said Calvi deprecatingly, shocked at the other's suggestion. 'They are entirely innocent.'

The Comisario eyed him keenly. 'So this was the special item of cargo?'

'Yes, señor Comisario.'

'How did you get on to this?'

'There is much detail I will not trouble you with.' Calvi examined his fingernails with studied preoccupation. 'But I can say that the agent of the U.S. Narcotics Bureau was invaluable.'

'Who was this agent?'

Calvi hesitated. Even now he would have preferred not to divulge it, but circumstances were such that he must. 'Señorita Valez,' he said in a subdued voice.

The Comisario's cigar dropped as his mouth opened involuntarily, the deep-set eyes mirroring his astonishment. 'This agent is a young woman?'

'Yes,' said Calvi.

'Well I must confess I am surprised. You spoke to me the other day of arresting her with the others.'

The Capitan smiled apologetically. 'It was necessary, señor Comisario, to go to exceptional lengths to protect her.'

The older man ran a hand across his iron grey hair. 'You must remind me to acknowledge our indebtedness to her in the report to Madrid. They will convey appropriate messages to the people in the United States. Well, I must say this *is* a surprise. Now . . . about Kyriakou. She was close to him, of course. Is it as you suspected?'

'In every way,' said Calvi. 'He manages the drug ring. The caretaker became co-operative in the early hours of this morning. Made a full confession. We have arrested Kyriakou, Tino Costa and some of the pushers. Those involved at the Barcelona end have also been arrested. The evidence is complete. The racket is broken.'

'Splendid, Calvi.' The Comisario tipped the ash from the cigar into the glass ashtray. 'And what of the Englishman, Charles Black?'

'I am coming to that.' Calvi paused, frowning at his thoughts. 'There have been extraordinary developments.'

For some time the Comisario listened while Calvi reported the night's events: the abduction of van Biljon and Manuela Valez, and the escape of Black and his companions in the *Snowgoose*. Calvi told him, too, how the housekeeper had driven the Land-Rover down from Altomonte and tipped off the police at the road junction, and of the chase which had followed but petered out.

Later, the farmer and his son had reported the truck hold-up to the police at San José. At much the same time a courting couple who had been in a car parked behind bushes at Cabo Negret had driven into San José to report what they had observed: men on the beach with a woman, a man being carried, torch signals from the beach answered from seaward; the entire party embarking in a boat of some sort, it was too dark to see, and abandoning the farm truck.

'*Extraordinario!*' The Comisario sat back in his chair, his head sunk on his chest, deep in thought. Then, as if he suddenly remembered where he was, he jerked upright, dusted the cigar ash from his tunic and said, 'What action have you taken?'

'Van Biljon's boat—the *Nordwind*—put to sea soon after two o'clock this morning. It is the fastest craft in harbour. His crew are on board, with three of our men, all armed. I reported at once to Palma and Madrid. A naval aircraft from Valencia, carrying out a search exercise off Alicante, was diverted and made a sighting at about half past three this morning which may be the *Snowgoose*. The vessel behaved suspiciously, reversing her course. Unfortunately the aircraft was low on fuel and couldn't stay in the vicinity, but the pilot radioed the position to the *Nordwind*. We hope that with her superior speed, and radar, she will make contact soon.'

The Comisario shook his head, his eyes reflecting his bewilderment. 'What d'you make of this, Capitan? Is it any way connected with the drug smuggling?'

'No. Definitely not. I thought at first that they might be a gang of international art thieves. But only one picture was taken from the gallery. A valuable one admittedly. But if that had been the object, there were many others, some more valuable. It looks to me more like kidnapping. Van Biljon is a rich man. We expect a demand for ransom. They are probably making for Oran or Algiers.'

'Tell me. Why did you have the police at the foot of the Altomonte road last night?'

'For two reasons, señor Comisario. We thought van Biljon's servants might be involved in the drug running. We wished to watch their movements at the critical time. Secondly, Señorita Valez had told me that she was going to Altomonte with Black, to dine with van Biljon. This was unusual because, as you know, he does not permit visitors. It suited us well to have Señorita Valez out of town while the arrests were taking place, and to have Black under her direct observation. So I agreed to her going. But she did not know that the police

car on duty at the road junction had orders to call at Altomonte if they had not observed her make the return journey
by midnight. Unfortunately our efforts to protect her were
insufficient.'

The Comisario walked across to the window and looked
down on the Avenida Ignacio Wallis and then across to
Talamanca where the first faint streaks of daylight were
showing in the eastern sky.

'This is extremely serious, Capitan,' he said. 'If she comes to
any harm we are accountable to the U.S. authorities.'

'I am aware of that, señor Comisario. I feel personally responsible. She worked with me. Took considerable risks. It
was not easy or agreeable for her.'

'Will she reveal her identity to these people?'

Calvi shook his head. 'Under no circumstances. She could
never be used as an agent again, if she did. Also, she has no
means of knowing that the operation has been successfully
completed: the arrests made, the ring broken. These agents
make many enemies. If they reveal their identity they en-
danger their lives.'

The desk telephone rang. The Comisario picked it up.
'Hallo. Yes, he's here.' He passed the instrument to Calvi.
'For you,' he said.

Calvi spoke in monosyllables, grunting approval. He put
the phone down. 'It is the harbourmaster's office. There is a
radio signal from *Nordwind*. She has sighted a schooner which
she believes to be the *Snowgoose*.'

Chapter Twenty-Seven

The wind was increasing, spray sluicing back over the schooner as she drove into the head sea, occasional rain squalls sweeping the cockpit, the rain beating into cold faces, prickling like fine needles. In the eastern sky the beginnings of daylight struggled against scudding clouds.

But it was astern, to the north-west where the night was giving way to a storm-dark dawn, that those in the cockpit were looking. 'There!' said Helmut. 'See that flash of white? It's a bow hitting the sea.'

Wedged in a corner of the cockpit, resting his elbows on the after coachroof, eyes pressed to binoculars, Black steadied himself against the motion of the *Snowgoose*.

'Ah,' he said. 'Got it! Must be something travelling fast. Bumping the head sea.'

'Think it's *Nordwind*?' Francois was unable to keep the anxiety from his voice.

'We'll assume it is,' said Black. 'But it could be several things. The Marseilles-Algiers ferry. A naval ship making for Algiers. Even a fast freighter. Won't be long before we know.' He went across to the chart-table. The deck-watch showed 0633. The log repeater read 12.4 knots. Wind and sea had brought the speed down. With the dividers he measured off the estimated distance travelled since the last dead-reckoning position. Then he measured the distance to Rendezvous Delta. It was just over seven miles. At twelve knots that meant another thirty-five minutes. If it was the *Nordwind* they'd sighted astern she'd have, weather for weather, a ten knot advantage.

In thirty-five minutes she could gain six miles on them. Everything would depend then on two factors: how far astern she was now, and whether *Snowgoose*'s dead-reckoning position was reasonably correct. If it were not, the difficulty of making the rendezvous with Weissner on time might be considerable.

He called to the others. 'See anything yet?'

221

Helmut shouted back, 'Still only occasional splashes
spray, but they're getting bigger.'

Black knew that the vessel astern would already ha
Snowgoose in sight, silhouetted against the light to the sou
east, the direction in which Black hoped that Weissner wou
show up soon. He said to Francois. 'Check over the automat
rifles. Spare magazines. The lot. Put them at the foot of t
forward companionway.'

'So you think it is *Nordwind*?'

'I don't think anything,' snapped Black. 'But it might be.'

To Dimitrio and Helmut he said, 'Keep a good lookout f
Weissner. Ahead, and on either bow.'

Helmut swore. 'These bloody rain squalls don't help. Vis
bility keeps changing.'

Black, wedged against the cockpit coaming, was lookir
astern again. 'If we don't find Weissner, he'll find us. He's g
radar and sonar.' He began to hum *Colonel Bogey*. The do
to the companionway opened and shut and someone came in
the cockpit. It was Manuela. She had on the brown suède co
she'd worn to Altomonte. He said. 'Hallo. You'll find a
oilskin in the saloon locker. It's wet here.'

She went down the companionway again without replyin
Soon she was back wearing an oilskin several times too bi
But she kept away from him, leaning against the doghou
clear of the worst of the spray.

Daylight was coming rapidly. Once again he raised h
binoculars and looked for the vessel astern. But a squall
rain had shut out visibility and there was nothing to be seen.
it were *Nordwind* she had radar, and evasive action no
would be a waste of time. As when the Zephyr had broke
down the night before, Black felt the cold douche of failur
But pursuit was a risk they had always considered in the
plans, and there was no shock or surprise. If only he kne
it were *Nordwind*. And where Weissner was. It was six fort
seven. Thirteen minutes to the rendezvous.

There was no point in sending the MAYDAY signal if th
vessel astern were the *Nordwind*. It would have to wait no
until they'd sighted Weissner. The rain had shut in around th
schooner and nothing could be seen in any direction. Eve
if they could make radio contact with him, there was nothin
to be gained by asking Weissner for his position, since the
were unaware of their own except by dead reckoning. ZID

gnal had said that Weissner would make the rendezvous by even o'clock. Black knew that meant he'd be there. Weissner was Weissner. The problem was, would they? His thoughts were interrupted by a shout from Helmut. 'It *is* a motor cruiser. She's gained quite a bit.'

He swung round, focusing the binoculars, trying to steady himself in the lurching cockpit. To the north-west the rain had cleared, and he could see the vessel astern with the naked eye. He was about two miles away. He saw the white bows lift to the sea, the red boot-topping showing for a moment, then disappearing as a cloud of spray leapt skywards to be carried away by the wind. For a few seconds the motor cruiser was sharply focused in his binoculars. He saw the radar scanner turning, the glass-fronted wheelhouse, the raked aerial mast. It was the *Nordwind*. A knot of anxiety formed in his stomach, and his mouth and throat felt dry. Van Biljon's men would be in the motor cruiser. Perhaps the police. The last thing he wanted was a shooting match. Kagan had given strict instructions that Spanish lives should not be endangered. But if they started shooting? The rain came again, a screen of wet grey mist which hid the motor cruiser.

Black looked at his watch. It was eight minutes to seven. He heard Helmut calling.

'What d'you say?' he said dully.

Helmut shouted. 'It's the *Nordwind*.'

'I know it is,' said Black. 'Don't shout.'

A desperate feeling of impotence possessed him. Where the hell was Weissner? They should have sighted him between the squalls by now. Was *Snowgoose*'s D.R. position so hopelessly out?

Weariness pushed his mind to the edge of fantasy so that the rain which enveloped the schooner became a grey nylon bag from which escape was impossible, and the deep note of the diesels the sound of distant guns. He shook his head in an effort to clear his mind. There was nothing he could usefully do now but wait and watch while the schooner flung herself into the short seas, the bows coming clear, hanging in the air, the hull shaking like a dog shedding water then, as the spray came blanketing over them, plunging into the next sea.

'It's clearing astern,' called Helmut, and Black turned, wedging himself once more, holding the binoculars ready.

The rain squall was moving to the west like a stage curtain revealing first the sea on the port quarter then, with chilling predictability, the white bows of the motor cruiser. But it was larger now, the detail of the forward superstructure clearly visible to the naked eye. Black felt an almost overwhelming desire to scream.

The plunging bows of *Nordwind* had a hypnotic effect and his mind numbed as he looked across the broken sea, so that he did not register the sudden boil and froth of water, the hissing eruption in the wake of the schooner, until a dark shape emerged, foam and white water cascading from it as it grew rapidly larger.

He jumped up from his crouching position and shouted, his voice touched with hysteria. 'Weissner, by God! Helmut! Transmit that MAYDAY.' As Helmut went down the forward companionway, Black called to Dimitrio at the wheel. 'Slow ahead together. Tell Kamros to stand by the seacocks.'

The note of the diesels dropped, and the hull vibration diminished. Francois came up the after companionway, his dark eyes full of inquiry. 'What is it?' he said.

Black pointed astern. 'Weissner's arrived. Get the old man ready.'

Francois disappeared and Black turned to Manuela. 'Stand by for another dinghy ride, my poppet.' He smiled uncertainly, wondering if he were forgiven, trying to make peace. 'Be rougher this time. But with real sailors.'

The submarine was fully surfaced now, the long black hull moving to windward, short sea slopping over the bows, spilling across the casing and falling away into the troughs. On the gun-platform men could be seen standing by the twin Bofors while others manhandled an inflatable dinghy.

The conning-tower loomed tall and sinister, the wet steel reflecting the greys of sea and sky. A man there took off his peaked cap and waved it at the schooner, and an Aldis lamp began to blink.

Black, focusing his binoculars, shouted into the wind 'Weissner, you old bastard! You were nearly late.'